The Adventures of
Buff, Gray, & Chocolate

Bringing Down the House

Lionel James

The Adventures of Buff, Gray, & Chocolate
Bringing Down the House
Second Edition

ISBNs: 978-1-7344873-2-9 (paperback)
       978-1-7344873-0-5 (hardcover)
       978-1-7344873-1-2 (eBook)

Published by:
4 Leggs & Me
A Dillon's Doggie Creations Company
www.DillonsDoggieCreations.dog
Valley Village, CA 91607

4 Leggs & Me rev. 2/9/2018
www.4leggsandme.dog
Dillon@4leggsandme.dog

Interior design by Jera Publishing

Printed in the United States of America.

ABOUT THE AUTHOR

Dillon and I would like to thank you for purchasing "Bringing Down the House," and we hope you enjoy reading it as much as we did writing it. I would like to just mention that "Bringing Down The House" is actually a reprinted version of my first book "Behind The Secret Wall," which we removed from the market a year after the first publication in order to further develop the story. So, if you had the chance to read and enjoyed the first edition, then we hope you also enjoy reading the next book in the series of, "The Adventures of Buff, Gray, & Chocolate," coming soon.

I was born in Richmond, Virginia, and raised with a strong Christian foundation. I attended the Richmond City Public School System until 1976, when I relocated to Los Angeles, California, and studied computer programming. My passion for westerns started at a very young age, and I favor the earlier period of the American West.

I have always shared my love with animals, but just never had one of my own until February 16, 2013, when this little 4-legged Cockapoo came into my life and started stirring things up. I named him Dillon, and I believe he is a gift from God. Dillon was born on December 21, 2012, and when he came to live with me, he brought with him the idea for "The Adventures of Buff, Gray and Chocolate."

It is our belief that all things are possible through Christ, who strengthens me.

Lionel James & Dillon
See you Soon

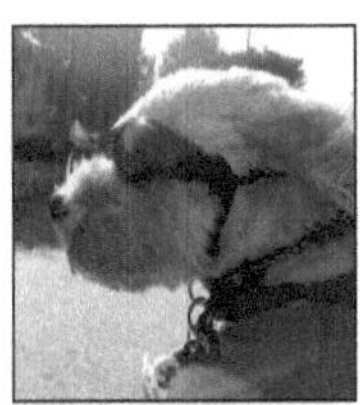

Dillon

THIS BOOK IS DEDICATED TO...

Dillon Copeland – the Cockapoo who entered my life with unconditional love. You changed my world! You are the love of my life.

My mother, Athylone Copeland, who passed away in 2003; her memories are with me forever more.

My sister, Renee Copeland, I love you with all my heart.

My father, Roy L. Copeland, who passed away in 1996; may you rest in peace.

To my beloved brother, Abner Copeland, who left us November 2013 – far too soon! You will forever be in my memories and my heart always. I pray you will eternally rest in peace.

"We love and miss you so much Peanut"

Abner Copeland
1964-2013

CONTENTS

PROLOGUE

PEOPLE MAY SAY "The Adventures of Buff, Gray & Chocolate" is a series of books intended only for children or certain young adult age groups, or that it should be in this genre or that genre just from looking at the cover or reading its metadata. But truth be told, "The Adventures of Buff, Gray & Chocolate" is a series of books that will complement many different genres, to say the least. It was written as a series of books for entertaining the entire family.

While there is truth in fiction, let it also be in "The Adventures of Buff, Gray, & Chocolate." Our story begins in the early American West pioneer era with famous, colorful events and inspired by people who led the way; people like Wyatt Earp, Johnny Ringo, the Daltons, Bat Masterson, Belle Star. And we mustn't leave out Wild Bill Hickok, John Wesley Hardin, Jesse James nor Pat Garrett and Billy the Kid. But for us that is where the truth ends, and our fiction begins, through stories and allusion told by animals of all breeds. "The Adventures of Buff, Gray & Chocolate" bring to you a wonderful fiction of truth in this colorful canine western, honoring famous characters such as Marshal Matt Dillon, Bret and Bart Maverick, Paladin, Victoria Barkley, Ben Cartwright, Cheyenne Bodie, the Rifleman and a host of other delightful characters.

We ask readers of all ages to please sit back and get to know some of our colorful and delightful fictional cast of characters like, The Red Basset Gang, The Morgan family, Sheriff Jack Russell, Warden of Canine Territorial Prison, Marshal Logan of Pittsville, The Middleton Detectives, Dollar Five, and the whole Nokota Territory. Let the Logan brothers, Buff, Gray, and Chocolate Logan, and a star filled cast of animals, influenced by animal breeds from around the world, take you on a journey through the Old West, beginning with, "The Adventures of Buff, Gray & Chocolate; Bringing Down The House."

"Woof, Woof...Woof, Woof."

The New Settlement Territory Map

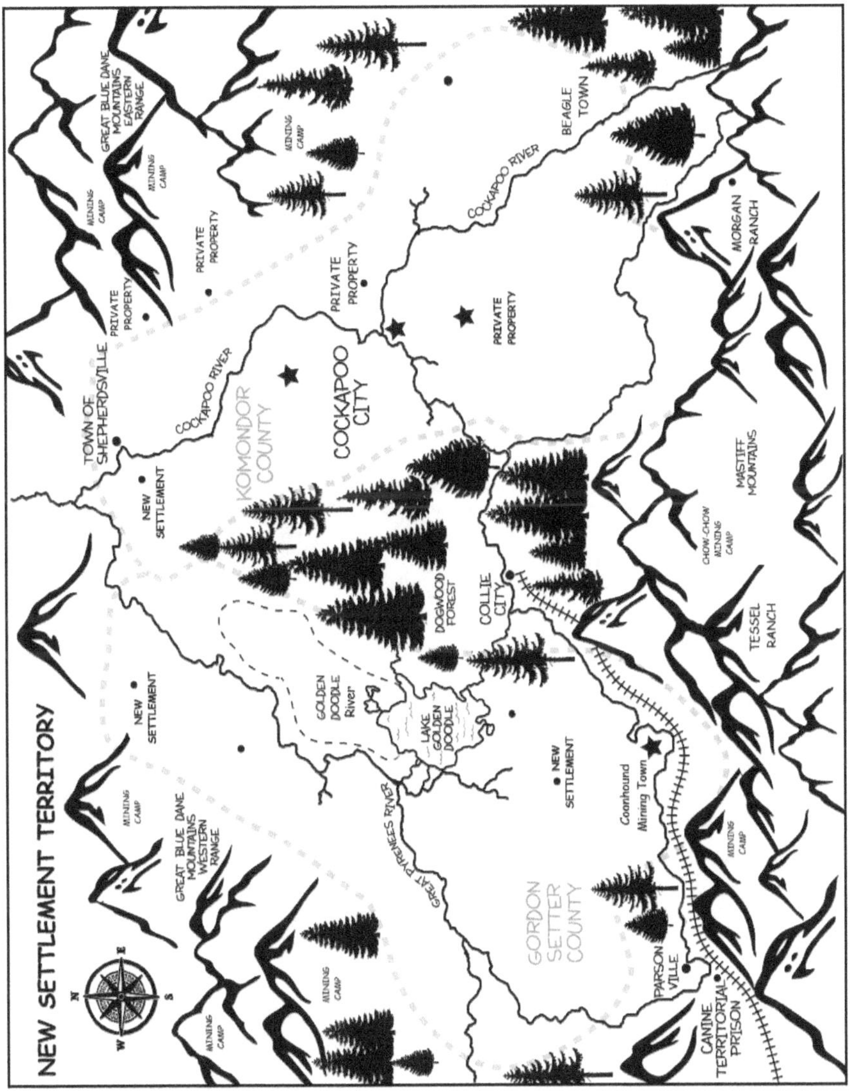

1

They Went South

MINER LAKELAND BINDER and Ben Wheaten Elam were born and raised in the Hills of the Coton De Tulear Mountains. Other than his wife, Beulah Feist Binder, and their son, Kaleb Lakeland Feist Binder, Miner Binder had no other kin. Ben was married to Mathilda Entlebucher Elam and they had a little girl named Harriet Entlebucher Wheaten Elam. Ben's only other living relative was his brother, retired wagon master Seth Wheaten Elam, and his wife, Isabel Appenzeller Elam, in Shepherdsville. Binder was a medium build bowlegged man with black and tan hair, with a dog named Spirit. Ben was also a medium build man with rust color hair, with one leg a hair shorter than the other. Both men stood a few feet above knee high and enjoyed the thrill of hunting fresh game.

Mountain life was all any of these two families ever knew. Mountain life was a rough and rugged back breaking kind of life, and a woman had to be her man's equal. Beulah and Mathilda, with no doubt, were as equal to their men as a wife could be. Beulah was once quoted as saying, "The only good thing about living in these hills is the smell of the fresh pine air." Ben and Binder were no strangers to good, honest, hard work—if you considered moonshining to be good, honest, hard work. But next to hunting game these two ol' mountain goats acquired fame and money to provide for their families by being known as the best moonshiners in the hills of the Coton De Tulear Mountains.

Ben's and Binder's lives were shattered by a yellow fever outbreak that swept through the Coton De Tulear Mountains like a cyclone. With the nearest doctor being in the town of Shih Tzu, five miles away, the fever took Ben's wife and his little girl, and took Binder's wife, too, leaving his young son Kaleb without his Ma. Ben and Binder became two lonely and hollow men.

After living on the edge of barely living, Ben and Binder decided to prospect for Gold. But in order to do that it meant leaving the Coton De Tulear Mountains, the only home they'd ever known, and head South to a little mining settlement called Chow-Chow over in Komondor County Ben had heard talk of. Ben said, "You know, Binder, I hear tell down there prospectors was gettin' rich. Why, Binder, between the two of us we could dig up enough gold to make our mules walk bowlegged. Yep, Binder, it's Chow-Chow Town for us, or bust," Ben told Binder with a laugh.

Ben was right, too. There was much gold being discovered in Komondor County and Gordon Setter County, too. In fact, folks were flocking west in search of that solid, yellow rock called gold.

"But, Ben, what we gonna do with Kaleb?" Binder asked.

"Why, Binder, you can leave Kaleb with my brother in Shepherdsville. Him and Isabel would be happy to look after the little rascal, and with some luck we just might be able to join up with a wagon train heading to Chow-Chow," Ben replied.

"That's a right good idee, Ben, right good," Binder agreed.

So, Binder left his four-year-old son, Kaleb, behind with Ben's brother, retired wagon master Major Seth Elam, and his wife Isabel. Binder said, "Kaleb, yer Pa gotta be leavin' you for a spell, so you gonna go stay with uncle Seth and aunt Isabel. And Kaleb, I don't know how long I be gone, but I'ma promisin' you I'll get someone to write some letters for me to send you. And be a good boy now, Ok, son?"

"Okay, Pa. Now, you promised," young Kaleb replied.

So, Ben and Binder started packing up everything they had left in the world that meant something to them and started out for Shepherdsville, with Kaleb in tow. After a few days of eating Isabel's cooking, Ben and Binder started feeling alive again. Seth said to Ben, "You know, Ben, I did some checkin' around town the other day and found out that a friend of mine, a Major Porter, is coming through town in the morning with a wagon train heading south, and if you two old goats get into town tonight, You can join that wagon train in the morning. But Ben, yer gonna need a wagon and some food," Seth told his brother.

"Well, Seth, me and ol' Binder here got some money for a grubstake, but we ain't got any for gear," Ben told his brother.

"I figured on that Ben, and that was my second reason for going to town the other day. I want you and Binder to take this here money, and when you get to town go to the livery stable. I've got a good friend, Sam, who came out here with me a long time ago, and he'll have a wagon for you and Binder. And if you strike it rich, then you can pay me back. And if you don't, then no matter. Same goes for you, too, Binder. And don't worry about Kaleb, we'll take care of him as if he was our very own. It should only take a week or so for you to reach Chow-Chow," Seth told the two wanna-be prospectors.

"And here's enough food to get you through," Isabel offered.

Ben and Binder thanked them both. They said goodbye to little Kaleb, and off to town they went to hook-up with Major Porter's wagon train. After sleeping the night in a hotel bed, Ben and Binder heard the wagon train as it pulled into Shepherdsville early that morning. Ben and Binder checked out of the hotel and went to see Major Porter.

"Major Porter, Major Porter," Ben called out. Walking up to Major Porter Ben said, "Major Porter, my name's Ben Elam, Seth's brother. And this is my good friend, Miner Binder. We want to join your wagon train, that is, if'n your heading south to Chow-Chow Town."

"You say your brother's name be Seth, retired wagon master?" Major Porter asked.

"Yep, I sure do, and he told me you was coming through here this morning," Ben replied.

"Well, Ben, you and yer sidekick fall in line behind my wagon. And this is my sidekick, Nauseous. Say hi to Ben and Binder, Nauseous," Major Porter said.

"How yah fellas doin'?" Nauseous asked Ben and Binder.

"Doin' just fine now, Nauseous, now that we found this wagon train," Ben and Binder replied.

"Say, Nauseous, can I ask you a question?' Binder said to Nauseous.

"Sure, Binder," Nauseous replied.

"How'd you get a lead name like that?" Binder asked.

"It's like this, Binder," Nauseous replied. "Leeroy is my handle, but folks call me Nauseous cuz I have a sensitive stomach."

"I see," Binder responded with a chuckle.

Ben and Binder were happy as two ol' goats could be, and thanks to Seth and Isabel they had some beans, some meat, coffee, and a good grubstake, and were on their way. Having a retired wagon master for a brother gave Ben the edge, so he handled the team of horses. Sitting in the seat with Ben, Binder was just grinning from ear to ear. Binder said, "You know, Ben, maybe we should have had Kaleb with us."

"I think you did the right thing, Binder, because if something happened to me or you, there would be no one to take care of the little one," Ben told Binder.

"Yeah, I think you're right, there," Binder agreed.

Nauseous rode up beside their wagon and asked, "Say, how you boys making out?"

"Doing just fine. But Nauseous, how long will it take the wagon train to get to Chow-Chow mining town?" Ben asked.

"Well, Ben, it's a pretty far piece. Oh, it looks close on the map alright, but it ain't so. But we'll be there before you can blink an eye. We'll make some stops along the trail to rest us and the horses and get in some hunting. They got plenty of good game on the prairie," Nauseous, the trusted scout, replied.

After several weeks of travel, Ben and Binder heard Major Porter calling out, "Circle the wagons, circle the wagons."

It wasn't one of Major Porter's biggest trains, but it was big enough—fifteen wagons in all. When they stopped, Binder was glad to be off that wagon.

"Binder, I'll get the bed rolls and you get wood for a fire, and get some beans and bacon going. I could eat a bear," Ben said.

"Ya know, Ben, we owe Seth and Isabel a lot. We got to do somethin' nice for them when we get all that gold. They done right by us, all this food. We got us a good grubstake, Ben," Binder said with a smile.

Ben replied, "Yeah, we'll get them somethin' real nice like. We'll get Isabel somethin' real soft and pretty."

Major Porter rode up to their wagon and said, "You know, Ben, Nauseous is taking some of the men out to do a little hunting for some meat and I thought one of you might like to go with them."

"I'll go, Ben, be good to get away and stretch my legs for a while," Binder replied.

"That's a good idee. If you go, Binder, I know for sure we'll have some fresh meat for supper. And, Binder, if'n you don't catch no meat, you can just keep on riding," Ben said, laughing as Binder rode off with Nauseous.

As he watched them ride off, Major Porter said, "You know, Ben, the west is filling up right quick. Folks are coming from everywhere and there's plenty of new towns springin' up. I hear tell in Komondor County folks are getting along right good. Some folks had some really big gold strikes, Ben. You and Binder can do the same, then buy a patch of land and farm it. Why, folks is buying up land out on the open range left and right, and starting to build ranches, and big ones, too. We'll be heading south and passing through a town called Cockapoo City. It's not that big yet, but it's the biggest one around so far. So, if anybody wanna send a letter or wire, Cockapoo's the place. And it's the best place to register your claim. Too many crooks in Chow-Chow Town. They got a stage line, too."

"Well, I sure pray Binder and me can make our strike," Ben replied.

Ben and the Major sat there talking the whole time the hunting party was gone. Before long Nauseous rode back into camp with the men and everyone was toting meat. Binder, Nauseous, and two other men shot bucks, and the rest of them shot rabbits and squirrels.

"See, Major, I knew I sent the right man. Is that what I think it is, Binder?" Ben asked.

"Sure, is, Ben," Binder replied.

Soon the smell of meat cooking began to fill the air. Some folks made beef, rabbit or squirrel stew but Ben roasted deer over an open fire while Binder, Major Porter and Nauseous waited impatiently to eat. Once their bellies were filled it was clean up time and off to bed. Just like every morning from the time they'd left Shepherdsville, Major Porter was up at the crack of dawn saying, "Rise and shine folks, it's time to get packing. We're moving out. Come nightfall we should be pulling into Chow-Chow Town."

After what seemed like a year to some folks, they were finally coming to the end of their journey. Once they were all packed and ready to go, Major Porter said real loud like, "Wagon's Roll," as he raised his right paw high above his head, pointing straight ahead and the wagon train pulled out. It wasn't too much further to go, and in just a little over an hour the Major and Nauseous were pulling the train into a clearing just outside of Chow-Chow. Major Porter gathered the folks on his train together in a circle once again, only this time it was to give them his last piece of advice.

Once all the folks were together Major Porter said, "Now I know many of you bought land out here before coming, so my advice to you is check in with the land office and locate your property. And folks like my friends, Ben and Binder, here, whose main reason for coming was to prospect for gold, should just set up camp some place and start searching for a claim to stake. And let me just say that it's been a pleasure taking your money and having you on my train. Good luck to all of you nice folks. I hope you all live long and get fat and rich."

As they started looking around, Ben said to Binder, "There ain't too much to look at Binder, but I see they got a Big Top Saloon, the Assayer's office, General Store, Barber Shop and bath. What do you want to do first?"

"Well, like the Major said, let's find us a place that looks lucky and start digging for our fortune," Binder replied jokingly.

After a short time of searching around the Mastiff Mountains, Ben and Binder each found a place that looked lucky to them and staked it out, each with their own mark. Day after day they would blast and dig, blast and dig, working their tails off looking for that shiny yellow rock.

"Ben, when we gonna register our claims?" Binder asked.

"We gotta find some gold first, Binder, before we register our claims with the assayer office, and make it legal like. Seth told me that once," Ben replied.

Finally, all those days of blasting and digging paid off. Binder and Ben both struck gold. Remembering Major Porter's suggestion, Ben took Binder to Cockapoo City where they registered their claims. Ben wrote Binder's first and only letter to Kaleb for him, and with the letter they mailed Binder's registered claim papers. What Binder didn't know then, was that he had registered one of the richest strikes in Komondor County.

When they arrived back in Chow-Chow they ran into Major Porter and Nauseous and took them to the Big Top Saloon for a nice tall glass of broth to celebrate their good news. The Major said, "Me and Nauseous are real happy for you fellas, and don't go letting folks know your business. We'll be pulling out come morning, so you fellas take care."

Ben woke up one bright sunny morning to the smell of bacon, biscuits and gravy. The smell filled the whole settlement. He looked around for Binder, but Binder was up early and gone to work his claim. He had just lit the last charge of dynamite he'd set and high-tailed it out of the mine. When the dust from the blast had settled, Binder went back into the mine to discover he'd hit the mother-load. Binder started to do a little jig right there in his mine. He loaded up a small pouch with a few gold nuggets and headed over to Ben's claim. When Binder arrived, he called out, "Ben, Ben, where ya at, Ben?" but Ben was still at the settlement.

Binder turned his horse, Pearl, around and headed toward the Settlement. He rode into the settlement yelling, "I'm rich, I'm rich," as loud as he could. He got off his horse and walked into the Big Top Saloon, owned by Bobcat. With one paw raised high in the air, waving one of the biggest gold nuggets anyone had ever seen, Binder walked up to the bar and the bartender, Jonesy, said "Well, now, Binder, what'll it be?"

"Well, Jonesy, let's see," Binder said as he placed the gold nugget in Jonesy's paw and asked, "You think this here nugget will buy a round of drinks for the house?"

"You know, Binder, this nugget I'm holding will buy quite a few rounds," Jonesy jokingly replied.

"Then set 'em up, Jonesy," Binder said.

Jonesy got a bottle and held it up high and said, "Listen up, men, Binder just bought drinks for the house, so step on up to the bar."

Jonesy had taken a liking to Ben and Binder, and he leaned over the bar and quietly said to Binder, "I'd be careful showing off all that gold around here, Binder. Some people around here can't be trusted."

Indeed, Binder was the center of attention. He took a seat in the back corner of the saloon, poured himself another drink and pulled his pouch out. Ben walked in and saw Binder sitting in the corner and walked over and said, "Mind if I have a seat, Binder?"

Binder looked up and said, "Hey, Ben, sure, pull up a chair. I went by your diggin's, Ben, but you weren't there."

Ben took a seat next to his old friend. Ben covered the bag of gold nuggets with his paw and said, "You know, Binder, you shouldn't be sitting here showing all your gold like this. Someone might get some bad ideas."

"You know, Ben, Jonesy just said the same thing. But nobody wants to hurt ol' Binder. Everybody loves Miner Binder," He replied.

"I didn't say someone wanted to hurt you, just that they might get an idee on taking your gold, Binder, that's all," Ben told his longtime friend.

Binder looked over at Ben and said, "You know, Ben, I better be gittin' some food in me. Broth for breakfast don't work too good."

Ben stood up with Binder and said, "Ok, Binder, let me walk with you."

"Oh, Ben, stop your mothering. I'll be just fine. I just need some grub, ok?" Binder replied.

"Ok, Binder," Ben said. "I'll check on you later. I'll just walk out with you."

As he left the Big Top Saloon with Binder, Ben headed out toward his own claim. He worked for several hours digging and blasting. When he finally looked at his pocket watch, it was way past noon. Ben thought it was time to see about Binder since he'd had so much broth. When Ben arrived at their camp Binder wasn't there. Ben looked around and asked if anyone had seen Binder, but no one had seen him since morning. Night began to fall and still no Binder. At that moment, Ben suddenly knew he might not ever see his good friend again, and he was right.

The weeks began to go by, and no one had seen or heard from Binder, and Ben couldn't stop blaming himself. He felt that if he had followed along with Binder that morning, maybe Binder would still be around. Ben knew in his heart Binder had met with foul play, even though some folks believed Binder sold his claim and left Chow-Chow.

Ben knew that it was time for him to head back to Shepherdsville and tell Binder's son, Kaleb, the sad news about his Pa being killed, and then head back to the Coton De Tulear Mountains a richer man. On his way out of Chow-Chow Ben rode through Cockapoo City, and he saw a man sitting outside the Bobcat Saloon playing a guitar. He couldn't tell right off who it was but when he got close-up, he could see it was Jonesy. Ben stopped for a minute to listen as Jonesy sang these words to a song:

Miner Binder: My Dear Ol' Friend

Miner Binder was a dear ol' Soul,
He came to Chow-Chow Town lookin' for Gold.
He named his claim the Kaleb mine,
Miner Binder was a friend of mine.

> Does anybody know how the story goes?
> Does anybody know if he had any kin?
> Whatever happened to his pot of Gold?
> Miner Binder was a dear ol' Soul.

When Jonesy finished singing his song, Ben asked, "Jonesy, where did you get that song you're playing on that there guitar?"

"I made it up, Ben," Jonesy replied.

"May I ask why you made up a song like that? It's so sad," Ben asked.

"Ya know, Ben, before meetin' you and Binder I got drunk one night in the Big Top Saloon, when I wasn't tending the bar. I was playing some poker and I got taken. I was gonna go home and get my pistol, then come back and kill that no-good cheating dealer Hollister Bobcat Cobb hired. But I didn't, I just let it go. Well, that day when Binder came into the Big Top with his pouch filled with gold, I told him what happened to me that night and not to talk about his strike so much. And you know what he did? He gave me one of the biggest gold nuggets that day I'd ever seen, and it was worth eight thousand dollars. And now, just like that, he disappears," Jonesy said.

"Yes, he was a good friend, wasn't he?" Ben replied as he rode out of the mining town, singing the Miner Binder song with tears in his eyes.

"Hey, Ben, wait a minute. Tell me something. Binder never did tell me why he called it the Kaleb mine?" Jonesy asked.

"Kaleb was his son," Ben replied.

Miner Binder

Nokota Territorial Map

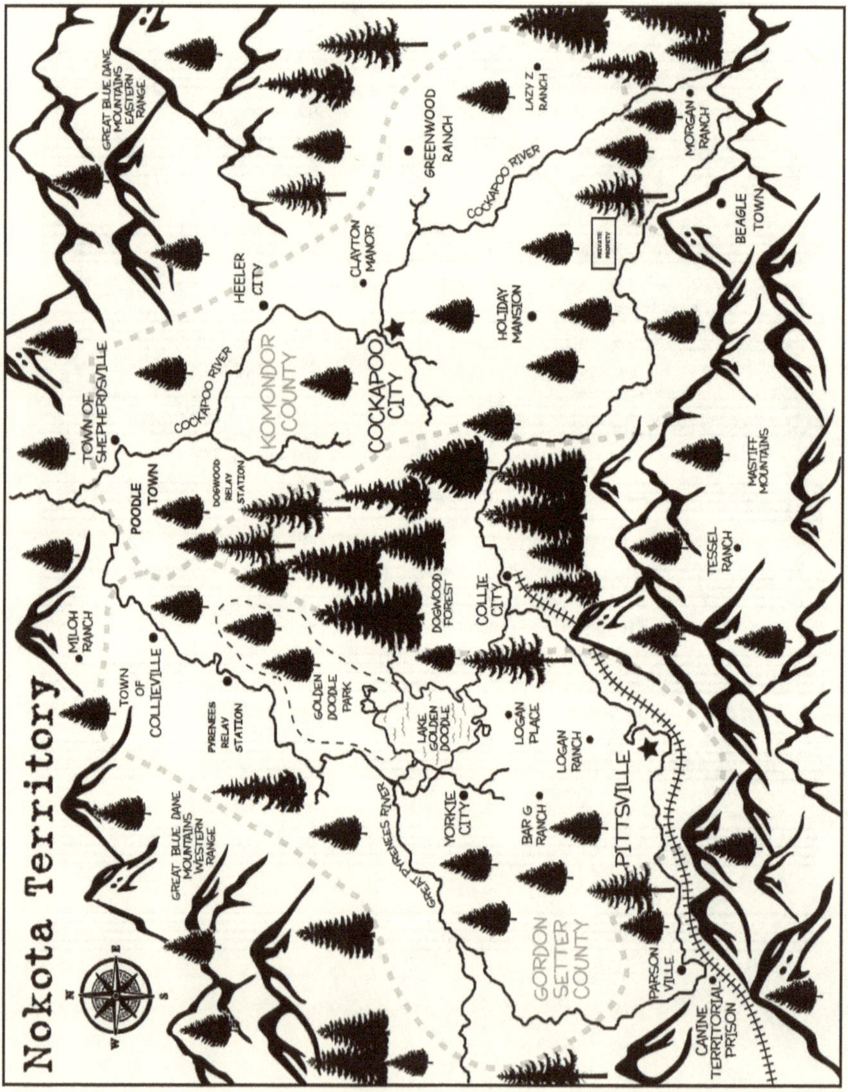

How Pittsville Got Its Name

WHEN NEWS OF a gold strike hit the papers in the East, folks came pouring into Gordon Setter County. Some came by horseback, some came by stagecoach, while others travelled in covered wagons. Folks came from all parts of the Nokota Territory to search for Gold in Gordon Setter County, even doctors and lawyers, and they were needed out west. It was just as Major Porter told it to Ben and Binder, who were with his last train to Komondor County. Folk's came with dollar signs in their eyes, high hopes, big dreams, and big ideas. The west was just right for folks looking to raise new families and set up new homesteads while trying to make a go of the land. Some of it was good land, while some of it wouldn't even grow weeds.

In the East folks were buying up Dime novels and reading all about the big gold rush out West in Gordon Setter County. But when news began to gather steam throughout the territory that a miner on Major Porter's last wagon train to Komondor County had met with foul play a few years back, folks began to fear for their lives, too. And when Major Porter and Nauseous learned that the man was their dear friend Binder, they were two heartbroken men. This wasn't the first time Major Porter had heard of something like this happening in a mining town, but this time it was Binder, and he was a good friend of theirs.

This journey for Major Porter was different than the others. It took several months on the trail for them to reach Gordon Setter County, and the months seemed to go by so much slower than before for Major Porter and his sidekick, Nauseous. Finally, the two men could see Coonhound mining town, and it was their last stop. Major Porter settled on some land he'd bought on his first trip to Gordon Setter County, and Nauseous stayed around the mining town searching for gold. He only made one strike, but it was enough for him to buy some land and build a little ranch on it.

With all the new folks that came on the wagon train the settlement began to grow. And since there wasn't any law to speak of, and no Major Porter, many folks felt alone and afraid and feared that the outlaws they'd read about in the dime novels would surely stage an attack on the settlement. Some folks paired up to protect what was theirs. Charlie Potts and Russell Logan were among the men that came on the wagon train with Major Porter. They also seemed to be two strong men who knew how to handle themselves as well as their pistols. So, the folks got together and approached Charlie Potts and Russell Logan and asked them to lead the new settlement. The two men accepted the request without having a second thought.

Someone spoke up and said, "Well, now that we have agreed on two good leaders, I suggest we change the town's name, too. I don't much favor the name Coonhound Town"

Just then a dog came running up to Russell Logan, and Russell said, "Down, boy, down." Russell thought for a minute to himself and he asked, "Whose dog is this anyway?"

"It's my dog, sir," said a little boy as he came running up to where Mr. Logan was standing to get his dog. "He's a good dog, too, sir, he won't bite. He just looks tough, that's all."

"And what is your name little boy?' Mr. Logan asked.

"My name is Peanut, sir," the boy replied.

"Well, tell me, Peanut, what kind of dog do you have there?" Mr. Logan asked the lad.

"He's a Pitt-Bull, sir," Peanut answered. "He's a tough dog, but he has a gentle soul, sir."

"Thank you, Peanut," Mr. Logan said. "I, Russell Logan, right here and now, claim that this settlement known as Coonhound Town, shall from now on be called the town of Pittsville."

"And I second it," Charlie Potts added.

Little Peanut started jumping up and down. Having a town named after his dog was cool indeed. As time went by the two men began forming a town council to help bring law and order and set up rules for the town to follow. Folks didn't waste any time. They started panning for gold and registering claims and right before their eyes, Pittsville had started to look like, and become, a good size town. Folks who made out better than some had started to build saloons, hotels, and eating diners. There was even a barber shop with a tub for those who favored baths.

It seemed like overnight there were new proprietors popping up. Those who struck it rich started to build big beautiful ranches all along the Pyrenees River. Folks were working the land, growing crops, raising cattle and fighting outlaws just to keep what was theirs. Some folks worked their tails off just to make ends meet.

As time went by Pittsville was on its way to becoming a wide-open town. The town was located southeast of the Great Blue Dane Mountains and southwest of the Grand Mastiff Mountains along the Pyrenees River, which ran throughout Gordon Setter County and right into the Cockapoo River. The view of the Great Blue Dane Mountains and the Grand Mastiff Mountains from the town of Pittsville was breathtaking.

You could see where the sky meets the tops of the tall, pointed Redwoods, Dogwoods, and Maple trees. The landscaping all along the Pyrenees River was magnificent with rows and rows of glorious evergreens, magnolias, and cedar trees. There were stunning lakes, running streams and creeks within each county. Some of the bigger cattle ranches even had large lakes on their property. Pittsville had the most wonderful view of the sunset anyone would ever want to see.

Like all the rest, Charlie Potts wasted little time and began digging for gold. He was from the purebred family called Poodle. Charlie was big and strong with shiny black hair. He was known for his many talents, but what he was known for best, was panning for gold. Charlie Potts found gold everywhere he sniffed. One day Russ said, "Hey, Charlie, haven't you sniffed out enough gold? Look at your nose. It's all dried up"

"My nose is just fine," Charlie replied cheerfully. "And when I'm finished sniffing around, that Prairie ain't gonna have a single gold nugget left for sniffing." The two men just stood there laughing.

Charlie had met and courted Marian Gates. They fell in love and were soon married. Marian's family was also purebred Poodle, only from the Miniature side, and she was gorgeous. She had beautiful curly black and white hair. In her youth, Marian was a former Beauty Queen, having won the title, Miss Pittsville, three years in a row.

Marian knew what it took to be a lady. She loved long walks in the morning just before breakfast. She felt it was a nice way to start her day. Marian loved remembering those days when she was a Beauty Queen, how young and beautiful she was then. But Marian was as beautiful today as she was years ago.

Marian and Charlie didn't know that Marian was with child when they started with the wagon train. But Marian soon gave birth to a little girl and named her Annie Potts. She was all Poodle. Annie had black and white hair just like her Ma. As the months went by Marian and Charlie watched their little girl grow a little each day. Annie was an amazing little girl. She had so many questions, Marian knew deep in her heart that if Annie took more after her than Charlie, that one day Annie might just want to see and travel the world.

Marian wanted Annie to be what Annie wanted to be, but Marian didn't want Annie to have the kind of life that she'd had. Although it wasn't a bad life, it was a demanding one. Soon Marian opened her own little dressmaker shop. It was the first and only one in Pittsville, and for miles around. She made dresses, blouses, pants and under garments for some of the richest ladies in town.

Many of the ladies who shopped there had once been beauty queens themselves, ladies like the Afghan-hounds. Now they loved sporting many colorful styles of hair and dresses which complimented their tall, statuesque figures Then there was the Standard Poodle, another beauty queen and a former contestant that had competed against Marian but lost. These ladies were also known for their stylish hair, favoring the colors black, white and tan. They were born to be on stage with bright lights and big-time music. They were smart and obedient with an adventurous spirt. It's no surprise they had won so many titles.

And let us not forget the sophisticated ladies; English Cocker Spaniels also were clients of Marian's. One of them had competed as a contestant against Marian for the crown, but also lost. These ladies, known for their social activities, moved rather quickly on their short legs. Many of them loved sporting stylish reddish hair, while others sported tan, silky and wavy hair. Whatever the color, black, white, red, or tan, or style, these beautiful ladies had one thing in common - their taste for new, fresh, colorful and quality clothing. And that's why these ladies came from all over the territory to shop at Marian's Dress Shop. Marian made her own clothes, so she always had something new and exciting for the ladies to buy.

Over the years as Annie grew up, she began to show an interest in her Ma's business. One-day Annie asked, "Ma, today's Saturday. May I come to work with you?"

This was a wonderful surprise for Marian because up until now Annie had shown no interest in her Ma's dressmaking business. Instead, she seemed to enjoy playing with dolls and baking with her best friend, Sophia.

Marian replied. "Of course, darling, and I believe today is payday, too!"

Annie was happy to hear this news. The first thing on Annie's mind was a bag of treats. But then she thought, and asked, "Ma, how can today be payday? This will be my first day."

Laughing quietly to herself, Marian replied, "Oh, honey, didn't I tell you? We pay a whole dollar in advance."

An excited little Annie could hardly contain herself. She said, "Oh boy, Ma! A whole dollar! Thank you, Ma, I believe I'm going to like working with you in the dress shop!" Annie's reply warmed Marian's heart.

"Nothing would make me happier, darling, than having you working beside me. You'll learn so much. One day when you grow up and marry, you might be making clothes for your little ones, too," Marian told her little girl.

"I love you, Ma," Annie said.

Charlie and Marian loved their little girl more than anything in the world, and the older Annie got, the prettier she became. Annie had the boys knocking down the door asking her Pa if they could call on Annie. Charlie knew most of those "no-goods," as he referred to those who came a-calling and wasn't about to allow Annie to throw her life away on any of them. There was one young man, however, that Charlie did like, and Annie did, too.

His name was Roy Logan. He was truly a gentleman with good manners. He would always say "Good evening" to Marian and Charlie and he always called them "sir" and "ma'am." Roy would often sit and talk with Charlie because, like most girls, Annie usually wasn't ready on time.

Charlie Potts knew Roy came from a good pair of genes. Roy was purebred Cocker Spaniel, just like his Ma and Pa. He had medium length wavy, silky, tan and cream hair. He was soft-spoken and cheerful most of the time and loved long evening walks. Roy was one of the most popular young men in all of Pittsville.

While Roy waited for Annie, he would tell Charlie all about the marshal business and how he wanted to be a good provider, just like his Pa. Roy loved everything about his Pa except one thing - his Marshal's badge.

One evening Charlie said to Roy, "Son, even though you have no interest in being a Lawman like your Pa, don't be in such a hurry to grow up. Take your time growing up, time flies when you reach your Pa's and my age, and there's always something you wished you had done."

"Yes, sir, Mr. Potts, I hear you," Roy replied.

Roy's Pa, Russell Logan, was voted to be the first town Marshal of Pittsville. Having quick paws made him perfect for the job. He'd struck it rich with his best friend, Charlie Potts, when Pittsville was just a boomtown. Russ had a nice big ranch and plenty of cowhands to work it, so he had time to keep peace in Pittsville. He had tan wavy hair, a nice muscular build, and good strong legs, which he needed when it came to chasing outlaws. Russ was an easygoing kind of guy, cheerful most of the time, and it took a lot to get Marshal Logan's dander up.

Roy's Ma, Sarah Logan, owned the only ladies hat shop in Pittsville. It was called Sarah's Bonnets. Sarah was also a former Miss Pittsville contestant, having won the crown once. Sarah only entered the contest to make her Ma happy and once was enough for Sarah. She realized early on how demanding a life it was and she wanted no part of it. Sarah had silky, cream-color wavy hair, and a gorgeous petite figure. Russ knew from the very beginning that Sarah was the one he would marry. One of the many things Russ loved about Sarah was the way she waggled her tail when she was on the move. He knew she loved his black wavy hair as much as he loved her wiggle. Russ and Roy visited the barber monthly for a haircut and trimmed paws. Russ could not allow his paws to go untrimmed because it might slow down his draw. Even though Roy wasn't much interested in being a lawman, having quick paws was the way of the West. Russ told Roy a long time ago, "Son, the faster your draw, the longer you live. It's just the way things are right now. "

Pittsville thought a lot of Marshal Logan. They thought he was one smart lawman and were glad he decided to wear the badge.

Logan's ranch was a beautiful place. Russ had it built from the ground up just for Sarah, as Charlie did for Marian, and as Roy would one day do for Annie. It was just down the road from Charlie's ranch, the Bar G, and G was for Gold. Russ Logan, being a soft-spoken man, was neat as well as organized and a true provider. He liked things peaceful at home, as well as in town.

Sarah would often say to Russ, "Russ, your bark is worse than your bite."

Russ's reply would often be, "Sarah, I think you're right."

Roy took after his Pa and rightly so; he was soft spoken, neat and well received by everyone in Pittsville. Russ would often say to Roy, "Son, respect isn't something that's given, it's something that is earned. Always remember that."

Russ and Sarah wanted the best for Roy, and they raised him well. Roy knew all about farming, cattle, and everything there was to know about running a big ranch. Roy was schooled from home and, like his Pa, Roy loved learning new things. But they differed in other ways. Unlike his Pa, who favored hunting, Roy favored reading. In fact, he loved reading Dime novels. They told true stories about the different Lawmen throughout the Wild West, like the one about Marshal Lance Colby.

Now Colby was one tough cookie. He kept peace in Cockapoo City, one of the roughest little towns south of the Mastiff Mountains. Then there were the novels about the Russell brothers, Jack I and Jack II, who were the first two Wardens at the Legendary Canine Territorial Prison. Jack III and Jack IV were the present Wardens, and those Russell boys were the real deal.

The prison was given the lead name Legendary, because the Dime novels told how it was the final resting place to some of the most famous and notorious outlaws who ever lived, like Frank and Jessie Terrier, and the heartless and despicable Al-Capone Hound from the hound family. They were all hanged and buried at Canine, just to name a few.

Canine Prison was located southeast of Pittsville, smack dead center in the hills of the Great Mastiff Mountains, overlooking the Pyrenees River. There was one long dusty road leading up to the Legendary Territorial Prison that was known for its escape proof record.

The one-man-cell prison was three stories tall, shaped like a square with five outlook towers, and all windows facing the courtyard. Each prisoner had a spectacular view of the gallows. The gallows platform where the prisoner stood with the rope around his neck waiting to be hanged had a trap door. The door lead to an eight-foot drop that would stretch anyone's neck. Each prison cell was six feet by eight feet and made of brick with an iron door containing a four inch by five-inch peep hole. Each prisoner was allowed one wash bucket, wash towels, and a bar of soap, along with three meals a day.

Unfortunately, one thing about the Dime novels Roy didn't care for was the fact that they printed true stories that painted a picture of outlaws who wanted to rule the West, and some did for a while. The Dime novels often told stories of the Nate Beagle, Havana Brown, and the Kitty Kat Gangs, three of the oldest established gangs in the West. They were hard to bring down and they were still giving the Middleton detectives a nightmare. Other old established gangs were the Red Basset and the Bloodhound gangs. There were many of them.

The Dime novel Roy treasured most was about his Pa. It was one of the most popular ones they ever printed. It told the real true story of Pittsville's Marshal Logan, who really gave the fast draw the new name "quick paws." Yes, sir, Pittsville was a right peaceful town, until that cold rainy night revengeful Gus Morgan came trotting into town.

Wanted: Outlaw Asa Morgan

SARAH ANN MORGAN was the school marm in Pittsville and she was a right friendly soul. She was from a long generation of English Spaniels. She was soft spoken, medium height, nicely figured with light brown wavy hair. She lived on a farm a few miles from town. Sarah Ann walked to school often, stopping to smell and taste the honeysuckles along the dusty road.

What the town folks didn't know about Sarah Ann was that she was the wife of the famous farmer turned outlaw, Asa Morgan. Asa wasn't an outlaw when Sarah Ann married him. He was a pig farmer with a few chickens and a milk cow. Asa gave his all trying to be a farmer, only it just wasn't in his heart to be one. He tried his best to get enough money together to buy some cattle, but one bad crop season after another had Asa looking for an easier, softer way.

Sarah Ann and Asa had a little girl named Sophia. Sad, but true, Sophia wasn't their natural child; she was an orphan. Sophia lost her parents on a wagon train coming west. They'd been shot and killed, so she was now living at the orphanage. One-day Sarah Ann saw Sophia walking down Main Street. The clothes Sophia had on were like rags, tattered and dirty. Sarah Ann took Sophia in and raised the little girl as her own.

Sarah Ann and Asa also had a little boy. His name was Gus Morgan, and he was their natural child. As the years went by Sophia was growing into a sweet little girl, but Gus, on the other hand, was turning out to be more like his Pa every day, cold, rude, and disrespectful. All the makings of an outlaw.

Asa, becoming fed up with farming, decided to try his luck at driving cattle for some local ranchers. At least that was the story he gave Sarah Ann. However, Sarah Ann's womanly instinct told her otherwise, and she was right. What Asa was really doing was rustling cattle from local ranchers with the Red Basset gang. When Asa finally told Sarah Ann the truth, she knew right then and there she couldn't go on living this lie, nor being the wife of an outlaw with a price on his head. Afraid of leaving Asa, Sarah Ann waited because she knew the time would come.

Asa left to rustle some cattle one day with the Basset gang and he never returned. This turned out to be a blessing in disguise for Sarah Ann. Asa Morgan was now on his own and had become one of the most wanted outlaws in the Nokota Territory. Asa held up banks, stages and even the passengers on the stage. Asa had indeed become a greedy man. He'd only shot one man in his life. It was the day he held up the stage from Yorkie City. The stage was carrying a strong box with ten thousand dollars in it, and a guard riding point for protection.

Asa rode out of a green pack of trees with his pistols drawn and firing into the air. He was wearing a red and white bandana over his face and a brown cowboy hat pulled down over his face. As the stagecoach came over the hill, the guard saw Asa coming out of a brush of trees. He took a shot and missed ol' Asa. Asa fired back at the guard, and he didn't miss, knocking the guard off the stagecoach and onto the dusty road. Judging from the amount of fudge the guard was covered with from Asa's pistol, there was no way he could have survived. Asa wasn't carrying his usual thirty-eight pistols with 10-point fudge pellets. He was carrying the deadly forty-eight with 15-point, which only lawmen and Government detectives like the Middleton's could carry. Somehow the Basset gang had gotten their paws on them. The forty-eight was given the nickname broken paws, because one shot in any paw could possibly render a cowboy's paws useless.

The people in the town of Pittsville liked things real peaceful like, and so did Marshal Logan. From time to time Marshal Logan had trouble with outlaws trying to make a run on Pittsville, but Marshal Logan's reputation preceded him, claiming to have one of the fastest and most intimidating draws any outlaw had ever seen. He could pull that forty-five and have it in your face before most pistol toting cowboys had their paws on theirs. In fact, most men didn't dare to take the big marshal on.

The stage-coach from Yorkie City finally pulled into Pittsville running almost 2 hours late with Pete, the stage driver, yelling, "Hey, Marshal! Hey, Marshal Logan." Leaving a cloud of dust behind it, the people and the Marshal knew something was up. Marshal Logan ran out of his office putting his hat on his head as he walked out the door and running over to the stagecoach.

The driver said, "Marshal, I quit! I quit! This is the third time we've been held up, and just five miles outside of Pittsville this time!"

"Same as always, Pete. Let's get a posse and go after them. But first, are you alright?" Marshal Logan asked.

"Yes, I'm fine, Marshal," Pete replied. "What tears it up is that Asa Morgan shot and killed Sam Marshal, the best riding guard and friend I ever had."

"Pete, me and the town are right powerful sorry about Sam, and we'll talk about you quitting later. Right now, we need to get Sam off the stage and to the undertaker." Marshal Logan called for some men to get Sam up off the stage. Then he turned back and asked, "Pete, you did say Asa Morgan, right?"

"Yes, Marshal, it was him. Asa Morgan seen me dead to rights, too." Pete replied.

When Marshal Logan got his posse together, he turned to the men and said. "Now I want all the men with wives and young ones to head on home and take care of your families. It's not your fight." But no one moved.

Marshal Logan repeated, "Go on home, I tell you. Now I mean it. I know how you feel, but Asa Morgan is a dead shot, and he don't miss much. Now I'm going to be right sorry if one of you family men stop one of his pellets. Now I ain't saying it again. Go on home."

Soon all the men with families turned their horses and headed for home leaving Marshal Logan with ten men, more than enough to chase down a gang of outlaws. However, Marshal Logan, like many others, had no idea the Red Basset gang had hooked up with the Bloodhound gang. Red Bassett and Cyrus Bloodhound, the leaders of their gangs, knew that together their gangs would be so big they could pull off three holdups at the same time in different parts of the territory. They also knew this would offer a great problem for lawmen all over.

Just as Marshal Logan was about to untie his horse and get his posse ready to ride, he looked over his shoulder and saw Sarah Ann Morgan walking along Front Street with Gus and Sophia, when she suddenly stopped. Marshal Logan stood beside his horse just watching them, he then saw Sarah Ann as she stopped again, only this time it looked like she was talking to someone, and she was. It was Asa. He was calling out to her from the alley. Sarah Ann turned to Asa with fear in her eyes.

"Leave us alone, Asa, please, just leave us alone," She told him.

Asa replied, "I'm sorry, sugar, but ol' Asa needs your help, and I see you have the two little ones with you. Now this is even better than ol' Asa could have ever dreamed."

"Asa, if you ever loved us, please, just leave us alone. Just go away," Sarah Ann replied to her outlaw husband.

Real soft like Asa said to Sarah Ann, "Fat chance of that happening, sweetheart. Now get over here and bring them young'uns with you. Now, Sarah Ann, or so help me I'll drop you and them young'uns right where you stand. I've got nothing to lose, now, baby."

Sarah Ann walked slowly into the alley, Marshal Logan was still watching it all, but Asa had no way of knowing that. Asa pulled Sarah Ann, Sophia, and Gus into the alley between

Marian's Dress Shop and Sarah's Bonnets and said, "Now, look, all four of us are gonna walk home real slow like, and Sarah Ann, if you so much as open your mouth, these little ones are gonna be needing a new Ma. You got that?" Asa told her.

With tears rolling down her face and the two little ones also crying, Sarah Ann knew she had no choice. So, she did the only thing she could do, and replied, "I understand, Asa. The Children and I won't give you any trouble, just please don't hurt us."

"Now why would I do anything to hurt you, Sarah Ann?" Asa asked. "You're my wife and those little ones and you are going to be my ticket out of this no good for nothin' town." What Asa didn't know was that his luck had just run out.

Marshal Logan turned to the posse and said, "Wait a minute boy's, somethin' up in that ally up the street. I'm not sure, but I believe it's Asa Morgan." Walking slowly out into the middle of Front Street, Marshal Logan yelled out loud and clean, "Asa Morgan, is that you in that alley between that hat shop and dress shop?"

Laughing back at Marshal Logan ol' Asa replied, "Yes, sir, Logan. It be me, good ol' Asa Morgan."

"Come on out, Asa, and drop those pistols," Marshall Logan commanded.

"I don't think so, Logan, at least not today," Asa yelled back. "Hey, Logan, before you start shootin' at me you better listen to me."

Marshal Logan replied, "Oh, yeah, Asa? And what is it you want me to know?"

"I'm not alone, Logan," Asa yelled.

With the barrel of his forty-eight, Marshal Logan pushed the brim of his hat back and said. "I know that, Asa. I saw you have Sarah Ann and the kids in there with you. Sarah Ann," the Marshal called out, "Are you and the kids alright?"

Sarah Ann yelled back all tearful like, "Yes, Marshal Logan, we're okay."

"Good," Marshal Logan replied. "Now, Asa, we can do this my way or yours, but hear me now Asa. If we do this your way, you might not live to see tomorrow."

Asa slowly came out on to Front Street from between the two buildings with both thirty-eights drawn, with Sarah Ann, Sophia, and Gus leading him, taking pot shots at Marshal Logan all the way. Asa said. "We all got to go sometime, Logan."

Marshal Logan dropped to his knees and fired both pistols hitting Asa in the leg. Asa fell backward leaving himself wide open. Marshal Logan shot again, dropping Asa Morgan right on Front Street. As he put his pistols back in their holsters, he walked over to Asa, where his son, Gus, knelt by his side with tears in his eyes.

Marshal Logan asked, "Why'd you make me do it, Asa, why?"

Asa said, "I tried, Marshal, I really did, but I just wasn't cut out to be no dirt farmer," then closed his eyes and died.

Gus Morgan looked up at the big Lawman and said. "Long as I live Marshal, I will never forgive you for shooting down my Pa like a dog, and right in the middle of Front Street."

Marshal Logan said, "Remember, son, yer Pa was an outlaw and drew paws first. Now go on home with yer Ma and let us take care of yer Pa."

From that day on, Marshal Logan felt bad about shooting Asa Morgan. Everyone in town knew it was a fair fight and didn't blame Marshal Logan for doing what they paid him to do. Marshal Logan tried his best to help Gus turn his life around. He took Gus fishing with him and Roy as often as they would go. Marshal Logan did everything humanly possible to keep Gus from becoming like his Pa, but Gus Morgan was too much to handle, even for the big lawman.

Marshal Logan even gave Gus his own Marshal badge, which made Roy a little jealous, so he had to give one to Roy, too. As the years went by Gus Morgan got older and a lot meaner. Gus could never see past that sunny day when his Pa fell to his death in the middle of Front Street in Pittsville. From that moment on Gus Morgan had a Pellet in his thirty-eight meant for Marshal Logan.

It wasn't long after that Gus left home. No one in Pittsville, not even Sarah Ann, ever saw him again. As time passed, Marshal Logan received several wanted posters for Gus Morgan. Marshal Logan knew all about Gus Morgan and what he was up to all those years. It was his job. Somehow, though, the Middletons and Marshal Logan had lost track of Gus.

On one cold and rainy night, in fact it was one of the coldest nights Pittsville had ever seen, Marshal Logan was just about to start making his rounds when the rain began to pour down. It was good in a way because it hadn't rained for some time in Pittsville. Even with all the rain, Marshal Logan still had to make his rounds, like he did every night, making sure all the merchants locked their doors. He never forgot to check Sarah's Bonnets, Marian's Dress Shop, and the Bank.

As Marshal Logan walked out of his office to start his rounds, he looked up into the dark sky. With the rain falling on his face, it reminded him how much he and Sarah loved to snuggle up to their marble stone fireplace with a bottle of red wine. He was also thinking of Roy and Annie because they were to be married very soon.

He remembered it was right after that incident, having to shoot Asa, when the Pittsville Bank was held up by the Red Basset gang. The gang had been robbing and stealing West of the Cockapoo River and East of the Pyrenees River near Poodle Town and Collie City, but somehow, they had now made their way south to Pittsville.

Suddenly the rain began to pour even harder. Marshal Logan saw a rider trotting slowly into town. As the man on the horse got closer the Marshal could see that the man trotting into town was Gus Morgan. He'd wondered what happened to Gus Morgan, and there he was, trotting toward him.

As Gus rode by, Marshal Logan looked at him and threw up a paw to say hi, but Gus just rode past the Marshal with a dazed look on his face, as if he were in another world. Suddenly Marshal Logan heard a pistol being cocked, he turned and looked behind him and saw that Gus Morgan had his pistol drawn.

Marshal Logan dropped face down on muddy Front Street, rolling over on his stomach with both paws drawn, aiming his forty-eight at Gus Morgan, shooting him right off his horse. Gus fell in the mud right on Front Street, just like his Pa had fallen that sunny day.

After the smoke cleared, Marshal Logan slowly walked over to Gus with one pistol in his paw, just in case Gus still had some fight left in him. The closer Marshal Logan got the better he could see Gus lying there hardly moving. Gus had been shot three time in the stomach from the amount of fudge from the pellets of Marshal Logan's pistols. The Marshal knew there wasn't any chance left for Gus.

Walking over towards Gus the Marshal reached down and picked up Gus's pistol. He heard Gus say softly, as he breathed heavily in and out, "I never did like you Logan, and I will never forgive you for killing my Pa. And my sons will never forgive you for killing me. You'll remember us Morgan's for the rest of your life, because for every son your sons have, there will never be any rest for us Morgan's until they're all dead. That's a promise from Gus Morgan." Morgan then closed his eyes as he took his last breath.

Marshal Logan looked at Gus and said, "Rest in peace, Gus."

4

A Killer's Final Threat

JUST AS THE rain began to clear up, the town folks began opening their doors to see Marshal Logan on his knees in the middle of Front Street with Gus Morgan's head resting in his arms. Those cold and heartless last words from Gus Morgan sent a cold chill all through Marshal Logan as he thought to himself, if it weren't for his quick paws, it could have easily been him lying there dead on Front Street instead of Gus Morgan.

As he called out for help to get Gus' body off Front Street and to the undertaker, Marshal Logan remembered how much he had tried to help Gus Morgan. Marshal Logan knew this was how it would always end for Gus. There was just too much Asa, the outlaw, in him to turn Gus around. But knowing all this Marshal Logan still felt that there should have been something he could have done or said to get through to Gus.

Once he had Gus taken care of Marshal Logan knew there was nothing more he could do, so he started heading for home. His heart was filled with grief and in some way, he still couldn't believe that what had just happened on Front Street, really had happened. Killing Gus was too much for him. He knew that all this came with the territory. He had looked upon Gus not so much as a son, but more than an outlaw. He had felt a sense of closeness to him, which made this even harder for him to accept. Marshal Logan only wanted to help Gus, but instead he was forced to take his life. Now with death on his paws Marshal Logan knew it was time to take off the badge.

Marshal Logan always enjoyed the ride to and from his ranch. He loved its scenery and it made him feel good inside, but this time he didn't even notice. Finally making it home he didn't even notice Roy and Annie sitting on the porch and rode right past them.

Roy was down on one knee and holding Annie's paws tightly in his. Looking up at her Roy said, "Annie, will you marry me?"

With tears of love in her eyes Annie said, "Yes, yes, Roy Logan, I will be your wife." Roy took Annie in his arms as they kissed passionately. Roy and Annie ran into the house to tell his Ma.

When they told Sarah their good news, Sarah said, "Well, it's about time."

Marshal Logan rode into the barn, took the saddle off his horse and put it in its stall. He slowly made his way to the house. When he walked in Roy turned and said, "Pa, Annie said yes. She said yes, Pa."

"Yes?" he asked.

"Pa, Me and Annie are getting married, that is, if her Pa approves of it," Roy replied laughingly.

"Russ, Russ, did you hear what Roy just said?" Sarah asked her husband.

"I'm sorry, son, I'm sorry, Annie. I'm sure Charlie will approve, son." Russ replied.

Sarah said, "Russ, what's wrong honey? I know some-things wrong."

"Sarah, darling, it'll keep. It'll keep. Son, would you bring your ol' Pa a good strong glass of Broth, please?" Russ asked Roy.

Knowing that something was heavy on her husband's mind Sarah said to Roy, "Honey, I have a wonderful idea. Why don't you take Annie home and have a talk with Charlie and Marian and get their blessing?"

Roy didn't waste any time getting to the Bar G. When they arrived, Roy helped Annie down from the buggy and they both ran into the house. Charlie was sleeping in his favorite chair and Marian was just cleaning up the kitchen. Annie rushed over to her Pa and said, shaking her Pa on his shoulder, "Pa, Pa, wake up, Pa."

Charlie slowly opened his eyes and said, "Oh, Annie, your home. Roy, you've never had Annie out this late before, is everything ok?"

"Well, Mr. Potts, I do need to be getting home soon my Pa seemed to be pretty upset about something when he got home. But Annie and I have something we want to ask the two of you," Roy replied.

"Marian, you'd better get in here. Something's up," Charlie said to his wife

Marian walked into the parlor and said, "Ok, honey. I'm here, dear, now what is this all about?"

"I don't know, ask Roy and Annie," Charlie replied.

"Mr. Potts, sir," Roy said, "I've asked Annie to marry me and we've come here to ask for your blessing."

Charlie just sat there looking at Roy. Then Marian said, "Roy, you and Annie have our blessing. Now when do we start planning for it? There's been enough time wasted already."

"Well, Mr. Potts?" Roy looked at him and asked.

"You heard my wife. What more is there for me to say, son?" Charlie said laughingly to Roy.

They had a toast of sparkling broth to celebrate this long-awaited occasion. When Charlie made his toast to Annie and Roy he said, "Roy, you been calling on Annie for nearly two years now and I was beginning to think you would never get around to asking her to marry you. I'm so glad I was wrong, son. Welcome to the family, Roy."

After the toast Roy again said he needed to get home. As Charlie walked him to the door, he asked Roy, "So, Roy how's your Pa? I heard from one of my ranch hands that was in town tonight that your Pa shot and killed Gus Morgan on Front Street. I haven't said anything to Marian yet. I thought it would be better if I had a talk with your Pa first."

"Oh, no," Roy replied. "For real, Mr. Potts?"

"Now, son, my ranch hands wouldn't joke about somethin' like that." Charlie answered.

"Mr. Potts, will you please tell Annie that I love her? I better be gettin' on home right quick and see about my Pa. I know he's taking this pretty hard," Roy said to Charlie.

"Yes, son, I know. You go on home now. Annie will understand, you know she will," Charlie said to Roy.

Roy turned that buggy around and within a few minutes he was riding up to his stable. He unhitched the horses and put them in their stalls. When he walked in the house, he saw his Ma sitting on the sofa with her arms around his grieving Pa. Roy didn't enter the room, he just stood outside it not wanting to interrupt his Pa. Russ was sitting in a chair just shaking his head, he said to Sarah, "You know, Sarah, it started off just like any other cold and rainy night. I was sitting behind my desk looking over some wanted posters when I looked at my pocket watch. I could see it was time to make the last round before heading home, so I put on my hat and duster, locked up and left the office."

"I headed down Front Street like always," he continued, "but as I looked up, there was a man riding towards me real slow like. It looked to be Gus Morgan, but I couldn't tell right off, so I threw up a paw to say hey as he rode by me. And thank God I was still close enough to hear his pistol click. Sarah, I turned just in time to shoot him before he shot me, and right in the same spot where I shot and killed his Pa. Sarah, if it were not for my quick paws, that could have been me lying dead in the middle of Front Street tonight, instead Gus."

"Oh, Russ, honey I'm so sorry. Honey, I know just how much you thought of Gus and the high hopes you had for that young man, but Russ you can't do this to yourself. That young man turned bad all on his own," Sarah replied, trying to help Russ make sense out of all this.

Roy finally went into the parlor and asked, "Pa, I know what happened in town tonight, are you ok?"

"No, son, no, I'm not okay," Russ answered as he walked over and stood in front of the looking glass. As he stood there looking at his reflection, he removed the badge from his shirt and laid it on the table below the mirror. He said to Sarah, "Honey, I'm done. Pittsville will just have to find a new Marshal."

"Pa, can I get you another glass of Broth?" Roy asked.

Russ turned to his son and said, "Yes, son, another glass of Broth would be nice, thank you. And make it stronger than the last one."

"Sure thing, Pa, coming right up," Roy replied.

"Roy, son, how did you hear about what happened in town tonight?" Russ asked his son.

"Well, Pa, I been standing out there in the hall for some time now and I heard you telling Ma. I didn't want to just come in and interrupt, so I waited. But while I was at Annie's, Mr. Potts told me one of his ranch hands was in town tonight and heard about it. Knowing how you felt about Gus and everything you tried to do for him, I knew you'd be upset, so I came home as fast as I could, Pa." Roy gave his Pa a big hug after telling him what Charlie had told him.

"Son, I'm so sorry for snapping at you the way I did earlier," Russ said.

"Pa, I know you were just upset," Roy replied.

"So, you and you're Ma are okay with me turning in my badge, then, right?" Russ asked

"It couldn't be soon enough for me, Pa," Roy replied.

"I second that, Roy," Sarah said with a look of relief.

"Then, when I go before that committee to give them my report, I'll also give them my badge. Now, what's for supper, honey? I'm starved," Russ asked Sarah.

"Come on, ex-lawman, let me get you something to eat. How about you, Roy?" Sarah asked her two handsome men.

"No, thanks Ma, I'm floating on a cloud, right now," Roy replied.

Russ asked, "So, Roy, what did ol' Charlie have to say?"

"Pa, he made a toast to me and Annie with a glass of sparkling Broth, and Mr. Potts knows I don't take to drinking," Roy told his Pa.

"Well, Roy, I hope you didn't disappoint Charlie?" Russ asked his son.

"No, Pa, me and Annie both had one toast, and then I left."

"Oh, my, I better go and see Marian tomorrow. We have a wedding to start planning for." Sarah was pleased, about Roy's and Annie news.

But Russ didn't tell Sarah or Roy quite everything. In fact, it was the first-time he could ever remember keeping anything from Sarah. But he felt that a threat from a killer was better left unsaid, at least for now. The next morning when Marshal Logan returned to his office, he found the town committee members waiting.

As the Marshal walked in he said, "Good morning, gentle-men. Up 'till now I'd forgotten about you." The men all laughed. Marshal Logan sat down in his black leather chair, behind his big brown oak desk.

He said, "I guess ol' Gus must have been drunk on Chicken Broth last night, and it gave him courage to come into town with a Pellet with my name on it."

As Marshal Logan started to give his account for last night, he told them that he'd always wanted the best for Gus ever since he shot Gus' Pa, Asa, in the same spot he'd shot Gus there on Front Street. The Marshal didn't have any answers for them. He just couldn't believe, until now, that anyone could carry around that much hate in them for so many years. He explained to his good friend, Charlie Potts, and the rest of the committee members how he saw a man trotting into town, not knowing that it was Gus.

Marshal Logan said, "It wasn't until the man rode right up to me - then, and only then, could I see clear, and I still wasn't sure it was Gus Morgan." Marshal Logan told the committee to the best of his knowledge, no one had seen or heard from Gus in years. The Marshal said that he knew Gus was wanted by the Middleton Detectives. He showed them the reports he'd gotten from the Middleton detectives which told the story of Gus Morgan's life.

Gus was from the Schnauzer family and he was a giant. He took after his Pa, Asa. He even had coal black hair with distinctive eyebrows and beard, just like his Pa. He was bold, aggressive and drank all the time after his Pa died. He took to robbing and holding up a bank or two, that is, until one day he walked into the Bobcat saloon in Cockapoo City.

Gus met Floleen, a saloon girl, that day. She was ten years younger than Gus, who was forty-eight. Floleen was from the English Sheep family from up north, and that was all she ever told about herself. She took the job in the Bobcat saloon because it came with room and board, but truth be told, Floleen hated saloon work, and she hated Hollister Bobcat Cobb even more. She found out things about Bobcat that went way back, thing's that could get her killed, so she knew it was time to move on. She was getting right tired of smiling at every cowpoke that walked in the saloon anyway. When she walked past Gus sitting alone, he offered to buy her a drink. When she got a look at his roll of money, Floleen knew in that moment Gus was her ticket out of that rat hole, and she took it.

She only married Gus for his money, love had nothing to do with it. Gus managed to buy a small farm with the money he got from robbing banks and holding up stage coaches before he met her. Floleen didn't care so long as she was out of the Bobcat. She gave Gus four boys during the time they were together. The oldest was named Pace, then Lace, Bo, and Billy Bob, and they all favored old Gus. Each one was tall with a muscular build, long black hair with thick eyebrows, just like their Pa. However, Bo and Billy Bob had a little English Sheep mixed in from Floleen, and they had black and white hair. Maybe that's why they didn't turn out like their brothers, Pace and Lace.

After years of living with Gus, Pace and Lace were getting more like their Pa, meaner and meaner every day. Floleen knew she had to make a move soon or Bo and Billy Bob were going to end up just like the rest, and she wasn't about to allow that to happen. Floleen knew she couldn't make right the big mistake she'd made in marrying Gus, not to mention having four kids by him, but she knew she didn't have to stay in the mess of a marriage the two of them had made.

Gus woke up one morning and Floleen was gone. She took Bo and Billy Bob with her and she never looked back. Floleen knew that one day Johnny law would come to arrest Gus and those no good for nothing boys, Pace and Lace. Pace even attacked her one night, and stupid Gus, worried about other men, couldn't see, or didn't want to see, what his own son had done.

Floleen knew no one had known where she was from, and more than anything, she was glad she'd never told anybody. So, she took her two youngest sons back to her home in Heeler City near the Great Blue Dane Mountains. You could get lost in those mountains, and that's just what Floleen did.

Now that the council had all the facts about the Morgans, or at least Gus Morgan, Marshal Logan gave them the news right there about his decision. Looking to the future, he told them that they needed more than his badge. What they should think about was looking for someone younger with quick paws and hiring two or three wouldn't hurt. Or at least someone good with a pistol.

He left his badge on the big brown oak desk. He turned to the council and said, "If I were any one of you, I'd get me a Middleton man." Then he walked out of the Marshal's office leaving it all behind and looking forward to the biggest wedding the town of Pittsville had ever seen.

Marshal Logan knew it wasn't over, and somehow, he had to tell Roy and protect him at the same time. This wasn't an easy thing to do with Roy building his new home. Russ figured the best way to help Roy was to teach him quick paws, and with all this free time now, he could work with Roy on the house and with his draw at the same time.

Russ knew that having a good friend like Jonah Middleton, founder of the Middleton's Detective Agency, was a plus because it would help him to know the whereabouts of the Morgan brothers. And Jonah would be a big help in getting a new Marshal for the town. So, it would be a win-win situation for all involved.

However, even with the information Jonah could provide, Russ Logan still wasn't convinced it would keep Roy out of harm's way. Russ knew that his son would have to meet his fate one way or the other. He only hoped that it would be face-to-face and not in the back, the way Gus Morgan tried to shoot Russ down that cold rainy night on Front Street.

The concern for Roy's safety reached the ranch hands as well. The men told Russ they knew that very soon now, Roy would need to hire new ranch hands to help run Logan's Place, and they planned to be right there alongside him, looking out for him when that time came. It's a lonely place to be when your paws are tied and there's nothing you can do to help the ones you love, and Russ Logan was the loneliest man in Pittsville right now.

It seemed like yesterday to Russ Logan, but it had been months since he turned in his Marshal badge. Up until now the only person Russ Logan knew he could trust to tell about Gus Morgan's threat was his good friend Charlie Potts. And one day while out at the Bar G Ranch, Russ told Charlie Potts what Gus said to him before he died. Charlie knew all along that there was more to all this, only he just didn't know until now. Right then and there the two men both agreed that, considering the affect this news would have on Sarah and Marian, that it would be best not to say anything about this to either them, for the moment. Charlie said to Russ, while sitting in Charlie's backyard, "Russ, you know, I never did like anything about that family."

"You never told me that before," Russ replied.

"Don't you remember all the trouble we started having after Asa and his family joined the wagon train?"

"I remember some, but that was a long time ago, Charlie," Russ replied.

"Not to me. It seemed like every time something went missing, one of them Morgan's was somewhere close by," Charlie reminded Russ.

"Now, I remember, Charlie," Russ replied, "but that don't make a whole family guilty, now, does it?"

"It does in my book; the apple don't fall far from the tree, you know," Charlie turned to Russ and said.

"You know Charlie, Asa was just like all the rest of us when we arrived out west, with nothing but what we came with. That is, until some of us struck it rich," Russ replied.

"And that's another thing I never told you. You know that Asa tried to jump my claim once. Man, I almost shot that fool.

If he had worked hard like the rest of us, he would have made out alright. But no, he had to drink up what little money they had. You know Russ, I really believe Asa had something to do with the disappearance of Miner Binder, although no one could ever prove it."

Russ said, "You know, Charlie, being reminded of all this, I think we need to talk with the new Marshal of Pittsville."

"Now you're talking, Russ," Charlie answered.

So, Bright and early the next morning the two rode into town to see the new Marshal. His name was Nauseous. Charlie and Russ both remembered him as Major Porter's scout on the wagon train they'd come out west with. When they walked into the Marshal's office, Nauseous said. "Well, now, if 'n it ain't Mr. Potts and Mr. Logan. Howdy, men. You know I heard you was the first lawman this town had, and a pretty darn good one, too, I hear told."

Charlie said, "I'd second that."

"Well sit down, take a load off. Now, what can I do for ya?" Marshal Nauseous asked.

Russ started to tell the Marshal all about the cold, rainy night and the threat from Gus Morgan. This was no surprise to Nauseous because he knew who was behind all the trouble he and the major had had on that wagon train. As Charlie said, it was the Morgan's, Asa and his son, Gus, stealing anything that wasn't nailed down, only they could never catch them at it. The Marshal told Russ that the first thing he should do is tell his son, Roy, and prepare him for what may lie ahead. He also told him that it was okay, for now, to leave the wives out, that nothing would be gained right now by upsetting them. But he said that they would need to know at some point, but he should tell Roy soon, before he runs into someone he least expects. And Nauseous told Russ that he would be on the lookout for any strangers in town.

# 5

He Rode A Sorrel Mustang

RUSS KNEW THAT Charlie and Nauseous were both right and that he really needed to tell Roy, only Russ just didn't know how. One evening Russ was sitting in the parlor smoking a cigar gazing out the window. Roy walked over and knelt beside his Pa and asked, "Pa, is everything ok? You've changed since the shooting." Roy could not remember ever seeing his Pa this way.

Russ turned his head and looked right into his son's eyes, tears rolling down his cheeks. For the first time in his life, the once big lawman cried on his son's shoulders as he said, "No, son, everything's not okay."

Russ told Roy they needed to talk, so the two men went outside and took a long walk. Russ began to tell his son the load he had been carrying all this time. Roy just shook his head in disbelief. He asked, "Pa, why didn't you tell me this a long time ago?"

"Son, all I could think about that night was how I was going to protect you," Russ answered.

"But, Pa, you've been holding this inside all this time, worried about me all by yourself?" Roy asked.

"I wasn't alone, son. Charlie knows, too. I just want you to be careful, Roy, that's all."

"Pa, Annie, and I will be careful, very careful, but we're going to live our lives as we planned," Roy replied. "Now, Pa, I want you to stop worrying, okay? Now promise me, Pa."

"Okay Roy, I promise. But one thing, promise me you'll keep practicing your quick paws," Russ told his son.

"Okay, Pa, if you want me to. Now listen, Pa, the ranch will be finished in about a week. Why don't you come ride out in the morning and bring Charlie with you and see the place?"

The next morning Russ and Charlie rode out to see the new Ranch. Roy had a big wooden sign above the entrance on the property that said, Logan Place. Roy was at the ranch that morning just as the sun came up, just him and a few ranch hands from his Pa's ranch. They had fallen a little behind schedule in completing the ranch because of all the practicing his Pa had him doing, but the men were almost done. It was finally coming together. Roy built the ranch right on the edge of Golden Doodle Pond just for Annie. It ran right into the Lake at Golden Doodle Park, where they were to be married. He and Annie fished at the Pond often.

Logan Place was a beautiful two-story grey house with white trimming, a wrap-around porch, and sash windows with white painted shutters that could be closed and locked from the inside. Four tall white columns stood on each end of the house, with a white and grey wood railing that ran between each column, and an entrance way to the porch on all four sides. There was a big brown plank door with a gold metal knocker in the center. When you walked through the doorway there was a beautiful crystal chandelier hanging over the entrance, and right in the center was a wide, white and brown stairway leading to seven big and beautiful bedrooms, with two full baths on the first floor and three full baths on the second floor. Not many folks were as fortunate.

There was a dining room to the left with walls covered in Burgundy and gold striped wallpaper, a beautiful hand carved wooden fireplace and mantel with a polished finish. Roy had made it just for Annie, which was sure to take her breath away. There was a long oak table and chairs that could easily seat twelve. There was a large sitting room to the right of the stairway with blue and white striped wallpaper. There were colorful throw rugs over most of the polished wood floors throughout the house. Near the stairway there were coat racks, hat hooks, and a boot rack. There was a rather long hallway behind the stairway leading to the kitchen, a wash room, and a parlor. Logan Place was something to see. The landscape on Logan Place had large, tall willow and oak trees, with a white picket fence running all along the property.

As Roy was coming out of the barn he glanced over his left shoulder. Out of the corner of his eye he could see a lone rider trotting up to his ranch. As the man got closer Roy could see clearly that it wasn't anyone he had seen before. The ranch hands also saw the man as he continued to trot his horse up to Logan Place. Roy thought to himself, what a beautiful horse the lone rider was riding. Horses were Roy's other passion, next to Dime novels.

Roy knew everything there was to know about horses. His Pa raised horses and cattle when they first came to Pittsville before the town council asked him to be the new marshal. Roy knew the horse the lone rider was riding was a Mustang, and very close in color to his reddish-brown Chestnut Quarter-Horse. Roy could see the Mustang was a dark and reddish Sorrel color with a lighter, reddish mane and tail, but still close in color to his Chestnut Quarter-horse. The only difference between the two was the white markings on Roy's horse's four legs.

As he rode up to Roy, the rider said, "Good morning, my name's Chad, Chad Shepherd."

"Nice to meet you, Chad, I'm Roy Logan," Roy responded. Rubbing the horse along its face Roy looked up at Chad and said, "That's a magnificent Sorrel Mustang you have there, Chad Shepherd. Why don't you climb down off it and give it a rest?"

Chad noticed right off that Roy loved horses just as much as he did. Chad stood tall for a shepherd, a little taller than Roy; he had black hair and wore a brown duster and brown cowboy hat with a nice brim that easily blocked the sun.

"I'm going to wash up and have a bite to eat. Care to join me, Chad?" Roy asked him.

Chad replied, "I could stand a little food right about now."

Roy looked the tall man over. He thought to himself that the man calling himself Chad didn't look like a killer, and he seemed to be dressed rather well for the prairie.

Roy said, "So, Chad, what're ya doin' out this way, I mean, are you just passing through? This isn't a place you just stumble across, ya know."

Chad looked at Roy and laughed a little, then said, "You have a lot of questions. Can't a man just be taking a ride? After all, it is a nice day."

Roy wasn't afraid of this tall stranger calling himself Chad, but he was a might curious, so Roy said to the tall stranger, "Well, Chad, this is my soon-to-be ranch. I'm getting married in a few months and I'm just about finished building this house for my soon-to-be wife, Annie."

"Well, I'm sure she'll love it," Chad said.

Roy went on to say, "We're not done, yet. Still have the bunkhouse to build and the smoke-house, and right there near Golden Doodle Pond, a little gazebo."

Roy told Chad that he planned to bring her here for their honeymoon. He told Chad how Annie didn't want anything big for their honeymoon, and how he planned to blindfold Annie, then drive her out here to Logan Place. He said he hired some folks from town that Annie didn't know to be servants for about a week or so, then when she's ready to pack and leave, he'll surprise her and tell her she's already home. Chad thought this would really make her happy.

Roy told Chad to pick a soft spot of grass while he fetched the big lunch Annie had made him. Chad took off his duster and laid flat on his back on the grass with his paws behind his head. Roy came back with a big picnic basket. "Let's eat, Chad."

Chad had his nose moving around in the air sniffing and he said to Roy, "Is that apple pie you got in there?"

Roy smiled as he said, "Your favorite, too, I see."

"You bet," Chad said rubbing his paws together and licking his lips. Looking at Roy, Chad said, "Man, I'm glad I follow the golden rules,"

Roy asked, "The golden rules, what's that Chad?"

"Well, the first one is, always follow your first mind; you can just about bet you'll be right every time," Chad replied, laughing so hard.

The two men talked for hours while getting acquainted and filling their bellies at the same time. Chad asked, "Roy, did you name your horse?"

"Yes, her name is Nugget," Roy replied. "Did you name yours?"

"I did, and her name is Lady," Chad answered.

Roy questioned Chad about himself. Chad told Roy he'd been on his own since he was fifteen and that he never knew his Ma or Pa. He told Roy he ran away from an orphanage. He got tired of the food, so he set out on his own travelling across the prairie, taking jobs here and there. He told Roy that the prairie was no place to be alone without a big canteen of water and a horse, and he'd had neither. Chad told Roy he was near dead when Warhaw stumbled on him.

"Who's Warhaw, Chad?" asked Roy.

Chad answered, "Warhaw was a ranch hand for Mr. Miloh, of Miloh ranch, a big spread north of here, up near Collieville. Mr. Miloh took and raised me. I set out on my own about 4 months ago. Mr. Miloh told me I could come back anytime I want. He done me a good turn; taught me how to ride, hunt, shoot and I had some schooling. He was like a Pa to me, I guess. Lady is my first horse."

Chad told Roy that Mr. Miloh raised horses, and cattle. He bought and sold mostly Morgan horses and Quarter horses.

"Now here I am, sitting here with you, eating some apple pie," Chad said.

Roy looked at Chad and asked, "You afraid of work, Chad?"

Chad looked at Roy and they laughed. He said, "No, Roy, I'm not afraid of work, but I'm not looking for work, either. I never could seem to stay in one place for long, Roy."

Roy looked at Chad and simply said, "This might be it, Chad." Roy explained to Chad that he wouldn't be chasing down Mustangs out on the open range for a living, but he'd be breaking in new bucks occasionally, and since he knows the prairie so well, he could help in planning the cattle drives.

Chad said, "It's a nice place, Roy, but how ya know we gonna get along?"

Roy said to Chad, "My Pa and I don't see eye to eye all the time now. You're a horse man like me, and I'll bet on a horse man every time."

Chad said, "Okay, Roy, let's give her a try."

As Roy looked over his shoulders, he noticed his Pa and Charlie walking towards them. As they approached, Roy said, "So, you two finally made it."

"Yeah, ol' Charlie and I took our time enjoying the view," Russ replied, then asked. "Who's this young fellow, Roy?"

"Pa, meet my new foremen, Chad Shepherd," Roy announced.

Russ said, trying to be as calm as he could, "Nice to meet you, Chad Shepherd,"

"Nice to meet you too, Mr. Logan, and just call me Chad, sir," he replied.

Russ asked Charlie to show Chad around the ranch while he had a talk with Roy. When Charlie and Chad were out of earshot, Russ began to question Roy about the stranger.

Right off, Roy said, "Look, Pa, I understand your concern and I know how much you love me, but, Pa, you've got to learn how to trust again. You can't look upon every cowboy I encounter as someone out to get even with us."

Russ looked at his son and all he could say was, "I guess I need to take some lessons from you."

Roy replied, "No, Pa, you look just fine from where I'm standing."

Russ said, "You're right, son," and gave him a hug.

Over the days and weeks that were left, Russ and Charlie, along with the cowhands, worked as fast as they could to get the bunkhouse ready. Roy and Chad worked on the gazebo together, and in a short time grew to be as close as brothers. Russ and Charlie started to feel the same about Chad as Roy did. But more importantly, Chad unknowingly showed Russ how to trust again and this made Roy one happy soon-to-be groom. But for now, the night was setting in and it was getting along supper time.

The men got washed up, got on their horses and rode to Logan Ranch where Sarah, Marian and Annie were waiting. When Charlie walked in, he took one look at the three ladies and said, "Ya look hungry. Are we late?"

The women laughed, but Marian looked at Charlie and said, "Oh, sit down and eat your steak, Charlie."

Roy gave Chad a bedroom next to his. It was like it was meant to be. Chad fit right in with the Potts and Logan families. There was no question that Roy's best man would be Chad when that time came. For the first time in his life, Chad felt a part of a family, and he began to feel closer to Russ than he did to Tom Miloh. Russ knew for sure that he was his old self again and it was time for a wedding.

Having all these wonderful things happening all at once was the best thing ever for Russ, but still in the back of his mind he felt that he would feel a sight better if he just knew the whereabouts of some of the Morgans. So, Russ put in a call to his good friend, Jonah, of the Middleton's Detective Agency, and Russ learned plenty. Jonah told Russ that Pace and Lace Morgan both left home after Russ killed their Pa and joined up with a gang. Russ found out the gang's leader was, in fact, Red Basset's son, Red Jr. Red had retired and gone into hiding. Jonah also told Russ that he heard that Pace and Lace had married and were believed to have four sons between the two of them. Russ thanked his good friend for the news.

Russ knew that Roy believed, just as his Ma did, that everything in life happened for a reason. But one day when they were out at Logan Place, Roy looked at his Pa and said, "Pa, what happens if they shoot me in the back?"

Russ didn't have an answer. He just looked at Roy and shook his head. All he could think to do at that moment was what his wife Sarah said to do when things weighed heavy on one's mind. Russ began to pray and ask God to protect his only son and the Logan and Potts families.

Till Death Do Us Part

A S THE EARLY morning sun rose over the Great Blue Dane Mountains, it lit up Annie's bedroom with the most beautiful shade of orange light. Annie had been waiting for this day ever since Roy Logan came calling.

Marian knocked on Annie's door and asked, "Annie, are you awake darling?"

Annie replied, "Yes, Ma, I am. Come on in."

Marian entered the room with a big smile on her face. She walked over and sat beside Annie and said, "My little girl isn't so little anymore, is she, daughter?"

"No, Ma, she's all grown up, now. Is it time for our talk?" Annie asked.

Marian said, "Yes, honey, it's time for our little talk."

The two of them sat side by side on Annie's bed and talked about the things every girl should know from her Ma on her wedding day. "You know, Ma, I wonder if Mr. Logan is having this talk with Roy right about now?" Annie asked.

"Well, if I know Russell Logan, him and Roy may not be having their talk right now, but I promise you, they will, if they haven't already," Marian told Annie.

The Golden Doodle Park where Annie and Roy were to be married could not have looked any lovelier. With all the support from the town folk, Golden Doodle Park looked like something right out of a fairytale. Chad was up and out early that morning, making sure every chair had been painted white, and in each chair a thank you note from Annie and Roy. The gazebo where the bride and groom would stand to say their vows, and all throughout the park, even the lake, were decorated with the most beautiful red and white roses, Baby's Breath, and rose buds all over the grounds.

The park was filled with many trees—dogwoods, maples and beautiful cherry blossoms. The grounds were even filled with mouth-watering walnuts that had fallen from the two walnut trees in the park. Chad was about to leave the park and head home when he met up with Charlie. Charlie invited Chad for breakfast, not knowing if Chad knew of the death threat Gus Morgan placed on their families. But Charlie felt since Chad was a part of their families, he had the right to know.

Charlie wasn't about to let anything spoil Roy and Annie's wedding day, so while they were having breakfast, Charlie began to tell Chad about the cold rainy night. Before Charlie said anything, Chad spoke up and told him that he had heard all about the cold rainy night before leaving Mr. Miloh's ranch. While Charlie and Chad sat and had their breakfast Chad looked over Pa Potts' shoulders. He said, "Pa Potts, look behind you out the window. If I'm not mistaken, that's Pace and Lace Morgan riding into town."

Charlie turned around just as Pace and Lace Morgan were trotting into town and went into one of the saloons. "So, that's what they look like. Now what are they doing here? They couldn't possibly know about the wedding," Charlie said to Chad.

"I don't know what they're doing here, Pa Potts, but I got a story to tell you about those two wanna-be bad boys," Chad replied.

Charlie asked, "Wanna-be bad boys? Whatta ya mean, Chad?"

Chad began to tell Pa Potts how Pace and Lace both drew down on him up near a place called Heeler City in Komondor County. Chad told Charlie he worked for a man named Miloh, who had raised him.

Chad told Charlie he and Warhaw, the foreman of Miloh ranch, delivered some horses to a relay station near Heeler City. After the drive they rode to Heeler City for a bottle of Sarsaparilla, and that's when he saw the Morgan brothers. They were poking fun at Chad because he drank milk. They called him a tenderfoot. Then the barkeep whispered in one of the brother's ears.

One of the Morgan brothers stepped out and said, "I'm Pace Morgan. I hear you got quick paws."

Chad told Charlie he stood there and looked Pace in the eye and said, "Anytime you want to find out, look me up at Miloh Ranch." Then Pace backed down and walked out.

Charlie asked Chad, "Do you have quick paws, Chad?"

Chad said, "Yes, Pa Potts, I do. You see, I grew up pretty much on my own until Warhaw stumbled upon me laid out there on the prairie one hot day near dead."

Charlie asked, "So tell me how you got quick paws."

Chad explained to Pa Potts, "Warhaw used to be an outlaw who ran with the Basset gang, only he wasn't wanted. Warhaw just got tired and he took a job on the ranch. He had quick paws, and every day for an hour he would take me out and teach me everything there was to know. He even taught me about the man holding the other pistol."

Chad was one of the fastest men alive. Chad told Pa Potts not to worry about Roy, that he was keeping an eye on him, too. He told Pa Potts that the Morgans don't even know Roy.

Charlie's reply was, "Yes, but by the time they come out of that saloon they might."

Chad put his arms around Pa Potts and said, "Look, it's almost noon and we've got a wedding to go to." The two men rushed home to start getting ready.

When Charlie arrived home, Marian had an impatient look on her face for him. "Charlie Potts, you get dressed now," she said.

"Marian, on my walk I ran into Chad and I took him to breakfast and time just ran over. Getting dressed now, honey," He said.

The ranch hands on the Bar G ranch got all gussied up, got on their horses, and headed for Golden Doodle Park to get a good seat. It was just past noon and the wedding was to start at two. Even the ranch hands from Logan's Ranch were all leaving for the park.

With Charlie all dressed up now and waiting for Annie, he asked one of his hands to drive Marian in the other buggy and take the lead. Charlie looked up and saw Annie coming downstairs. He turned to Marian with a tear in his eye and said, "Marian, I don't believe you've ever made anything as lovely as Annie's gown."

Marian looked at her husband and said, "You know, Charlie, I believe you're right."

Annie had on the most beautiful white gown. The Veil was made of a see-through white cloth with a sprinkling of gold, as well as on the gown. The train was at least six feet long. Sophia was her Bride's Maid. She had on a pale blue gown, as did Marian and Sarah. Marian had made all the dresses.

So, the Potts were now off to Golden Doodle Park and the day the town of Pittsville had been waiting for was about to start. The park started filling up with ranch hands from both ranches. They had set up tables with punch bowls and glasses. The bakery made three four-layer cakes, one on each table.

The men of the wedding party were all dressed in black tuxedoes, white shirts, and black bow ties. Russ even had a smile on his face while he was standing next to Sarah. Russ saw his son trotting up to the park with Chad. They looked like they had just stepped off the cover of a dime novel.

Roy and Chad walked over to the Parson and took their places for the arrival of the bride.

Roy turned to the Parson and said, "She'll be here, Parson."

The Parson looked at Roy and said, "Mr. Logan, your bride has just arrived."

Roy turned around and saw Annie getting out of a beautiful buggy driven by two white horses, with her Pa.

Marian was escorted down the beautiful trail by one of the ranch hands. There were three flower girls and one little boy carrying the ring. He approached Chad, gave him the ring, and stood firmly next to him. Sophia then walked the trail and then Annie's music began to play.

Everyone turned and looked as Charlie led his little girl into the park with the sun shining ever so brightly, and just a little light breeze. Two little girls carried the train of Annie's wedding gown. As Charlie approached Roy, he gave him Annie's paw as she took her place beside her soon to be husband.

The park was quiet as the Parson began to read from the bible. Roy and Annie looked at each other with smiles on their faces. When the ceremony was completed, the Parson said, "Roy, you may kiss your bride." Roy lifted the veil and kissed Annie, and everyone in the park stood up and cheered as they started for the tables, laughing and talking. They all began celebrating Roy and Annie's wedding.

No one even noticed, not even Chad, that Pace and Lace Morgan were standing on the edge of Golden Doodle Park taking it all in.

It was a day to remember, with lots of the town folk square dancing in the park. Annie called all the ladies over because it was time to throw the bouquet. She turned around, closed her eyes, and threw the bouquet. Sophia caught it.

"My turn," Sophia said with a laugh.

After a few toasts to the bride and groom, Roy and Annie left the park. When Annie arrived home, she opened the door to her bedroom and saw her Ma sitting on her bed.

Marian said, "Well, you didn't think I was going to say goodbye to my little girl in front of all the guests, did you?"

"Oh, Ma, thanks so much for everything, and this lovely wedding dress. I do declare, I don't think I ever want to take it off," she said as she twirled around the room.

"Then wear it on your honeymoon if you like, dear." Marian replied to Annie.

"Oh, stop it, Ma," Annie said while she started packing for her honeymoon. Everyone except Annie knew where Roy was taking her for the week.

There was a knock at Annie's bedroom door. "Who is it?" she asked.

"It's your Pa, the one that paid for that big wedding you just had,"

"Oh, Pa, come in," Annie said.

"How's my little girl?" Charlie asked.

"Pa, if I had discovered one of your gold mines right about now, I couldn't be any happier."

Charlie told Annie, "That's just what I'm giving you and Roy for a wedding present, from your Ma and me."

Annie was lightly jumping up and down as she said to her Ma and Pa, "I declare, newlyweds, and rich ones at that, all in one lovely afternoon. What more could there possibly be?"

Just then, Annie heard Roy calling for her. "Annie May Potts Logan, you better get down here," Roy yelled. Then Marian, Charlie and Annie came downstairs. Roy said, "Oh, I'm sorry, Ma. I'm sorry, Pa Potts. I thought Annie was alone."

Roy walked in with his Ma, Pa, and Chad, and they all had a private family toast to the bride and groom, all three ladies crying. Roy said as he put down his glass, "Come along, Annie, let's go before the three of you start to cry me a river." And off they went.

When Annie arrived at Logan Place, she had no idea that she was about to walk into her new home. Roy had Chad and the ranch hands remove anything that might give their week away. They even took down the sign at the entrance to the ranch. Roy hired some of the far away kin of a few town ladies to work out the week at the ranch for him and Annie. He had someone to do the cooking, the cleaning, the washing, and they were even served breakfast in bed each morning. After breakfast they would take a walk along the creek not far from Logan Place.

In the evenings, Roy loved to take a walk before he would go to bed. Each evening he and Annie walked around Logan Place, looking up into the dark sky trying to find the North Star. Roy just loved the way it sparkled so bright.

Annie asked Roy, "How did you ever find this place, honey? I don't even think I've ever been out this way before."

Roy said to Annie with a smile, and it was a big smile, too, "You know, honey, Chad and I were riding one day, and we came out this way."

He told Annie that he knew the place was here because his Pa told him, but he had never seen it until now. He said to Annie that tomorrow was their last day, and that in the morning he wanted to take her riding. He knew how much she loved riding.

The next morning the early sun shone through the windows of Logan Place. Annie was up early and had begun to pack. Roy stopped her and said that they were going riding first and there was plenty of time for packing later.

Roy took Annie horseback riding on a trail that he and Chad had cut out. It started out behind the barn, went along the creek, and ended up back in front of Logan Place. It was about a two-mile-long ride. Annie fell in love with the place. As she rode up in front of Logan Place and got off the horse, she knew her honeymoon was coming to an end, but their life as man and wife was off to a wonderful start. Roy asked Annie, "Honey, I know you didn't want a big honeymoon, but did I do alright?"

Annie said, "Roy, darling, if you gave me one wish right now, you know what it would be?"

"No, honey, I don't. What would it be?" Roy asked.

Annie said, looking at her husband, "That we would never, ever have to leave this place. That's how alright you've done, Roy Logan."

Roy said to Annie, "Okay, honey, your wish is granted."

"Oh, Roy, stop being silly. Let's go inside and pack," She said.

When Annie opened the door, and walked back inside she looked for the housekeeper, but couldn't find her. She went into the kitchen. There was no cook and it was as clean as could be. Annie looked at Roy out of the corner of her eye then asked, "Roy, where is everyone?"

Roy said, "I guess you must have made that wish I gave you."

Annie started to scream. Roy hated her scream it was so loud, "Please, honey, don't scream anymore," he asked.

"Roy, this is our new home?" Annie squealed.

"Yes, honey, it's your new home."

Just about that time there was a knock on the door. Annie opened it and it was the whole family. It was truly a wonderful surprise. Everyone stayed way past midnight. Sarah and Marian were helping Annie all that afternoon putting things up and opening presents. Roy even had a portrait painted of Logan Place hanging over the fire place.

Sarah and Marian were dead tired, so Russ and Charlie thought it would be best to take the ladies home because come morning, things were back to normal. As time passed, Logan Place became one of the biggest ranches in Pittsville, and they were about to start moving the largest herd of cattle Roy ever had.

Annie knew it meant driving cattle to market for Roy this time because the herd was too large to ship by rail. Annie hated cattle drives. She remembered back when she first came to Pittsville, Roy's Pa was into cattle. She remembered it so well because her Pa went on a few drives with them. She thought her Pa would never get back and she was not looking forward to it again.

Roy told Annie the night before that his Pa and hers were going along with him and Chad, but it was more than just the cattle drive on Annie's mind. Annie had visited Doc Ollie the day before. He told Annie that from her size she was going to have a big childbirth. She was expecting and had planned to tell Roy that night at supper.

Now her plans would have to be changed. She could still tell him tonight or wait until he returned from the cattle drive. Annie called her Ma to help her decide what to do. Marian told Annie that it would be better to tell him before he left, it's all a part of being married. Sometimes you must take the good with the not so good and still make things work.

After talking with her Ma, Annie decided to make one of Roy's favorite suppers, and he had many, but she decided on fried chicken. Then she would tell him he was going to be a Papa. Marian and Sarah were the only two who knew Annie was expecting.

Roy finally got home. Annie had been cooking most of the day since her call to her Ma. Roy walked over to Annie, kissed her on the lips and said, "You always seem to know what I want for supper. How do you do it, honey?"

Annie smiled and said, "It's the woman's instinct in us."

Roy said, "Annie, this is our biggest herd and we're going to drive it to Cockapoo."

Annie said, "Cockapoo! Roy, that's on the other side of Collie City, and it's at least a two-and-a-half-day ride,"

Roy replied, "Yes, I know, honey, and it well be longer with the cattle." Roy explained to Annie that the Cattlemen's Association of Komondor county was meeting in Cockapoo City and he was offered $600,000 for his cattle. Roy explained to Annie that with the money he would make on the herd, he wouldn't ever have to drive cattle again. He and Chad could just do the ranch and crops.

Annie still didn't like it but there wasn't much she could do about it. Roy got washed up for supper, after which he had his usual pipe in the study before a fire. Annie came in after she'd finished cleaning the kitchen. She sat down next to Roy, and said, "Honey, I didn't want to tell you like this but, I'm expecting."

Roy couldn't believe his ears. He kissed Annie and told her that they would celebrate when he returned.

Roy turned in early and he did so with a smile. He was happy as any man could be about the news Annie just gave him. Annie sat up for a long time reading because she simply couldn't sleep. She just didn't feel good and didn't know what it was, but it was enough to keep her from the rest she now needed, and more so than before.

She finally did fall asleep, only it was pretty much time to get up. Roy was up already packing food in his saddle bags. Charlie was driving the cook wagon, and he was a good cook, too. The men gathered out near the barn waiting for Roy and Chad. Chad came downstairs and Roy looked at him and said, "Buff, Gray, and Chocolate."

Chad said, "Buff, Gray and Chocolate! What's that?"

"They're the names of my three boys. Annie is having trip-lets," Roy said, and then ran up the stairs to give Annie a big kiss goodbye.

Annie came down with Roy. Marian and Sarah were in the kitchen talking, and Marian said, "Annie will be staying with us until you return, Roy."

"Why don't you all stay here? It's bigger," Roy replied. Roy gave Annie one long kiss on the lips then ran out the door of the kitchen, jumped on Nugget, and joined the other men.

"Let's move this beef to Cockapoo City," he said, and off they went.

7

Stampede

ROY CALLED OUT, "Head 'em up, move 'em out!" as he trotted along, waving goodbye to Annie until she faded from his sight. Russ was handling the team of horses and chuckwagon like an old pro, while Charlie was sitting beside him nibbling on a bag of lamb and turkey bits.

"Hey, Pa, you sure you know what you're doing with my chuck-wagon?" Roy yelled jokingly at his Pa as he rode by trying to catch up to Chad.

Russ yelled back, "Why, boy, I was moving cattle before you were born."

"You got things under control, Chad?" Roy asked as he trotted up alongside his brother in name only.

"Yep, got it, brother," Chad replied. Roy rode up ahead to make sure everything up in the front was going smoothly too. The weather was very kind to Roy and the men. It wasn't too hot, but then it wasn't to cool either. It was turning out to be a nice spring like day. A nice breeze filled the air, and there was nothing but miles and miles of good green grazing grass on the trail ahead. Roy's herd was sure to be nice and fat before getting into Cockapoo City.

Riding back towards Chad Roy gave him a thumb up. "You know, Chad, so far it looks like you picked us out a pretty good trail," Roy said.

"You know, Roy, Warhaw showed me all these trails. There's a line shack we can bed down in as well. I even know a short cut to Cockapoo City, and it won't cause a problem for the herd, either," Chad told Roy.

"A line shack. You sure, Chad?" Roy asked.

"Sure, I'm sure. I told you, Warhaw used to ride with the Basset gang. Boy, there ain't no place in this territory Warhaw don't know about," Chad said.

"Chad, how long you think we been moving this beef?" Roy asked.

"Well, Roy, judging from the sun, I'd say we been pushing beef well into evening time. In fact, it's gonna be getting dark soon, and if I got my bearings right, we should be riding up on that line shack pretty soon, brother dear," Chad replied.

"That looks like Pa riding this way," Roy said to Chad, and it was. Russ rode up to where the boys were, and Roy said, "Hey Pa, what're you doing on that horse?"

Russ replied, "I had to stretch my legs boy. Charlie can handle that team every bit as good as I can. Besides, I wanted to ask, don't you fellows think we need to be finding a place to rest for the night?"

"Chad and I were just thinking on that very same thing, Pa," Roy answered.

Before long the boys and Russ, riding side by side, finally spotted the line shack Chad was talking about, and it was in good shape, too. When they rode up to it Chad got off and went inside. "C'mon, fellows, let's see the inside," he said. "Hey, ya know, this place ain't half bad."

Looking around Roy said, "Well, at least it's clean. I wonder whose land this is?"

"I'm sure someone must be still using this line shack, maybe even Mr. Miloh's men." Chad replied.

"You think so, Chad?" Roy asked.

"For sure, Roy. Ol' man Miloh don't be driving beef any-more himself, but he's got a big ranch like you and he feeds a lot of people back east with that beef, just like you'll be doing with this herd."

Chad said, "You know, Roy, come to think of it, we could be just coming to the end of your land."

"No way, Chad," Roy replied.

"Oh, yes, there is a way. You know, Roy, when I came across your ranch I was coming from the North. You're moving North East of your ranch, so we need to look over the map, because your property would end just about where we are," Chad replied to his brother.

"I don't know, Chad. Of course, I was a lot younger when Pa decided to take the wagon train west, but him and Charlie did buy up a lot of Government land deals," Roy said to Chad.

Russ walked up and said, "So, whatta you boys think of the drive so far?"

"Oh, it's going great, Pa. But, Pa, answer me a question," Roy asked his Pa.

"What is it, son?" Russ replied.

Roy went on to say, "Well, Pa, whose land you think we're on right now?"

"I'm glad you asked that, Roy. I was really hoping you would take an interest. It's our land, Roy. In fact, this line shack is in the middle of Dogwood Forest, and just about a mile or so East of here we'll still be in the Forest, but off your land and half way to Cockapoo City," Russ replied.

"And once I throw in my shortcut, we'll be there in about another day's ride," Chad added.

"This is insane," Roy said to himself. "How can one man own so much land?"

"You know, Roy," Russ answered him, "that was the great thing about coming out west. You see, son, when the Government opened all this territory, they saw a way to make money. And when the news got out about the Gold being found out here, the fever hit like a ton of trees, and Charlie and I went for it. And now we're up to our tails in money."

"Don't forget the outlaws," Roy replied.

"Well, now, that depends on how you look at things, Roy. We may not have called them outlaws in the East, but there was just as much trouble there as there is here," Russ explained to his son. "C'mon, now. Charlie says grub's ready."

So, after finally arriving at the line shack, the men were all bedding down and getting ready to eat, some inside and some outside the line shack. "Hey, Charlie," Russ said, "what ya cooking up over there? Smells pretty good in here."

"Something quick and easy Marian showed me how to make," Charlie replied.

"Well, does it have a name, Charlie? I'm sure Marian called it something," Russ replied.

"Oh, yeah," Charlie replied laughingly. "It's called rabbit stew."

"Rabbit stew!" Russ said. "Charlie, are you sure? Where'd you get rabbit from? We didn't stop anywhere on the trail."

Charlie replied, "You know, Russ, I remember a few cattle drives when all we had was beans and beef. So, I did a little hunting and trapped me a few rabbits, enough for the trip. I got some eggs and bacon, some jerky, chicken, and fixin's for biscuits, too."

"You see boys," Russ said. "Now you know. When you're moving cattle, always make sure you got someone like Charlie, who enjoys cooking and eating just as much as you do, and you can't go wrong."

Roy said, "I think you got a point there, Pa." And Chad seconded it.

Roy walked outside to the chuck-wagon where Charlie was cooking over an open fire. Sniffing the cooking odors in the air he asked, "Is it ready yet, Charlie? I'm hungry enough to eat a bear."

"It's ready. Just get a plate and some bread and fill it. I've got some hot coffee on the fire, too." Charlie replied.

So, all the men sat down and filled their bellies on the wonderful meal Charlie had prepared.

Looking up at the clouds Russ said, "You know, Charlie, those look like some awfully dark thunder clouds, and you know what that does to cattle."

"Yeah, and the last thing we need is a Stampede," Charlie replied.

With their bellies filled and some good hot coffee to finish off the meal, the men started getting comfortable on their beds. Russ, Roy, Charlie and Chad slept in the line shack with two others, leaving four men to watch over the herd. Roy started to tell them about the babies but decided he would wait. It had been a long, hot, dusty day, and Roy Logan was beat, but he couldn't really sleep. He tapped Chad on the shoulder and said, "Chad, Chad, you asleep?"

"Well, I'm not now, Roy. C'mon, Roy, can't you go to sleep?" Chad asked.

"No, Chad, I can't sleep." Roy said to Chad.

"Have you tried counting sheep?" Chad replied.

"I'm, serious Chad. I got things on my mind, like what I'm gonna do with all that money from the cattlemen in Cockapoo City. $600,000 dollars. Man, whoever thought beef could pay so much?" Roy said to Chad.

"Whatta-ya gonna do with all that cash, Roy?" Chad asked.

"Annie, Chad, Annie. I'm going to make sure she never wants for nothing, or my children. And I'll put some away, give some to the Parson. I'm so wired up, Chad, I think I'll go outside for a bit." So, Roy got up and put his boots back on and eased out the door. He looked up to the sky and thought how pretty the dark sky was, all lit up with stars. As he stood on the outside step of the line shack, he just couldn't get his mind off Annie and what she must be doing right at this moment. With this being his first cattle drive, Roy felt as tall as his Pa. He felt like the luckiest ranch owner alive, with a beautiful young wife about to give birth, and a nice big ranch.

Roy knew inside that most of these things were just that - things, and you don't put value on things is what his Pa told him. But when he thought about Annie, his face just lit up. He thought about how much they were in love, and he couldn't wait to sell this beef and get home to the woman he loved. The night air was getting colder by the minute, so Roy eased his way back inside, took off his boots, and laid back down next to Chad and the warm fire.

Roy laid his head down on his saddle and pulled the blanket over his head. The men were all asleep, except those watching the cattle, keeping them calm. The least little sound could set them off. Suddenly from out of nowhere there was the sound of pistols being fired. "Stampede! Stampede!" someone called out.

Chad was the first to jump up, followed by Roy, Charlie, and then Russ. The men reached for their pistols and saddles, threw open the door of the line shack and ran toward their horses.

They threw their saddles over their horses, jumped up on them and started running down the herd, with Chad and Roy leading the way. They tried their best to turn that big herd and get them into a circle. It wasn't easy, but they finally got the herd under control. Chad came riding slowly into camp, he looked around for Roy, but he didn't see him. Chad called out for Roy repeatedly. He saw Nugget, Roy's horse, but no Roy. Chad knew this wasn't good. He walked and walked until the dust began to clear, and right there at his boots he saw Roy's hat, and it was covered with blood.

Chad dropped to the ground with tears in his eyes. "Someone's gonna pay for this, I promise you, Roy. Someone will pay."

Charlie and Russ rode up on Chad and they knew right off something had happened. Russ got off his horse and went over to Chad, pulled him up and turned him around, and asked, "Chad, where's Roy? Where's Roy, Chad?"

Rocking back and forth and crying, Chad replied, "I don't know, Pa Logan."

Charlie went over to Chad and said, "Chad, son, come on, sit down by the fire." Chad got up and put his paws over his face. Russ said, "Come here, son," as he put his arms around Chad, and with both paws rubbed up and down Chad's back. Russ stayed with Chad while Charlie and the others searched until the sun came up, but Roy was nowhere to be found. The men were devastated.

When he could finally speak, Chad said, "Pa Logan, you do know this was planned don't you?"

Russ replied, "Yes, son, I know it was planned, just like I've known all along this would happen sooner or later. And there was not one thing I could do to keep it from happening. Not one single thing." Russ went on to say, "Well, I guess now, at least, I don't have to worry about my boy's life any longer." Having said those words gave Russ's heart some relief, but still, he and all the men stood there in a circle, heads bowed deep into their chests, with tears rolling down their faces.

Chad said to Pa Logan and Pa Potts, "There may not be anything you can do, but there's plenty I can do, once we get Roy's cattle to Cockapoo."

Russ and Charlie both told Chad that his way wasn't the right way,

Chad's reply to Pa Logan and Pa Potts was, "It's the only way I've ever known."

Russ told Chad that they would just let the Middletons handle this. They had a longer reach and can track better than they could. Chad wasn't hearing Pa Logan and he said to him, "Pa Logan, the Middletons couldn't even find Asa or Gus Morgan before you had to shoot them both down. So, you tell me, just how they gonna find Pace and Lace before they find out about the babies?"

Russ and Charlie looked at one another and said, "Annie is with child, Chad?"

"Yes, Roy told me just before we left on the cattle drive, and he was hoping for boys."

This was even worse, Russ and Charlie thought. But Russ wanted to know something, so he asked Chad, "How did you know about Asa and Gus?"

With tears, still in his eyes Chad said, "Pa Logan, when a lawman as big as you is being hunted down by two big name outlaws, now that kind of news spreads fast." Chad told Pa Logan that he knew all about him and the Morgan's before he left Miloh ranch.

Russ said, "Chad, you never told me you worked for Ben Miloh,"

Chad said, "I didn't think it was important, Pa Logan. But Roy knew. He knew everything, everything about me."

Charlie told the men that plans were changing, that he and Russ would be heading back to the ranch in the morning to give the girls the news, while Chad and the men finished the drive to Cockapoo. Russ pulled Chad aside and told him, "Now, son, listen to me, now. I don't want you going off half crazy."

Russ told Chad that once he got to Cockapoo to make sure his head was on right, and then look up Thaddeus Clayton, Thomas Greenwood, or a Richard Holiday.

He told Chad that those three men were the top leaders of the Cockapoo Cattleman Association and they can best settle with him on the price they agreed with Roy for his cattle. Chad told Pa Logan that he knew of those three old wise men and he knew they had founded Cockapoo. Chad said that he had also been there before.

Charlie spoke up and said, "Chad, please, if you or any of the men run up on a Morgan, please send someone to get the Marshal. We don't want to lose you too, son."

Russ and Charlie gathered up all of Roy's belongings. After spending hours and hours searching for Roy they just couldn't think straight. Not knowing where Roy was, or if he was even still alive, was just too much to bear. Chad had more on his mind than driving a bunch of steers to Cockapoo, that was for sure. He was on a hunt. Chad knew without any doubt that a Morgan had pulled the trigger on his brother, and he wasn't about to rest until he pulled his trigger on them.

Before the men parted ways, it was Pa Potts' turn to try and calm the anger that was raging within Chad minute by minute. Charlie pulled Chad aside and walked him about ten feet away from the men before he said, "Chad, you remember that breakfast we had on Roy's wedding day?"

Chad answered with his eye still filled with tears, "Yes, sir, Pa Potts, I remember. But this ain't Komondor County and we ain't headed toward Heeler City, and poking fun at me is one thing, but Pa Potts, this is another."

Charlie saw in Chad's eyes what Russ couldn't see, and he knew there was no way to reason with Chad. Chad and Roy were like brothers. Charlie looked at Chad with tears in his eyes and said, "Chad, you are like a son to us all, and Annie needs you now more than she even knows. Chad, whatever, or however, this goes down, please stay within the law. We can't afford to lose you, too."

Looking at Charlie Chad said, "Thank you for understanding what I must do. And I promise, Pa Potts, it will indeed be within the law, because this is going down my way."

With only an hour or so before sunup the men gathered their things and started heading toward Cockapoo, while Russ and Charlie headed back to Pittsville without Roy, to give the girls the sad news.

Like A Brother

RIGHT AFTER RUSS and Charlie left the line shack, Chad had the men do another search for Roy's body. He just couldn't think of leaving without his brother.

Several more hours of searching the prairie for Roy had passed. Nick went to Chad and said, "Chad, it looks like rain." Chad just stood there. "Chad, I know it's hard. It is for us, too, but we've got to get moving. Mr. Logan is going to be upset if we don't get this herd to Cockapoo City, Chad," Nick said, looking Chad right in the face.

With a tremble in his voice Chad looked Nick right back in his face and said, "Don't you think I know that, Nick? That's my brother out there somewhere."

"Chad, we've searched and searched. You know that prairie better than anyone I know. Now there's no telling where the cattle could have dragged him. And if the blood on his hat is his, that means Roy could have been ambushed. And if he was, he's most likely dead now, Chad. C'mon, Chad, we gotta get moving," Nick stressed to him.

"I will never believe Roy is dead, Nick. He's alive, you hear me Roy Logan is still alive, and if it takes my whole life, I'm going to find him, after I settle up for him," Chad replied to Nick, then added, "Are the men ready, Nick?"

Nick replied, "Yeah, Chad, they're all ready and waiting for you."

Chad jumped up on Lady and said, "Well, I guess there's nothing more we can do here," as he looked around shaking his head from side to side. Then with a hard, strong voice Chad said, "Head 'em up, move 'em out!"

It started out being a beautiful morning despite the fact there were dark clouds up ahead. Chad and Nick rode side-by-side for miles saying nothing, but each of them had one thing on their minds - finding the coward, or cowards, responsible for this.

Pulling himself together, Chad finally got the herd moving. They had started driving the cattle shortly after sunup and it was now coming up on noon. Nick, riding ramrod, bringing up the rear, noticed one of the cowhands was trying to get his attention. Nick rode over to see what the ranch hand wanted. When he was close enough Nice could see that it was Jason.

Jason asked Nick, "When is Chad going to take a rest? We've been pushing this herd since sunup."

Nick looked at Jason and replied, "Jason, my boy, I have a question, too. How bad do you want the one, or ones, behind all this?"

Jason replied, "Just as much as you and Chad."

"Is that a fact?" Nick said. "Well, Jason, Chad believes we'll find them in Cockapoo City, and so do I. So, do you see any cattle falling out anywhere?"

"No, sir," Jason said.

"Then Chad's doing mighty fine, cause we're only a few miles outside Cockapoo City. We can rest the herd when we get there," Nick said.

Looking back Chad saw Nick and Jason talking, so he rode up to where they were and asked, "What's going on, fellas?"

Nick said, "Nothing, boss man. Just Jason here thought we might need to rest the herd."

Chad looked at Jason and said, "We got some settling up to do, Jason, and it's in Cockapoo City. The cattle ain't gonna drop that many pounds. Now, let's ride."

Roy's herd wasn't the only thing gathering up steam. Chad had the men so fired up all they were talking about was settling this for Roy.

"Tree Cockapoo! Burn it to the ground," The men were saying,

But Chad made a promise to Pa Potts to keep things within the law, so he wasn't about to let the men tree Cockapoo, but he sure as heck felt like it.

It was getting close to nightfall when they hit Cockapoo City limits. Chad took Nick, Jason and three other men and rode into town, while the other men bedded down the herd just outside the town limits. Chad went to see the Marshal first. The name on the building said, Marshal Lance Colby.

Chad opened the door and walked in. The Marshal said. "What can I do for you, young fella?"

"Marshal, can you tell me how to get to the Cattlemen's Association Bank?" Chad asked.

Marshal Colby replied, "Yeah, it's about four buildings down on the left side of Front Street."

"Thanks, Marshal," Chad said, then turned and walked out of the Marshal's Office and over to where Nick and Jason were standing. He motioned for Nick and the others to follow.

When Chad located the building, he and Nick walked inside. Chad asked the desk clerk if there was a Mr. Clayton, and the clerk told Chad to wait there. When the clerk returned, he had an older man with him.

The man said. "I'm Mr. Clayton, Sr., son. What can I do for you?"

"My name's Chad, Mr. Clayton, and we've been driving cattle from Pittsville to Cockapoo for Roy Logan, to deliver to you, sir."

"Come with me into my office, son." Mr. Clayton replied.

Chad and Nick followed Mr. Clayton back to his office. When they entered, there were two men sitting in his office already. Mr. Clayton introduced Chad and Nick to Mr. Holiday and Mr.

Greenwood. He said, "Please, have a seat. Now tell me, did you happen to lose any cattle on the drive here?"

"It's possible Mr. Clayton, you see sir. Some men stampeded our herd and maybe ambushed Roy Logan, and right now we don't know if he's alive or dead. So, we split the men up, and drove the herd here to keep Roy's agreement with you. Then we're going to head back to Pittsville. As to the number, I'm sure we lost a few, maybe ten or fifteen, there 'bouts," Chad replied.

"We're powerful sorry for your loss, son. I tell you what, here's what we'll do." Mr. Clayton handed Chad a check for $600,000.

"Mr. Clayton, I can't take this sir, it's for the full amount," Chad replied.

Mr. Clayton said, as he gave the check to Chad, "Son, it's only money, and what's money compared to a human life? And besides, it was the price that Roy and I agreed upon. So, please, Chad, take the check."

"Thank you, sir. That's very kind of all of you."

Scratching his scalp with his paw, Mr. Clayton remembered something. He said, "Sit down, please, both of you. You know, Chad, I didn't think much about this until just now. But just before your arrival here, my son, Thad, was here a bit ago and he told me something he'd heard as he walked by the Bobcat Saloon. He said he saw, two men going into the saloon talking extremely loudly. My son said that he wouldn't swear on it in court, but that it sounded like, 'Pace, my brother, us Morgan's finally got us a Logan tonight. Grandpa Asa would have been proud.' And that's what my son heard." Mr. Clayton told Chad.

Chad replied, "Do any of you know if they're still in the Bobcat?"

Mr. Holiday replied, "Well, son, I rode past there about a half hour before you got here, and they were still there drinking, it looked to me."

Chad accepted the check and said, "Thank you, Mr. Clayton, Mr. Holiday, and you, too, Mr. Greenwood." When he and Nick got outside, he looked at the men and said, "They're here."

Jason asked, "Who, the Morgan's? No way."

Chad said, "I told you we'd find those back-shootin' cowards here."

Chad, Nick and the four other men walked until they found the Bobcat saloon. Before going inside, Chad said, "This is my war, boys. I know how y'all feel, but they're all mine."

"Fine, but we're coming in behind you," Nick said.

"That's fine, just stay out of my play," Chad replied.

As Chad walked through the Bobcat saloon doors, he waited until Nick and the others took a seat. He walked over to the bar and ordered a glass of milk. Holding the glass in his paw, Chad turned and lifted it into the air, and with a loud voice said, "I hear there's a celebration in here tonight."

Pace and Lace turned and said, "Indeed there is, sir, indeed there is. We got us a Logan."

"Ok, fella, take it outside my saloon." Bobcat said, but it was a little too late.

Chad's anger rose into his throat. With his glass of milk held high into the air, he spat right on the floor of the Bobcat saloon and said, "I know you did, you back shootin' cowards, I was there. It was my brother you two shot."

Pace went for his pistol and so did Lace. Chad dropped to the floor, rolled over onto his belly and with his quick paws, he drew both pistols. Chad's first shot hit Pace Morgan killing him instantly. His second shot hit Lace in the shoulder. Chad got up and looked around. He saw Mr. Clayton and said, "Can you please fetch the Marshal for me, Mr. Clayton?"

When Marshal Colby got there, he asked. "Who's responsible for this?"

"I'm afraid I'm the guilty one, Marshal," Chad confessed.

"Someone get the Doc. And I'll take those pistols, son," Marshal Colby said, looking at Chad. "I know these two boys, and they're bad ones. In fact, the whole family is, if you ask me. And you cut them both down to size. You must be right quick with those paws, young man."

"No, Sir, it was just luck," Chad replied.

Marshal Colby asked, "Did anyone see what happened here?" but no dared to speak out against a Morgan.

Then Mr. Clayton spoke up and said, "I saw it, Lance, and that young man, Chad, shot in self-defense."

Marshal Colby told Chad, "Ok, quick paws, it looks like you're free to go. And if you got any buddies with you, you can take them, too. And keep clear of Cockapoo City. We don't need your kind of play in our town."

"Well, Marshal, maybe you should do your town a favor and take out the trash more often," Chad said to Marshal Colby.

"That will be enough, boy. I run this town my way, and if you don't want to see the inside of my jail, you better get along," Marshal Colby replied with a look of anger on his face.

"Gladly, once I deliver this herd," Chad answered.

Chad, Nick and the others left the Bobcat and headed back to the herd. Mr. Clayton said, "Wait a minute, Chad. I'll send some of my ranch-hands with you, so you fellas won't need to come back. It's not that I don't want you to, it's just easier that way."

"Thank you again, Mr. Clayton. Now we can just head straight for home. Come on, boys, we got work waiting for us. Let's ride," Chad said.

9

The Annie Potts Logan Story

LIFE ON THE western frontier was rough and hard for any man or woman. A woman needed to be just as bold and daring, with a fearlessness equal to a man. Annie Potts Logan was such a woman, but Annie was beside herself when her Pa told her that Roy had been shot during the Cattle drive, and that his body had been trampled over and dragged away by a stampede of cattle.

Annie just could not bring herself to believe Roy was dead and gone. Annie couldn't explain to her Pa why she felt the way she did, but nevertheless it was how she felt. Marian asked Annie, "Annie, darling, how do you want to handle Roy's home going?"

Annie replied, "Ma, you and Ma Logan can plan things, can't you? I just can't plan something I don't believe has happened and won't believe until I see Roy's body."

Marian told her daughter, "Annie, honey, the sooner you accept this the better things will be. Annie, you're about to have children. You've got to pull yourself together."

"Ma, I've told you and Pa I'm fine. I just don't accept it. If Roy is dead, Ma, then where is his body?" Annie answered her Ma.

"Annie, honey, the men told us all of that over and over. He was trampled to death by the cattle, honey." Marian explained.

Annie remembered back to the day of the Cattle Drive and she smiled as she remembered the look of excitement on Roy's face about the deal he'd made with Mr. Clayton. The reality of never seeing Roy's big, beautiful, green eyes ever again was overwhelming for anyone, and Annie was no different. Only thing was, Annie wouldn't allow herself to dwell on it. Perhaps this was the reason for Annie's inner strength, because all her life, as far back as she could remember, it was never easy for Annie to say goodbye.

Having finally made it back from Cockapoo City, Chad was keeping himself busy with the chores around the ranch, and there were many. Chad was coming in from the barn one day when he saw the Parson walking up to the front door. He ran over to greet the Parson and show him inside. Chad showed the Parson into the parlor where Charlie, Marian, Sarah, Russ, and Nick were sitting and sharing stories about Roy.

"I don't see Annie. Is she receiving callers?" the Parson asked.

Chad said, "Just a moment, Parson, I'll get her for you." Chad went to Annie's room, and knocked gently on her door.

"Who is it?" Annie asked.

"It's Chad, Annie. The Parson is here, and he would like to have a word with you."

Annie said, "Chad, will you please kindly show the Parson into Roy's study and tell him I will receive him there?"

Chad returned to the parlor and showed the Parson to Roy's study. Annie was sitting near a window in a lovely oak rocking chair Roy had made for her. The Parson walked into the study and looked around. "Oh, my, so many books. I knew Roy loved reading, but I guess I never knew how much," he said, laughing, and so did Annie. "Yes, Roy loved and favored Dime Novels. He also enjoyed other authors' works, as well," Annie told the Parson.

The Parson walked over to her and said, "Annie, I wish I could somehow make this easier for you."

Annie got up from the rocker, and as she turned to face the Parson she said, "Parson, is it not true that people can accept sad news in different ways?"

The Parson replied, "Yes, Annie, this is true. However, a person can also be in denial when it comes to sad news such as this, Annie."

Annie said to the Parson, "I will tell you as I've told my family, I really am fine."

"Have you started to plan a service for Roy, Annie? And will you be attending?" the Parson asked.

"No, Parson, I have not. Roy's parents are taking care of all the arrangements, and yes, Parson, I will be attending the services," Annie replied.

"Very good, my child. Well, I'll say goodbye for now and see you at the services," the Parson replied. He left Annie alone in the study and went back to the Parlor.

Sarah told the parson they had decided to have the service in two days, which would make it Sunday. The Parson marked his book, then said his good byes and took his leave.

Those were the longest days of Annie Potts Logan's life. She wanted so much for Sunday to arrive, not to hurry things along, but to put closure to all that had happened. She felt like she would give birth at any minute.

The days went by a lot faster than Annie thought they would, and before they all knew it, Sunday had arrived. It was indeed a busy day for the Logan and Potts families, and it wasn't any easier for any of the cowhands from either ranch. The towns people of Pittsville, as well, were truly in mourning over the loss of Roy Logan.

The Parson lead the service and he allowed those who wanted to speak about Roy, to do so. Annie sat with a white handkerchief in her paws and close to her face, and all eyes were on Annie. It wasn't a very long service because the Parson knew how this was affecting Annie, but he still wanted to make it a memorable day for the Logan and Potts families. The Parson said, "Before asking everyone to stand and hold paws, I want to share a story with you," He said. "I recently visited the Logan family's home. Now like many of you, I knew of Roy's passion for Dime Novels and I heard that his favorite was the story about his Pa, the great lawman, Marshall Russ Logan. But you know, I think Roy had collected every Dime Novel in print," The Parson said, laughingly.

Then the Parson asked if anyone else needed to say any last words. There were none. The Parson asked everyone to bow their heads as he started to read the last words over Roy Logan from the Holy Bible, as the family had requested. He said;

"Rest in Peace, Roy Logan."

"The Lord is my shepherd; I shall not want. He maketh me to lie down in green pastures: he leadeth me beside the still water. He restoreth my soul: he leadeth me in the paths of righteousness for his name's sake. Yea, though I walk through the valley of the shadow of death, I will fear no evil: for thou art with me, thy rod and thy staff they comfort me. Thou preparest a table before me in the presence of mine enemies: thou anointest my head with oil, my cup runneth over. Surely goodness and mercy shall follow me all the days of my life and I will dwell in the house of the Lord for ever. Amen."

"May you forever rest in peace, Roy Logan, and may your family and friends move forward in their respective lives with their memories of your warm soul, your heart of gold."

10
My Pride And Joy

A S TIME WENT by Annie started looking and feeling normal again. Although she still felt a deep sense of loss, she and Chad both accepted, at least for the time being, that Roy could possibly be dead. Each day brought a new meaning, a fresh new start. With the babies on the way, Annie had been making baby clothes for some time. Annie learned so much from working in the dress shop with her Ma when she was little, and it helped to keep her mind busy.

With all of Roy's affairs in order now, and the family healing, Russ and Charlie rode over to have a talk with Chad. They felt now was a good time. But they also wanted to know how he and the men handled things in Cockapoo. After they tied their horses to the post out in front of Logan Place, they went inside to say hello to Annie. They each gave her a kiss. Charlie was very impressed at some of the clothes Annie had made.

Chad came in and said, "I thought I saw you two riding up. How's every little thing?"

"Just fine, son, just fine. We came by to say hello to Annie and the wives and see how you and the men are getting along," Charlie said.

"As you know, I'm not, nor will I ever be, the rancher you guys are, but I'm learning, Pa Potts," Chad said.

Russ said, "It takes time and some hard work to become a good rancher, Chad. And you know them both well, son. Just keep believing. Wow just look at this place - the grounds look very well kept up and the cattle look nice and fat. Wouldn't you say so, Charlie?"

"You're right about that, Russ," Charlie answered. "The cattle look really good. You may be ready to sell some off soon. I hear some buyers are coming to town soon."

"We'll be ready, Pa Potts," Chad said.

Russ asked, "Chad, has the doc been by?"

"He stops by every day and he should be stopping by pretty soon," Chad replied.

"Chad, come on, son, and take a walk with us," Russ told Chad.

"Sure thing, Pa Logan. Just let me get my hat," Chad replied.

So, the three men walked along the creek. Russ said, "Well, Chad, it's been some time now, and everything here looks great. And there doesn't appear to be any lawmen after you, so tell us, son, how did things go in Cockapoo?"

Chad said, "Well, after settling the payment with Mr. Clayton, I told him what had happened to Roy on the cattle drive. Mr. Clayton and the others offered their condolences. Then Mr. Clayton told me that his son, Clayton, Jr., told him that just before we rode in with the herd, Pace and Lace Morgan boisterously rode into town that night, rousing up the town and shooting their pistols in the air. There were fudge pellets everywhere."

Chad continued, "He said that the Morgans stormed into the Bobcat Saloon yelling how they got themselves a Logan. When I heard that I just stood there and my whole body started shaking. Mr. Clayton asked me if I wanted him to get the marshal, and I told him yes, but after I was done confronting them."

Chad then told them that he went to the Bobcat Saloon and confronted the Morgan brothers. He explained how he had shot and killed Pace and wounded Lace in a fair fight, as he had promised.

Chad went on to say, "I turned to Mr. Clayton and told him he could fetch the Marshal now. Mr. Clayton told Marshal Lance Colby the story and he let me go. But I know it's not over yet."

Charlie said, "Well, son, Russ and I are very proud of you for not only keeping your word, but for handling things the right way."

While the men were out on their walk, Doc Ollie had arrived and was with Annie when the men got back to the house. Sarah and Marian had been with Annie for the last three days and told the men just as they walked in that it was time for those babies to show their faces. And then the pacing started, back and forth, and after hours of pacing came the wonderful sound of babies crying.

When Doc Ollie finished, he announced, "You now have five new members to the Logan and Potts family tree; four boys and a girl."

Charlie asked Doc Ollie, "Say, Doc, in what order did the little girl come?"

"Charlie, I'm happy to tell you the little girl was the last one to show her face," Doc Ollie replied. And they all yelled out with joy because she was the youngest of the five, in perfect order.

Doc Ollie told the family that they could come in and see Annie. She was lying there with the five newborns in her arms. The men went to reach for the babies, but Marian and Sarah pushed them out of the way, saying, "Did you all wash your hands when you came in from outside?"

"No," the men replied.

Sarah said, "Well, please do if you want to hold these little darlin's. And wash your faces, too. Then cover them up and come back."

"Yes, Ma," they each replied.

Later, as Charlie, Russ, and Chad sat there, each with a baby in their arms, they thought of Roy, but neither one spoke his name until Annie asked, "You know, Ma, I wonder what Roy would have named them?"

Marian said, "You know, dear, I don't know, but I'm sure the names would have come from one of his dime novels."

They all laughed but Chad said, "No, I don't think they would have come from a dime novel. I know what Roy told me the day of the drive, what he would name them if Annie had three boys"

Annie said, "Chad, Roy told you about the babies?"

"Yes," Chad replied. "Right after you told him, he came out the kitchen door, jumped on Nugget, and said that if you had three boys, he would name them Buff, Gray and Chocolate Logan. But I guess he never thought you would have five."

Doc Ollie said, "I wasn't sure how many at first because the heart beats were so soft and so close together that I couldn't tell. I thought there was a good chance of five, but I didn't want to get everyone excited."

Annie looked at the babies and said, "Thanks to your Pa, we only need two more names now."

Annie asked them all to think of a nice name for a girl. She wanted something strong, yet soft, that would go with Logan.

Marian said, "I got it. Why don't we name her Fuchsia Logan?"

Then Sarah said, "Oh, I love that, Marian, and how about Clay Logan for the other boy?"

Annie said, "Yes, I love them both! Fuchsia and Clay Logan, how perfect."

It was a long day and it was looking like an even longer night, and the Logans, Potts, uncle Chad, and Nick played with the five new additions. Once the little ones were born, the weeks and months seemed to almost fly by, and the little Logans were growing by leaps and bounds. Grandpa Potts and Grandpa Logan didn't want to miss out on anything. They came by every day. They just couldn't get enough of those little tykes. Marian and Sarah combined their businesses together and called it Pittsville Hat & Dress Shop. They did it so they would have time to help Annie with the "little people" as Charlie called them.

In the first year of the Logan babies' lives, Sarah and Marian took turns staying with Annie, one week each. They even hired a lady in town to help run the shop for them. Yep, Annie had plenty of help raising the "little people" and Annie welcomed it.

Charlie and Russ, along with uncle Chad, had much on their minds, like how to protect their family. So far, the men agreed that as the children got older, they would not be allowed off the property.

Charlie hadn't realized it until now, but he was glad that Roy built Logan Place twenty miles from town. It was private, for one thing, and the only two, other than the family, who knew about the children was Doc Ollie and Sophia, and they both knew what the cost was if any of this ever got out too soon.

Every time the grand parents came to visit, they mostly came at the same time, making sure they each got equal time with the little ones before they put them down to nap. As soon as the children realized who was who, every time the grand parents came, and they saw that horse and buggy pull up, they became excited.

It was show time for the grandparents. The little ones would crowd around the door jumping up and down, turning around in circles. Annie told her Ma on one of their visits that she believed Buff was her Pa's favorite, because he always went right for him when he came to visit. Marian told Annie that after one of their visits Charlie had said he truly believes Buff has a nose for gold, just like him, ever since Buff tried to get Charlie's gold and diamond ring off his paw. And for sure, every time Buff saw that big shiny diamond on grandma Potts' paw, he went for it, pulling and licking. And once he set his mind to something, it was a done deal for sure.

Fuchsia was so cute and being the only girl in the whole lot just made her even more special with four brothers to look after her. Annie knew Fuchsia would be well looked after. Annie told Sarah that all Fuchsia does is crawl around the floor taking her brothers toys, because she likes playing with their toys better than her dolls. She was a pretty little thing, curly white hair with shades of color that resembled pink. Little Fuchsia was something. You could tell Fuchsia was going to be one tough cookie.

Clay seemed to be like his Pa in many ways. Although he was too young to read, he always had a book of some kind up under his arms running around that big house. Annie said he loved to look at the pictures, so the grandparents always made sure to have new picture books for Clay on each visit.

Annie seemed to think that Buff, Gray and Chocolate had many of the same interests. Annie told her Ma that they loved to play bang-bang cowboys and that Clay played along sometimes. Annie told her Ma that Clay didn't seem too interested in all that running around and falling down stuff. Grandpa Russ got them each little cowboy hats. Fuchsia threw hers on the floor, but the boys seemed to like theirs.

Annie's little ones were soon talking and walking. Charlie, Russ, and uncle Chad would take the boys fishing every weekend, and sometimes Nick would come along. One time while they were fishing in Lake Golden Doodle, Clay wandered off, but uncle Chad had him in his sights the whole time.

However, uncle Chad wasn't sure just what had Clay's attention, so he walked over to where Clay was standing and noticed that Clay was very interested in the beehive in the tree above him, so interested in fact, that he had a stick in his paw trying to poke at it.

Chad ran over to where Clay was playing and said, "Clay, be a good boy and put down the stick, ok?"

But Clay had other ideas for that stick, and as he threw his little arms back as if to strike the beehive, uncle Chad dived towards Clay, picked him up and said, "Bad, Clay, bad. We don't throw sticks."

"Uncle Chad, I only wanted to see where the buzzing was coming from," Clay said.

"Clay, next time you want to know something, you ask me or Ma or your grandpa or grandma, Okay?" Chad replied.

"Okay, uncle Chad," Clay said. Clay wanted to know what was wrong with playing with the beehive, so he asked uncle Chad, "Why can't I play with the bee's, uncle Chad? Why? Why can't I play with the bees?" Clay started to rub his eyes with his paws and began to cry.

Uncle Chad explained, "Clay, remember the rubber band hitting your face?"

Clay answered, "Yes, sir, Uncle Chad, I remember,"

"Remember how bad it hurt your face?" Chad asked.

"Yes, sir, Uncle Chad, I remember. And it hurt my face bad."

After explaining about how bees can sting, Uncle Chad said, "Clay, if I let you play with the bees, your face will hurt more than the rubber band. Do you want that to happen?"

"No, sir, uncle Chad," Clay replied.

"Now, no more playing with the bee's, right?"

Clay replied, "Right, uncle Chad."

"Now give me a big hug." So, Chad took Clay back over to where the others were fishing. Buff, Gray and Chocolate were running around playing bang-bang-bang, then Gray fell on the ground.

Clay ran over and jumped on top of Gray and said, "I got him, Buff! I got him, Chocolate! He ain't gonna get away."

Buff said, "Thank you, deputy. I take bad man now."

Russ asked Chad what happened, and Chad told him that Clay just got a lesson in beehives.

"He didn't get stung, did he?" asked Russ.

"No, I was watching him the whole time, but I don't think Clay's going near any beehives anytime soon," Chad said, and they laughed.

The men started to gather up their fishing poles and told the boys it was supper time.

"I don't want to go," Buff said.

Grandpa Potts replied, "Ok, Buff, you stay here and we'll all go eat. Bye, Buff."

Grandpa Charlie didn't get five feet away before Buff came running, yelling, "Wait for me, Grandpa, wait for me."

Grandpa Potts picked him up and told him, "We're not gonna leave you, Buff."

When they all came in Fuchsia said, "Go wash up, supper's ready, Grandpa. You're late. Grandma was waiting for you."

Annie said, "Pa, she's talking to you. Ma wanted to see you. Nothing big, she just had a question."

Charlie looked at Annie and said, "She's worse than you when you were little, Annie." Annie just shook her head.

After supper, the grandparents put the little ones down for the night. As usual, it was the best time of the evening for them both. That was also when they got to tell them a bedtime story. When it was Charlie's turn, he told them all about his gold mines, and he had a few claims across the prairie. When it was Russ's turn, he told them about his days as the Marshal of Pittsville, and Buff, Gray, and Chocolate were all ears. They loved grandpa Russ's story's about being a lawman.

While the men put the little ones to bed, Sarah, Marian, and Annie went to work on a quilt they were sewing. Sarah asked Annie what she was feeding the "little ones" they are growing so fast. Annie said she fed them the same her Ma had fed her, and the same thing she had fed Roy.

Sarah said that they must have improved on the formula because the other day Gray stepped on her paw and it hurt like the devil. "That boy is heavy," she remarked.

Marian said, "They all are, Sarah. Annie's growing an army here on Logan Place, didn't you know that?" And the ladies just laughed. When the men were done, it was time for the Potts to go. It was Sarah's week.

With the "little ones" all tucked in for the night, Annie and Chad talked about going into town for supplies in the morning. Annie suggested that Chad take the boys with him, but Chad said no. Annie told Chad that was the same thing Pa Russ and her Pa said, too.

Annie asked Chad what was wrong with putting the boys in the wagon and taking them to town. Chad said, "Annie it's just not a good idea, that's all. The town is no place for them. It's too rough. Maybe when they're older."

Annie said, "Well, maybe y'all are right. Pittsville isn't the safest place these days."

Annie said good night to Chad and went to bed. Chad sat there thinking how he was going to handle this the next time it came up. He thought about telling Annie about the mark that Gus put on the family, but he thought somehow, she would put two and two together and figure out what happened to Roy. But for now, it was taken care of.

Chad went to bed with much on his mind. He thought day after day, watching them growing, and thinking one day they will ask why they can't leave the property. He wondered if Charlie and Russ were doing the right thing in keeping this from the family.

Chad tried to see this the way Pa Logan and Pa Potts did, but he knew he could not. Living there watching the kids playing together, loving each other, helping anyone up who may have fallen, sharing the treats with one another, he felt that he could see things Russ and Charlie could not see. Chad felt that the only way to protect the family was to tell them the truth. He had a lot of respect for both Charlie and Russ, but he just couldn't see how to protect anyone without letting them know what they were being protected from. So, Chad planned to have a talk with Pa Logan and Pa Potts about the family secret in the morning.

Five Little Secrets

CHAD WAS UP early the next morning. He wanted to get the kids up and started on their chores first thing, but when Chad went to their rooms, he found their beds had been made. He could even smell breakfast, and he thought to himself, no, it can't be. When Chad walked into the breakfast room, which was just off the kitchen, he could see that it was food he was smelling, and it smelled good, too.

It was Buff, Clay, Gray, and Fuchsia. They all turned and said, "Good morning, Uncle Chad."

Scratching his head with his paw Uncle Chad said, "Good morning, kids."

Fuchsia replied, "Good morning, Uncle Chad."

Uncle Chad didn't know what to make of it all. "Alright, kids," he asked. "So, what's up with the food and what do you want?"

Gray answered his Uncle, "Now, Uncle Chad, why you just right off suspect we want something?"

"Well, isn't that usually the case?" Uncle Chad asked.

"Okay, Uncle Chad, maybe you have a point there, but this time it's a surprise, plain and simple, and no strings attached, honest," Gray replied. "See, Uncle Chad, Fuchsia made the eggs and Buff milked the cow. Clay took the bread from the warmer and I got the water from the well and prepared the stove."

Uncle Chad started laughing. It was, indeed, a surprise. Uncle Chad said, "Well, I guess the cat's got my tongue. But where's Chocolate?" asked Chad.

"Oh, he's still sleeping, Uncle Chad. Now come over here and sit down, we're going to serve you yer breakfast," Fuchsia replied.

"I still think you kids are up to something, just not today," Chad replied.

Then he sat just where Fuchsia asked him to. Chad looked the table over and said, "I'm so proud of you kids. You got up early, and no one had to tell you to. And on top of that, you worked together and made this wonderful breakfast." Then he tasted the eggs and said, "My, these eggs sure are good."

"Taste the coffee, Uncle Chad. I made it," Gray replied.

Uncle Chad took a sip of coffee and said, "Yep! Even the coffee's good, too."

As Uncle Chad sat there eating his tasty breakfast, he was thinking how much the kids had done this morning working together. It convinced him that somehow he had to get grandpa Logan to see that telling the family about the Gus Morgan threat would be the right thing to do, and the best way to protect them. He also thought it would be a good bonus to take the kids with him to visit the grandparents. And at the same time, it would reward them for making him this great breakfast. So, Chad said, "Well, to show you kids how thankful I am for this tasty breakfast, how would you all like to ride over and pay a visit to Grandpa and Grandma Logan after breakfast?"

"I'd like that very much, Uncle Chad," Buff replied.

"So, would I, Uncle Chad," Gray replied.

"You fellas aren't leaving me out," Clay replied.

Uncle Chad looked over at Fuchsia who was still eating her breakfast and looking to be deep in thought and said, "Fuchsia, we haven't heard from you, sweetheart. Would you like to ride over to Grandpa and Grandma Logan's house?"

"Well, it sounds like a man thing to me, but since I know grandma Logan has a new dress for me that Grandma Marian made, sure, count me in, too," Fuchsia replied, sticking her tongue out at her brothers. Once breakfast was over, Fuchsia made plates for Annie and Chocolate and put them in the warmer, and it was off to Grandpa and Grandma Logan's house.

Just minutes after they'd left the house, Annie come down stairs and saw the way things had been left, and it pleased her greatly. Annie called Chocolate to come down and have breakfast.

She could see all their chores were done so Annie said to her son, "Chocolate, when you're done with breakfast, look to see if one of your brothers fed the horses in the corral for you, and if not, you know what to do."

"Yes, Ma," Chocolate responded.

When he finished eating, Chocolate said. "Ma, may I please be excused?"

"Yes, honey," Annie replied.

The children always looked out for one another so when Chocolate got out to the corral, he could see that one of his brothers had indeed fed the horses. He ran back in the house to his Ma and said, "Ma, someone did feed them for me."

"Okay, now next time, you need to do something for them, right?" Annie told her son.

"Right, Ma," Chocolate replied.

"Now, Chocolate, I know your brothers and sister have finished their studies. Have you finished yours?" Annie asked. She knew Chocolate was just as smart as his siblings, but Chocolate's mind would wander off sometime. Chocolate loved to fantasize and make believe he was a detective, so much so, that he took after his Pa and had just about every Dime Novel written on the Middleton Detectives. Annie didn't necessarily think it was a bad thing but somehow it needed to be controlled. And the fact that Annie started home schooling her children from a very early age made this easy to handle.

Annie made straight A's all through school, and she was more than qualified to home school her children. Sometimes Grandma Potts and Grandma Logan would sit in for Annie. Classes on the Logan ranch were held one hour a day with her five young ones. Annie could see that her little ones were no longer little, and she felt the aid of a school Marm would help her out a lot.

Annie remembered that her very best friend, Sophia, was a school marm. She also remembered that Sophia changed her last name because it was Morgan, and Sophia wanted no part of the Morgan name. Sophia was very grateful to Sarah Ann Morgan for taking her in off the street of Pittsville, because she was surely on her way to becoming a saloon girl, but it made no difference. Sophia still didn't want to carry the Morgan name.

Annie didn't know how to reach Sophia on the dog-a-phone, but she did know where Sophia lived in town. So, with Chocolate being the only one around, Annie, with Chocolate's help, got the buggy ready for their trip into town to pay a call to her dear friend, Sophia, whom she hadn't seen since her and Roy's wedding day.

A funny feeling came over Annie when she arrived in Pittsville. She remembered that cold rainy night when Pa Logan was the Marshal and had killed Gus Morgan. Chills went through her and she was shaking. Annie thought to make a quick stop at the General store first, so she wouldn't have to stop in town on her way back to the Logan Place. Jonas, the proprietor, was a long-time trusted friend of the Logan and Potts family.

Annie was a welcome surprise for Jonas. No one, including Jonas, had seen Annie since the wedding. Most of the town folks knew of Roy's death, however Jonas was a bit taken when Annie walked in the store. Jonas looked around the store and then he took Annie by the hand and led her to his living quarters in the back of the store.

When they were alone Jonas said, "Annie, what are you doing in town, and alone at that?"

Annie looked at Jonas and said, "I don't understand your question Mr. Jonas, but I came to call on Sophia."

"Sophia?" Mr. Jonas replied. "Well, what on earth for, child?"

"I wanted to see if she would help me home school my children," Annie replied.

Mr. Jonas asked, "Whose little boy is that with you?"

"He's my son, Mr. Jonas. What's all this about?" Annie asked.

"Where is your buggy?" Mr. Jonas asked Annie.

"It's around the side of the store," she replied.

Mr. Jonas told Annie to wait right there and not to move. Soon Mr. Jonas came back with his coat and hat and said to Annie, "I will tell Sophia to call on you, but right now I'm taking you home."

Annie looked very upset as she asked, "Mr. Jonas, what are you doing? What's wrong?"

He replied, "Something I was asked to do, but never thought I'd have to do, Annie, getting you and you're son out of town."

Mr. Jonas had never even been out to Logan Place, but he knew the way. Annie sat there looking very confused, but she didn't say a word.

When Chad and the others got back to Logan Place with the grandparents. They all went inside. Chad called for Annie and Chocolate but got no answers. Chad went to Pa Logan and said, "Pa, I don't think they're here,"

"Where could they be?" Russ replied.

"I don't know," Chad said, "but it's not like Annie to just up and leave."

Russ started to sweat. Chad did, too. Charlie walked into the kitchen where Chad and Russ were standing and asked, "What's going on?"

"Annie and Chocolate aren't on the ranch," Russ answered.

"Where are they?" Charlie asked nervously.

Chad looked at Pa Potts and said, "We don't know yet."

The men were going out of their minds at Logan Place. They looked the whole ranch over and couldn't find hide, head, nor tail of Annie and Chocolate. While running through the house, Chad looked out the big bay window in the dining room and saw a buggy coming up the drive, only Chad couldn't tell who was handling the reins.

He slung open the front door and saw that it was Mr. Jonas from the general store with Annie. Chad ran out and helped Annie out of the buggy.

"Chad, what's going on?" Annie asked.

"Annie, please, just go in the house, please, Chad said. We'll talk about all of this in a minute."

"Okay," Annie said, and went into the house with Chocolate.

Chad stood out there talking with Mr. Jonas. He was thanking him for bringing Annie and Chocolate home. Mr. Jonas asked Chad, "Where is Russ?"

"He'll be out in a minute, Mr. Jonas," Chad replied.

Russ came out of the house and he walked over to Jonas and said, "Thank you, Jonas."

Jonas replied, "Russ, when you told me what Gus said to you, and asked me to be on the lookout for the family, I never thought this would happen."

"I know, Jonas, neither did we," Russ said.

"You mean you never told them?" Jonas asked.

Russ said to his trusted friend, "No, but after talking with Chad this morning, and now this, I'm going to take care of that."

"Russ, when you first came to me with this, I didn't like it then, and I like it even less now. You cannot keep your family safe without them knowing the truth. You must tell them, Russ." Jonas said.

Chad asked, "Mr. Jonas, did anyone see them?

"No, I'm sure of that. She came into town to see Sophia. Thank God she came to see me first. I told her I'd send Sophia out here, and then I put them in the buggy, tied my horse to it, and got them out of town as fast as I could."

"Thank you, Mr. Jonas," Chad replied.

Jonas got on his horse and headed back for town. He looked at Russ and said, "Russ, you must tell them about the cold rainy night."

Standing underneath the tall dogwood trees in the front of Logan Place, waving goodbye to his dear and trusted friend, Jonas, Russ Logan knew that he had come to the end of the road. He knew it didn't matter if he was ready or not, he had no choice now.

As Russ turned to walk back toward the house, he smacked his paws against one of the dogwood trees. He walked into the house closing the big brown plank door behind him and heard the gold metal knocker bang against the door. They were all gathered in the family room. It was another lovely room Roy had designed for Annie when he built Logan Place.

The walls were covered with hunter green wallpaper with a floral pattern. Above a gray stone fireplace Chad had hung pictures of the children showing them at different ages. The drapes hanging at the windows were a sunny bright yellow with a sheer center piece, and shiny, dark, oak wood flooring, with the most beautiful crushed blue velvet sofas and chairs, with matching cherry end tables and antique brass lamps.

Russ walked into the family room where Charlie, Marian, Annie, Chad, and Sarah were sitting patiently and closed the double doors behind him. "Family," he said, "I got something to say. First, I want to apologize to you, Sarah, Marian, but most of all, to you, Annie."

"Apologize for what, Pa Logan?" Annie asked.

As the tears started to roll down Russ' face, he said, "No, please, let me finish before you ask me anything. I've been keeping this from you Sarah, Marian, and you too, Annie, because I really thought I was doing the right thing for the family. Everybody was hurting somethin' awful after Roy was taken from us, and I just couldn't see putting fear on top of a mountain of family pain. You see, that night I killed Gus, what I didn't tell you was what his last words to me were. Gus told me that he never did like me, and he cared even less about my family. He said that he would never forgive me for killing his Pa, but that I would remember him. Then he said, 'For every son your son has, there won't be any rest for us Morgans until they're all dead.' I froze. I couldn't believe so much evil could be in one man, let alone an entire family, and in a dying man. So, I just couldn't bring myself to tell you this, Sarah, Marian and Annie."

Annie said, "So, Pa, you're telling us now that the Morgans were responsible for Roy's death?"

"Yes, honey, that's what I'm telling you," Russ replied.

"Well, tell me this, Pa," Annie asked. "Did Roy know about this?"

Russ answered her, "Yes, Annie, I told him. I didn't know how else to keep him safe."

Annie said, "Pa Logan, this wasn't you're doing. You did your job. I'm thankful to you for telling Roy so he didn't live in fear."

Chad said, "Pa Logan, I think you're leaving out something"

Russ looked at Chad then said, "Chad, maybe you should tell it."

"Okay, Pa," Chad stood up and said right out. "Annie, I shot and killed the man responsible for shooting Roy on the cattle drive. It was Pace and Lace Morgan, only I didn't kill Lace. I merely shot him in the shoulder, but he's alright."

For the first time in Annie's life she was filled with emotion for her children and outrage for her husband, like she had never felt before. Annie looked at Chad and said with anger in her voice, "So, you justify my husband's murder by shooting his killer in the back? Chad, we're Logans, and we don't handle our affairs that way!"

"No, Annie, it wasn't like that at all," Chad responded in a loud voice. "I was sick inside, Annie, and so were the men. When we got to town, I did everything Pa Logan and Pa Potts told me to do. But in my gut, I knew that we'd find them in Cockapoo. I know the Morgan's, Annie. They're killers."

"I told Mr. Clayton what happened to Roy on the drive," Chad continued, "and when we finished our business with the Cattleman's Association, Mr. Clayton told me that the Morgans came riding in and shooting up the town, bragging on how they got them a Logan. I stood there Annie, something came over me, and yes, I killed, but I didn't shoot anyone in the back." Crying like a child for his dear brother, Roy, Chad told Annie, "It was fair, Annie. It was fair, just like I promised it would be."

Annie reached over, put her arms around Chad, and held him in her arms. And as they cried together for their love of Roy, Annie thanked Chad, not only for seeing that justice had been done, but for handling it the right way. Annie told Chad how sorry and wrong she'd been to even think he would do such a thing. The most important thing now was keeping the children safe. Annie looked at Pa Logan and said, "But tell me, Pa Logan, how do we keep five children a secret?"

"No one knows about the children except Doc, Sophia, and now Jonas. That's an edge they will have. When the time comes all five of them will know what to do, and how to do it. I'll make sure of that," Chad replied.

"And Annie," Russ added, "to answer your question as to how I plan to keep them safe, it's simple. Just don't let them off the ranch, and Charlie and Chad both agree with me. And since the children are home schooled makes it all the better. There's enough on this ranch to be completely self-sustained. Roy built it that way."

But what no one was aware of was that not all the Children were in another part of the house. Chocolate was outside the family room window and overheard the whole thing. Young and frightened out of his mind by what he overheard, Chocolate ran to find his brothers and sister. With tear filled eyes, he ran straight to Buff crying profusely.

"What is it, Chocolate, and why all the tears?" Buff asked.

Chocolate told his brothers and sister word for word what he had overheard. Buff said, "Listen up," trying to calm the others down. "I said, listen up," Buff repeated loudly. "We're not little kids anymore, although sometimes Ma thinks we are."

"We're not grownups yet either, Buff," Fuchsia replied, with tears in her eyes.

"I know that, Fuchsia, but I want you to hear me," Buff said. "No more tears from this moment on. Clay and Fuchsia, you know your job for now is to take care of Ma and the ranch."

"Buff, you, Gray and Chocolate are leaving, aren't you, Buff?" Fuchsia asked, interrupting her brother.

"Yes," Buff replied, "Just as soon as we're ready, and we all know why. And if someone wants to kill another Logan, we'll play that hand when it's dealt to us."

Destiny Calls

AFTER LEARNING THE truth about Roy's death, things seemed a little easier for everyone. Russ seemed to be free of the heavy burden he should never have carried, and Charlie seemed to be feeling a little easier, too. However, with the truth out, Annie still didn't know for sure if Sophia Morgan knew one of the Morgans had murdered her husband, Roy. Annie hoped to at least restore their once treasured childhood friendship. Annie's prayer to God now was asking for his help in keeping her children safe.

For a while Annie thought perhaps Jonas had forgotten to ask Sophia to pay her a call. Several weeks went by before Sophia came to see Annie. It was a hot and dry mid-morning. Annie was sitting in the family room with the ceiling fans on, reading.

Chad came in and said, "Annie, you have a caller."

"Show the caller in, Chad, and thank you." Annie replied.

The caller was her dear friend, Sophia. "Well, come in," Annie said. "Don't just stand there with that schoolgirl smile on your face."

Sophia walked over to Annie, gave her a hug, and said, "You look as lovely today, Annie, as you did when we were little."

"As do you, my dear," Annie said joyfully.

Sophia said to Annie, "What a sweet thing to say. The truth of the matter is, I've been to hell and back more than once, Annie."

Annie told her friend, whom she hadn't seen in many years, "Sophia, I'll tell you what my Pa told me about visiting hell. He said to visit hell is one thing; to live in sin, now, that's another. He told me that hell is a place on earth that we can walk away from anytime we choose. Now, that's my lesson on hell," Annie advised her dear friend. Annie then gave Sophia a little tour of Logan Place.

Sophia said, "Annie, this is the most beautiful home I do believe I've ever seen in all my life."

"Yes, my Roy did a wonderful job. He was always good with his paws," Annie responded with a smile. Sophia told Annie that she had wanted to attend the services for Roy, but she understood and respected the family wishes for a private service.

"Sophia, would you like something to eat or drink?" Annie offered.

"Yes, thank you, Annie. A glass of water would be nice. It's a bit hot out today, you know."

"Yes, it is. Come with me, and let's get this girl a tall glass of water," Annie said.

As she sipped her water Sophia said, "So, Annie, Jonas said that you wanted to see me about something?"

"Yes, I did. Well, I wanted your help with schooling my young ones. I started working with them one hour a day when they turned eight, but now it's getting to be a little too much for me," Annie explained to Sophia.

Sophia said to Annie, "From what I remember about you and school, Annie, you made all A's. In fact, you might be more qualified than I am."

"Nevertheless, you're the teacher, I'm not," Annie replied. "And it would be helping me in a big way."

"Well, sure then, Annie. I'd love to help out," Sophia said.

The plan was for Sophia to teach on Monday, Wednesday, and Friday. This would leave Tuesdays and Thursdays for Annie to help them with their studies.

Sophia said, "Together again. It feels nice, Annie."

"You know, Sophia, we have a lovely guest house not far from the main house and you're welcome to use it while you're tutoring the children," Annie told Sophia. "You might even want to stay here, on the ranch. Would you like that?"

Sophia said, "Thank you, but no thank you, maybe later. For now, I'm enjoying being on my own. Tell me, Annie, how old are the children now?"

"Well, you'd think they were our age the way they act," Annie replied, "but they're fourteen years old now and growing fast."

Sophia said, "My, Annie, all those babies at once, oh dear. Well, we need to get busy then, don't we? My, Annie, where does the time go? It flies so fast. It's been lovely spending the afternoon with you, Annie, but I'd better start my drive back to town before it gets dark. And I'll see you in the morning."

"It's been lovely seeing you as well, Sophia," Annie replied.

She walked her friend to the door and waved goodbye. She closed the door and walked around the ranch looking for Chad. She found him bringing water up from the creek, filling the horse trough for the horses. "It's a hot day, isn't it?" Annie said to Chad.

"You got that right. So, your visit with Sophia went well I take it?" Chad asked Annie.

"Yes, she's coming tomorrow to take over schooling with the children."

"Annie, do you think that was such a good idea?" Chad asked. "Her last name is Morgan, you know."

Annie replied, "Chad, I understand your concern, but I don't see this as becoming a problem. The children know nothing, and neither she nor I plan to tell them anything."

Chad then asked Annie, "Annie, does Sophia know that her nephew, Pace, shot and killed your children's Pa, and that I killed Pace?"

"Sophia hasn't considered herself a part of the Morgan family since her Step Ma, Sarah Ann, died," Annie told Chad. "And when she could get away from them, she did. As for what she knows or doesn't know, I never questioned her. She and

I have been friends for years and she'd never knowingly hurt me or my children."

"Well, ok, I only hope you girls know what you're getting into. And let me know if you need help," Chad told Annie with concern in his voice.

Monday morning, nine o'clock sharp, Annie had the children in the study waiting for Sophia. Annie told them about Sophia and that she was coming to help her with finishing their schooling. When Sophia arrived at Logan Place, Chad led her to the study. When Sophia walked into the study the children stood, said good morning, and introduced themselves one at a time.

Gray was the last one to stand and say good morning to Sophia. He said, "Good morning, Ms. Sophia, my name is Gray Logan - no E."

Sophia smiled and said, "Okay, Gray, no E." Sophia looked at Annie and said, "He must be the smart one."

Annie just hung her head, laughed, and said, "Ok."

Sophia loved teaching but because of her last name she gave it up a while back. It wasn't until helping Annie that she realized just how much she had missed it. Now her days were spent giving piano lessons to some of the townfolk while trying not to be found by her adopted kin, the Morgans. Sophia enjoyed her lovely, lonely little hide-away, and looked forward to the day her last name would finally be changed.

Sophia was amazed just how much Annie had taught them about Math, English, Spelling, so she thought she would start with History. Sophia loved teaching the children, and as the months went by Sophia taught them everything that she learned in school. She gave them tests in history on the different dates and times of the events she taught them. There were tests in spelling, math, and even some science. Sophia even questioned them on famous lawmen, with their own Grandpa Logan heading the list.

Sophia took over for Annie and she grew to love them as if they were her own. They looked at Sophia as if she was an aunt, and the children weren't children any longer. They had grown into what Fuchsia often like to be called - young adults.

Charlie and Russ still came over just about every day after school to spend time with them.

Annie and Chad still made sure the children did their share of work around the ranch. Clay had started to go on cattle sales with Uncle Chad and Nick, while Buff and Chocolate and Gray showed a lot of interest in the Law. Fuchsia was looking more and more like Annie every day, and becoming a good cook like her Ma, too.

Buff was going with Grandpa Potts from time to time up to where some of his gold mines were hidden, but ever since Buff told his Ma they'd been shot at twice, Annie wouldn't allow him to go any longer. And she was a little upset with her Pa for not telling her.

When Chad learned Pa Potts and Buff had been shot at while at the diggings, Chad kept his promise to all five of the children. He took them out once a day after their chores and taught them how to shoot a pistol and rifle.

Buff, Gray and Chocolate and Fuchsia were all getting good. Clay wasn't too bad. In fact, he was good, but it was just not something he cared for. He didn't like pistols much. Like his Pa, he only wanted to know how to use one well, and that he knew.

Annie knew Roy would be proud of the kids. With their schooling soon ending, Annie had wondered about Buff, Gray, and Chocolate. Sophia gave her regular updates after class. She told Annie that from the look of things, she felt that Buff, Gray, and Chocolate had something strong on their minds.

It was the last day of class. All five of the Logans were in the study waiting for Sophia. The children made a card and Fuchsia made a cake for Sophia. Sophia walked in and said good morning. She went on to say that since this was their last meeting that she thought they would have a little party. Sophia said that she and Annie had made some nice treats and things for them.

Sophia said, "Before we end, I want to ask you each a question. Fuchsia let's start with you. Tell me, is there anything special you want to be?"

Fuchsia said, "I want to stay close to Ma and learn the dressmaking business, and maybe have my own shop one day." Sophia was very moved by the closeness Fuchsia had with her Ma.

She then asked Clay and he said, "I want to work the land like Pa did, become a big cattle rancher, and own a lot of land, maybe even build a railroad. The sky is the limit, Ma says."

Sophia said, "Very good, Clay, very good."

When Sophia called on Chocolate, she was a little worried. "Chocolate now tell me what you would like to become," she asked.

Chocolate stood up and answered her, "I want to work for the Middleton Detective Agency."

"Okay," Sophia replied. She knew from teaching the children that there was more to this Detective business, only she didn't know what. She turned to Gray and asked him what he wanted to be.

"I want to be a lawman," Gray blurted out.

"Okay," Sophia said. Then she looked over at Buff and said, "Lawman?"

Buff shock his head up and down and said, "Lawman."

Sophia thought this to be interesting, so she asked, "Can you three please explain to me why you want to be Lawmen?"

"It's simple," Chocolate answered. "We want to help bring peace to the West like Grandpa Logan and bring in all those responsible for killing our Pa, the Morgans."

And they all said together, "Yeah, the Morgans."

Momentarily taken aback at this, Sophia looked at Chocolate and asked, "Chocolate, how do you know it was the Morgans that killed your Pa?"

"We know," he said.

"I'll be right back," Sophia said, and then thought she'd better locate Chad.

When Sophia found Chad, she told him that she felt he should come in and have a talk with Buff, Gray, and Chocolate. Chad asked, "What for, Sophia?"

She replied to Chad the only way she knew how and said, "They knew it was the Morgans," and Chad was out of the stable like the wind.

On their way to the study Chad got Annie and the three of them went to have a talk with the children. Uncle Chad asked, "How do you all know a Morgan killed your Pa?"

Chocolate told his uncle, "Because I told them. I wasn't trying to listen in, but you see, I was coming in from the barn after feeding Lady Nugget when I walked past the open window and heard Grandpa Logan telling what happened."

"I'm sorry, Children, we should have told all of you long ago," Chad said, "but sometimes we grownups don't always have the right answers."

But this time uncle Chad did. He told them everything from beginning to end. Fuchsia went to Annie and said, "Ma, I love you, and I'm so sorry about Pa, but Buff, Gray, and Chocolate are going to clean up the West. You wait and see."

Annie hugged her sweet, caring daughter and said, "I just wish you could have known your Pa, just a little."

Fuchsia looked at her Ma and said, "But we do know Pa, Ma, and more than a little. He's everywhere on this ranch."

Annie had never thought of, or looked at things, in the way Fuchsia had just expressed it, but she knew she would from now on, because every word her daughter had spoken was true. Annie knew her boys had work to do and that their life was already laid out for them. It was getting on to evening time and the children had to get their chores done before supper.

Annie said, "You children hurry up and get those chores done. We're having pot roast tonight."

Annie knew Buff, Gray and Chocolate would be leaving. That was one of the reasons she'd made pot roast, it was a favorite of all her children. After supper Buff, Gray and Chocolate asked to be excused from the table and went outside to sit under the starry sky with grandpa Potts, grandpa Logan and uncle Chad. Clay also joined the men. Once the conversation got going the first thing Grandpa Logan reminded the boys of was that this wasn't about revenge - that they were called to do the same job he was called to do once, long ago. Grandpa

Potts told them to remember that trust is something that is earned and not just given. Clay told his brothers how proud he was of them and that he would hold down the fort until they returned.

Uncle Chad said to Buff, Gray, and Chocolate, "Boys, I've taught you the quick paws draw, how to fight, gamble, how to think like an outlaw. I have taught you all that I know, good and bad, and now, even if you don't know it, you boys are ready. Just don't forget what you've learned." Uncle Chad was one of the fastest, if not the fastest, most honest gunslinger around.

Grandpa Logan said, "And you know everything I've taught you about being a good, fair, and honest lawman. And remember, like uncle Chad said, never take a drink of broth, and to let the ladies alone. In other words, don't go looking for trouble because it surely will find you."

Grandpa Potts said, "And remember, Buff, Gray, and Chocolate, to always remember that this is your destiny. And don't ever turn your back because there are outlaws out there looking to hunt down and kill, or maybe even hang, the first Logan they see."

Grandpa Logan said, "I've been thinking on this and I believe I've come up with something that can really help you boys in your work. Now it's simple; I want you boys to change your last name. I know it sounds funny or even crazy, but look, no one ever knew your Ma had five children except Jonas, Sophia and Doc Ollie. So aside from them you boys aren't known anywhere, so it would give you boys an even bigger advantage."

"Change our last name, grandpa? To what?" Buff asked grandpa Logan.

"How about, Nagol?"

"Grandpa, is that even a word?" Chocolate replied laughlying.

"Yes, Chocolate it is, actually, it spells Logan when you turn it around." Buff said to Chocolate.

They sat there for a moment thinking and saying the name out loud. "Listen, I know it sounds a little strange boys, but I believe it's going to be a good thing in the long run. I mean, you're not hiding from anyone but there's nothing wrong with putting a plan together. And it will also give you boys a chance to find and deal with the Morgans," Grandpa Logan explained.

"You know, Grandpa Logan, you just might have somethin' there. Think about it, Gray and Chocolate, we'll be able to let others know who we are when we're ready. And most of all, we'll know the Morgan brothers before they know us, giving us the upper hand," Buff said to his brothers.

Gray looked at Chocolate and then back at Buff, and said, "Let's do it."

"Nagol it is." Gray replied.

"And on top of that," Uncle Chad said, "you three will be some of the fastest men alive, but I think it would be better if you sent wires only and send them in care of Mr. Jonas at the general store." Grandpa Logan and Grandpa Potts both agreed with Chad. That way no one could connect them to the Logan family.

"Now that we have things set, I believe you three are ready. You boys remember where you come from, don't be so eager to trust or make friends, and look out for one another. I guess what I'm trying to say boys is, just be Logans," Grandpa Charlie said, reminding his grandsons.

"Now go on up and say good night to yer Ma and give her a big kiss, boys. She's not taking this too well," Grandpa Logan told the boys.

It was the most touching moment in all their lives. When Annie awoke the next morning there were three roses on her pillow from her boys. As Annie came down for breakfast, she sniffed at the three red roses. This morning, to her surprise, everyone was sitting at the table in the breakfast room, waiting for her. Annie looked at her Pa as she held the roses to her nose again and said, "They're gone, Pa, aren't they?"

Charlie said, "Yes, daughter, they're gone, but we're all here."

Annie smiled and said, "And all of you are what keeps me strong."

Fuchsia kissed her Ma and said, "Good morning, Ma, how about some bacon, eggs and some coffee? Oh, and I made biscuits, too."

Clay said, "And, Ma, I made the coffee. Have a cup."

As Clay gave Annie the cup of coffee he'd made, she tasted it and said, "Oh, Clay, this is really good coffee."

"Thanks, Ma."

Marian walked over to her daughter and told her, "Annie, you gave birth to five little ones. Three of them from birth were ordained by divine purpose beforehand. But, honey, this is fate, not an accident."

Annie knew, as did the rest of the Logan family, that Buff, Gray, and Chocolate were here for a good reason. Clay said, "Ma, I can see it now,"

"What's that, honey?" she asked.

"The next headline of the Dime Novels," Clay said, holding his paws up together, and then spreading them apart as he said, "How the Logan Boys Tamed the Wild West."

They all smiled as grandpa Logan began to say grace and bless the food.

The Gray Logan Story

JUST BEFORE DAY break Buff, Gray and Chocolate rode off Logan Place riding three of the finest horses raised by the Logan and Potts family, branded with the same brand as the cattle, a paw shape engraved with the letters LP, Logan & Potts. The boys were singing some of their favorite cowboy songs. Each wearing their favorite Stetson cowboy hats with circular Conchos, colorful shirts and blue jeans. They were also wearing gold belt buckles engraved with their initials. Grandpa Logan had given each grandson one for their birthday. It was exactly like the one he had made for their Pa, Roy, on his birthday. They wore the belts proudly along with black, silver toe cowboy boots and long, leather dusters.

Buff was riding a Chestnut Quarter Horse with a little darker red body and lighter reddish mane and tail than the one his Pa had. He named it Nugget. Gray was riding a Quarter Horse with a gold and yellow body, a black mane, and a tail the color of Buckskin. He named his horse after uncle Chad's horse, Lady. And Chocolate was riding a Quarter Horse with a copper red body. The mane and tail were sorrel in color. He named it Lady Nugget. They were some of the finest horses to bear the Logan & Potts brand they'd ever raised

The brothers had one agenda: to bring peace, law and order to the western frontier, starting with bringing to justice the ones responsible for killing their Pa, and being hunted by the Morgan brothers made no difference. Having been taught the quick paws draw by the fastest man alive, their uncle Chad, the boys were more than ready. They awaited each challenge with the courage and wisdom given to them by Grandpa Logan, Grandpa Potts and uncle Chad.

When they came to the three forks in the road, Chocolate knew he was heading to Collieville, but Buff and Gray decided to flip a coin to see who got what. Gray got Poodle Town and Buff got Cockapoo City. They gave hugs to each other and off they rode. Now a young man and on his own, Gray felt tall in the saddle. Gray had many things on his mind. Having never been to a town before he wondered what the people would be like—kind, hard working? But Gray was sure of one thing; he knew he was ready.

Gray followed the stage route like Grandpa Potts told them, and he'd hoped he would have come across a relay station by now. He'd been riding his horse near three hours now, stopping a few minutes at a time to rest. Everything Grandpa Potts told them about the prairie was true - "Hot and dusty for miles and miles." Gray figured he'd come far enough for one day so he thought he should start looking for a place to set up camp before it got dark, but the sound of pistol shots changed all that. Gray noticed a stagecoach driver slapping leather, and man those horses were moving, with four riders on horseback riding down the stage. "They must be road agents, planning to holdup the stage," he thought. Gray froze for just a minute, not from fear, but he wanted to look things over and figure out his best move. After pondering what was taking place before his eyes, Gray felt the only choice he had was to ride in shooting, and that's just what he did. Shooting from the saddle with his left paw Gray picked off three of the would-be robbers, leaving the lone rider to do nothing except turn tail and run.

As Gray approached the stagecoach, the driver slowed down and said, "Man, where did you learn to shoot like that?"

"My uncle Chad taught me," Gray told the stagecoach driver.

The driver asked Gray, "Do you know who you just shot and killed?"

"No, I don't," Gray answered.

"Well, lemme tell you, buddy, you just stopped some of the Red Basset gang," the driver said.

Gray thought to himself, "Now on top of the Morgan's, I'm gonna have the Red Basset gang coming for me. It just ain't my day."

The stagecoach driver thanked Gray in a big way, and said, "I have three passengers with room for another. I'd be right proud to have you ride with me. I'll be making a layover at Dogwood Relay Station, then heading to Poodle Town early morning."

With his butt hurting from saddle sores, Gray was only too happy to accept the kind offer. "Why, thank you, sir, for your kind offer," he said. "I do believe I will accept, Sir."

"You can call me Hank," the driver said. "Tell me, son, what name d'you go by?"

"You can call me Gray. Nice to meet you, Hank."

"Nice to meet you, too, Gray. Just tie your horse on back of the stagecoach and climb on board."

It was Gray's first ride on a stagecoach. Sitting there with a big smile on his face from all the excitement, and having his first stagecoach ride, Gray knew he mustn't let it show. He also knew he mustn't bring special attention to himself by looking like a newcomer, so he pulled the four-inch brim of his brown Stetson down over his eyes and fell asleep, thinking to himself that his journey had just ended where his destiny began.

Before long Gray heard the driver say, "Dogwood Relay Station fast approaching, folks."

Gray woke up, took off his hat and ran his paw through his curly hair. Looking out of the stagecoach window Gray saw a sign which read, "Greenwood Brothers Stage Line…Dogwood Relay Station. Poodle Town 10 miles…Population 350."

Hank pulled up in front of the relay station and announced, "We'll be leaving for Poodle Town come daylight, folks, and breakfast is at 6am."

Gray had some food and got a room for the night, but not before getting Lady fed and settled down for the night. Come morning they were back on the trail heading to Poodle Town. It was a short trip, and before long Gray heard Hank calling out, "Poodle Town, folks."

When the stagecoach stopped, Gray was more than glad to get off and stretch his legs. He threw his saddlebags over his shoulders and walked over to Hank. "Say Hank," he asked, "is there a good place to eat and stay in town?"

"Sure, but first would you mind taking a walk to the Marshal's office with me?"

"Lead the way, buddy," Gray replied.

"Ya know, Gray, you're somethin' else with that pistol," Hank said.

"Thank you, Hank, it took a lot of practice, let me tell you." Gray replied.

On the way to the Sheriff's office Hank told Gray that the Basset Gang held him up once before, but there had been no money on board that day. "You just saved the town Ten Thousand dollars," he said. "When I get back from Cockapoo, I'd like to buy you a drink, Gray."

"I'd like to let you, Hank, but it's milk or sarsaparilla for me," Gray replied.

Hank opened the door to the Sheriff's office and said, "Sheriff Tull, they tried to hold me up again today, sir."

"You mean the Basset Gang?" Sheriff Tull asked.

"Yes, sir," Hank replied. "Sheriff, I want you to meet the man who saved us and the town's money."

Sheriff Tull got up from behind his desk and said, "What's your name, cowboy?"

"Gray, sir."

"So, Gray, what's your last name?" Sheriff Tull asked.

"Gray will do for now, Sir," Gray replied.

Sheriff Tull looked at Gray and asked, "So what brings you to our little peaceful town?"

Gray replied saying, "Begging your pardon, Sheriff, but I don't know if I'd call this a peaceful town. I mean, your stagecoach was almost held up by road agents, and from what

Hank here tells me, they've tried before. But to answer your question, you might say I'm just passing through."

Sheriff Tull got out his wanted posters.

"No, Sheriff, you won't find me in there," Gray said.

Sheriff Tull looked at Gray and said, "Well, I'm stumped."

Gray laughed and said, "No need to be confused, Sheriff. I'm telling you the truth. I'm from Pittsville, sir."

Sheriff Tull looked Gray up and down and asked, "Are you looking for work?"

"Now that depends on what kind of work your offering, Sheriff," Gray answered.

"Did you say Pittsville?" the sheriff asked.

"Yes, sir, I did," Gray answered.

"Where 'bouts?" asked Sheriff Tull.

"Nowhere particular, just here and there," said Gray.

"You ever hear tell of a Marshal out that way name of Logan?"

Gray pushed his hat back showing more of his face, and answered, "Yep, I heard of him. Last I heard he wasn't a Marshal anymore."

"I know, and it's too bad, too," Sheriff Tull said. "We could've used a few more like him. I heard what took place in Pittsville, how he shot and killed Asa and Gus Morgan. Now they're a mighty rough family. Anyway, I have a deputy sheriff job open if you want it, Gray. Why don't you think on it and let me know in the morning?"

"I will, sir. Is there a nice place where I could get a room?" Gray asked.

Sheriff Tull said, "Yes, and if you take the job, the rent is free."

"Well, that's nice to know," Gray replied with a smile.

The sheriff told Gray, "I'll walk you over to Ma Mollie's. Just let me get my hat. She has some of the best rooms and food in town. Her sister owns a boarding house just like this over in Cockapoo City called Bea's Place."

Gray asked the Sheriff where the stable was, and the Sheriff told Gray that Ma Mollie had a clerk that would take care of his horse for him, just be sure to get his bed roll and saddle bags. So, when they got to Ma Mollie's, Sheriff Tull introduced Ma Mollie and Gray. She took one look at Gray and said, "Now,

Alexander, this here is a good man. Just look at him, big and tall, looking well fed. Got to be a Mama's boy, for sure."

Sheriff Tull looked at Ma Mollie and said, "Ma Mollie, I done asked you not to call me Alexander."

"It's your name, ain't it?" she replied.

He looked at Gray and said, "Just call me Alec, please, Gray."

Gray chuckled as he looked at the sheriff and said, "Okay, Alexander."

Sheriff Tull flinched for a second before he saw the glint of humor in Gray's eyes, then said, "Well, it's getting along to supper time. You hungry, Gray?"

"Yeah, I could eat a little something," Gray replied to Alec.

Alec led the way and Gray followed him to the dining room while Ma Mollie brought them supper. It was beef stew. Gray was sitting there thinking how much he loved beef stew. Alec thanked Gray again for helping Hank, then he started telling Gray about some of the trouble in and around Poodle Town. Alec told Gray all about Ma Tessel and her three boys, Lucky, Sandy, and Zack, and her daughter Raina. They lived up in the Mastiff Mountains.

Gray asked, "What are they, cattle rustlers or somethin'?"

"Nope, just plain mountain folk, but those children of hers can't be trusted," Alec replied. He went on to say that their Pa was named Zachariah and the youngest boy, Zack, left home after their Pa passed on. Lucky and Sandy are bad news. They've had it in for Marshal Colby for some time.

"Who is Marshal Colby?" Gray asked the Sheriff.

"He's the Marshal over in Cockapoo," Sheriff Tull answered.

"So, what do you mean they've had it in for Marshal Colby?" Gray asked

"They tried to kill him once when they held up the Cockapoo City Bank."

"So, this Cockapoo is supposed to be a rough town or something?" Gray asked.

"No, not really," Sheriff Tull answered. "No more than this one." Then he filled Gray in on the Morgans. After Marshal Logan killed Gus over in Pittsville, they went wild. Word got around that someone had shot and killed Pace Morgan in what was once the Bobcat saloon in Cockapoo City. Alec said that he wasn't Sheriff when that happened, he was still trying to find his way.

Alec told Gray that he'd heard that Pace left behind a brother named Lace and three or four sons he'd had with some saloon gal. He wasn't sure and didn't know their names. He said that he saw them riding into town from time to time. This gave Gray much to think about. Alec told him all about the Basset and the Bloodhound gangs, too.

Gray learned that Alec had a great amount of respect and love for his Grandpa Logan, so much so that Gray almost gave in and told Alec his last name, but thought he'd better wait. Gray asked Alec where he could make a call or send a wire. Alec said he would show him in the morning but that it would have to be a wire. They didn't have the dog-a-phone in town yet. So, the two men ate a wonderful supper and Sheriff Tull showed Gray to his room.

As Gray lay there with his paws behind his head, he thought of Clay and Fuchsia, and how much he missed them already. Soon Gray closed his eyes and went to sleep. The next morning Gray was up early, as usual, looking to see if the wash pan had any water. It was filled to the top, so he started washing his face and getting his hair together, then got dressed. He smelled food and when he finished dressing, he put on his boots and went downstairs.

When he went into the dining room Ma Mollie said, "I had a feeling you were an early riser."

Gray replied saying, "I don't believe in sleeping late. I might miss something, Ms. Mollie."

"Now, I done told you, it's Ma Mollie," she replied.

"That's right. I'm sorry. Say, Ma Mollie, where can I send a wire?" Gray asked. "The Sheriff was to show me but he's still asleep."

Ma Mollie said, "The best place is at the newspaper office, son. That's what the Sheriff does. It's just across the street. Just tell him you're with Alexander."

"Maybe I should just say Alec," Gray said, laughing with Ma Mollie.

He walked out the door and across the main street to the newspaper office and asked if he could send a wire. Gray asked the clerk if he could please bring any reply to him at the Sheriff's office. Gray addressed the wire to Jonas, care of the general store in Gordon Setter County, Pittsville. That's what Uncle Chad had told them to do. The wire simply said, "Arrived safely."

Gray thanked the man and bumped into Sheriff Tull just as he was about to leave.

Sheriff Tull asked, "Did you get that wire off?"

"Yes, sir, I did," Gray replied. "And thank you for the job, too. When do I get my badge?"

Sheriff Tull looked at Gray and said, "You know, Ma Mollie's usually right when she calls a man out, and I got a really good beat on you, too, Gray, whatever your last name is."

Gray looked at the Sheriff and said, "I've got a really good feeling about you, too, Alexander."

Back at the Sheriff's office, Alec told Gray to raise his left paw and place his right paw on the bible and repeat the oath. Sheriff Tull said, "I, Gray.... by the way, what is your last name?"

"It's Nagol," answered Gray.

" . . . . promise to do my best to uphold the peace in Poodle Town and to serve the folk of this town to the best of my ability, so help me, God."

Sheriff Tull pinned the deputy Sheriff badge on Gray's shirt. Gray was all smiles because he knew destiny was calling. He thought to himself, "I wonder what Buff and Chocolate are doing right about now?"

Getting settled into the deputy job, Gray was in the sheriff's office one day reading the descriptions on some wanted posters. When he came across the Morgans, he finally got to see the faces of the two Morgan brothers who'd been seeking revenge on his family. Gray couldn't believe even with Pace Morgan now dead he still had a $7,000.00, bounty on his head. His brother Lace Morgan's bounty was worth even more - $8,000.00, and both were wanted dead or alive. A man could really get rich on bounty money, but his Uncle didn't accept the bounty, it just wasn't the Logan way.

As the days and weeks went by, Poodle Town seemed to be a quiet town just like the Sheriff had said. Gray and Sheriff Tull were taking a walk around town and Gray asked him, "Sheriff, you were right. This town is quiet, but what I don't understand is, why?"

Sheriff Tull said, "Gray, let me tell you how Poodle Town came to be. You see, Poodle Town was originally further south, just about at the foot of the Mastiff Mountains. And it wasn't called Poodle Town then, it was called Chow-Chow Mining Town. There were claims being jumped and miners being murdered for their gold. Folks was gettin' rich, but just wasn't settlin' down there. So, when all the gold was got, folks moved on. This was a mere stage stop between the mining areas of the Blue Dane Mountains, Cockapoo, Chow-Chow and Beagle Town, and that was the last town before the Morgan Ranch. And it almost got taken over by the Morgans. But then folks started buying up property around here and building ranches, and Saloons, of course, and this stage stop wasn't far from Cockapoo City. So, Gray, you might say that Poodle Town just sort of moved from the foot of the Mastiff Mountains to the foot of the Great Blue Dane Mountains."

"So, whatever happened to Chow-Chow?" Gray asked Sheriff Tull.

"It's nothing but a ghost town now and get this Gray, they say there was a prospector that just up and disappeared there some time back. Binder, I think, was the name."

"Well, Sheriff, if there's one thing I know, folks just don't up and disappear," Gray replied.

"Well, one day my smart young deputy, maybe you will solve the mystery of the so-called missing Miner Binder," Sheriff Tull replied, laughingly.

"You, know, Sheriff Tull, I might just do that. Yep, I might just do that," Gray replied.

Ties To Cockapoo City

AFTER PARTING WAYS with his brothers back at the fork in the road, a sense of loneliness came over Chocolate, probably because this was the first time he'd ever been away from his family. But like Buff and Gray, Chocolate was more than ready. Trotting his way over the prairie Chocolate's mind began to wander. It took him back to the day he was standing outside the family room window. Grandpa Logan had gathered everyone except the children in the family room. Chocolate hadn't meant to eavesdrop on Grandpa Logan, but when he started telling the family about the cold rainy night it sounded so interesting and important, Chocolate just couldn't help himself.

But after hearing everything Grandpa Logan told the family, Chocolate was very glad he had followed his instincts and listened in. Chocolate remembered how upset Grandpa Logan seemed to be. It was a side of his Grandpa he'd never seen before, and he was sure he had seen tears rolling down his Grandpa's face. But it explained why he had become so protective of the children and why they were never allowed off Logan Place. Chocolate knew his Grandpa loved being a Marshal and he also knew his Grandpa wouldn't shoot anyone without a good reason, or there being no other way. Chocolate believed every word his Grandpa Logan said about the killing of Asa and Gus Morgan, but more importantly, he knew his Grandpa wouldn't lie.

And just like his Grandpa couldn't believe anyone could carry a hateful and vengeful heart until they died, neither could Chocolate. Knowing someone is out to kill you isn't a good feeling, so Chocolate knew Grandpa Logan was right by having them change their last name, because it allowed them to be the hunter and not the ones being hunted.

As he rode along singing a song and looking out over the prairie, Chocolate could feel the sun on his back as the hot wind swiped across his sweaty brow. Chocolate reached in his pocket for his time piece that his Ma gave the boys one year for Christmas. His had a blue casing set with diamonds, and the time was noon right on the nose. He rode on and suddenly came upon the welcome sight of a local stage stop. As he rode up, the stagecoach driver was changing horses on the coach. It had Greenwood Stage line, Pyrenees Relay Station written along the top just above its doors.

When he was close enough, he called out, "Hey, driver, tell me, are you heading towards Collieville?"

The driver answered back, "No, I just left Collieville, but there's a stage due here in about an hour from Yorkie City, heading to Shepherdsville. He'll be stopping in Collieville if'n you're waiting on the stage, fellow."

"You know, that's not a bad idea," Chocolate replied. "Tell me, just how far is Collieville from here?"

"Well, riding horseback, sir, trotting or burning leather, it'll still be some daylight left when you get there. So, pay the fare and take the stage, and enjoy the rest of the way," the driver told him, drumming up business for the stage line.

Chocolate tied his horse to the hitching post and went inside. It was a right sizeable place. After taking a seat at one of the tables, a lady walked up to him and said, "Can I get you somethin', Mr.?"

He looked over at the black chalk board hanging on the wall behind the bar and said, "I'll have today's special, please."

"How do you want your steak, sir?" the lady asked him.

"Well done, please, with a glass of milk on the side. And thank you," he replied.

The lady yelled out, "One black board special, burn it."

"Can you tell me where I can wash up before I eat, ma'am? he asked.

"Sure, go right up them steps over there and take room number two. There's clean water and towels, and it'll be 50¢ since you won't be staying overnight."

Chocolate thanked her and went right up to the room. He got cleaned up and laid across the bed for just a few minutes before she came knocking on the door, letting him know his food was downstairs waiting. When he got to the table, she laid the plate in front of him with a glass of milk. Chocolate sat there looking at the piece of charred meat. He was so hungry he wolfed down the steak and fried potatoes, along with a piece of apple pie and a big chunk of cheese. He was so full and tired he asked the lady if she would let him know when the stage to Collieville arrived, and he went back upstairs to his room and laid down. He slept the whole hour, then came the knock on the door. "Hey, Mr.! Hey, Mr., the stage just pulled in."

"Thank you, ma'am," Chocolate answered back.

When he got downstairs, he could see out the window that someone had tied his horse to the back of the stagecoach. The man behind the bar told Chocolate that he'd had his son give his horse to the stage driver, and he tied it to the stage for him. Chocolate gave the lady two bits, then he turned to the little boy who was standing beside his horse and said, "Here's a dime little one, go buy some peppermint sticks."

"Oh, boy, thank you, mister. Thank you! Hey, mister, what's your horse's name?" the little boy asked.

"My horse's name is Lady Nugget," Chocolate told the young boy.

"Next up, folks, Collieville," the stagecoach driver shouted. And before long the stagecoach pulled out of the station. Chocolate was jerked this way and that way, up and down, but he was glad to be off his horse. At least he felt cool for the first time since leaving Logan Place. It was just him and another fellow on the stage. The other fellow looked like a gambler, all dressed up in dude clothes. He looked at Chocolate and asked, "What's your name, fellow?"

"It's Chocolate," he replied.

"You got a last name, Chocolate?" the man asked.

"Chocolate will do," he replied.

"You play cards, Chocolate? I guess you can tell by the way I'm dressed that I'm a gambler," he said.

Chocolate answered him and said, "No, sir, I don't play cards. And I don't gamble, either, but I would like to catch me a few Zzzz's, if you don't mind."

"Oh, I'm sorry, fella. Just making short talk. Enjoy your nap," the gambler replied.

Although the ride to Collieville was only about an hour and a half, it was long enough to fall into a deep sleep. As he tipped his Stetson hat down over his eyes and laid his head on the back of the seat, with the cool breeze blowing against his face he felt like he could sleep the entire trip, and he did. He had always been a light sleeper, so when he felt the stage coming to a stop he woke up. And sure enough, they were pulling into the town of Collieville, and Chocolate was surprised to see the town so full of folks.

The gambler looked over at Chocolate before getting off the stage and said, "You know, fellow, I smell a celebration of some kind. And where there's a celebration, there's money, my boy, money. See you around."

Chocolate got off the stage and got the small bag he had packed with just a few things. He asked the stage driver where he could find a good hotel. The Stage driver told him that Collieville had three hotels, and for sure they were all filled, but the livery stable was just down the street if he wanted to bed his horse down. And he was right on the money, the hotels were all booked. Chocolate unhitched his horse from the back of the stagecoach and walked her down the street towards the livery stable. When he arrived, he asked the little old stableman if he knew of any boarding house with rooms to rent. The stableman said he did, but that it was Founder's Day and he was sure all the rooms were taken. He said to Chocolate, "You're new here, ain't you?" young man.

"Yes, sir, I am," Chocolate replied.

The stableman asked, "So, where you from young fellow, and what kind of name did your Ma give you?"

Turning his face just a little away from the man so he wouldn't see him smile, Chocolate laughed to himself and said, "I'm from Pittsville, and my name's Chocolate, sir."

"Well, Chocolate, you seem like a nice enough young fellow, so I tell you what. I don't usually take in transients, but if'n you have a mind to, you can bed down right in here with your horse," he said to Chocolate.

The idea wasn't too appealing to him, but at least it was warm, and from the smell of whatever it was the old man was cooking, it just might turn out that he's one heck of a cook. So, Chocolate replied, "Sir, I will accept your kindly offer with hope of getting a room in the morning."

"Tell me somethin', Chocolate, are you any good with those pistols you're toting? You got two of 'em, that usually means a fellow's pretty good."

"Well, I guess I'm just as good as the next fellow, why?" Chocolate asked.

"Well, Chocolate, I'll tell you a little secret. Over to the Collieville Grand Hotel, whenever there's any kind of festival or dance the Grand Hotel always saves a suite. And it just so happens there's a Skeet Shoot going on today, and the fellow who wins the Skeet Shoot Contest, he gets to stay in the hotel suite for as long as he stays in town. Now, don't you let on I told you," the old man said.

"Well, now, thank you kindly, sir. I believe I will," Chocolate replied. "Say, by the way, what's your name?

"You can just call me Sam, like everybody else."

On his way out of the stable Chocolate turned and said, "See you later, Sam, and thanks for sharing the secret. I believe I'll head on over to the Collieville Grand Hotel."

Chocolate thought to himself, it couldn't be much of a secret with all the signs hanging in town saying Skeet Shoot Contest today, winner take all. From what Chocolate could tell, it was a nice sizeable town. There seemed to be a saloon on every corner, as well as two banks and a land office. He finally came across the Collieville Grand Hotel, and it certainly was something to see. It took up half of the block and sure enough, ol' Sam was right. The sign outside the Collieville Grand read: "If you think you got two good eyes and a fast draw, enter into the Skeet Shootout. Top prize is a suite at the Collieville Grand with a dog-a-phone and all the vittles you can eat." But it was only for a week, not for as long as your stay in town, like Sam had said. And that was fine with Chocolate because that stable didn't look any sweeter to him now than it did when Sam first told him about it.

So, he walked on over to the table and signed up. He noticed that some of the names had Middleton Man beside it, so he asked the man sitting at the table about it, and the man said, "Well, sir, if you are a Middleton man, then you need to say so right off. It's so that everyone who enters knows what they are up against, so you better be pretty darn good at Skeet Shooting."

Chocolate's first thought was that if he didn't win the Skeet Shoot and had to sleep in the stable, at least he'd found what he came to Collieville for, and that was the Middletons. So, he leaned down and wrote, "Chocolate Nagol from Pittsville," and checked his pistols.

When the contest started it made sense to him why the Middletons had to tell who they were. It was because the contest was broken up into two teams, the Middleton Men and anyone who thought they were good enough to out shoot Collieville's finest. It had gotten down to the fourth round and Chocolate was still in the running. He was paired against a good Middleton Man, but after an hour of Skeet Shooting it had come down to the final two, Chocolate and a Middleton Man. Chocolate had the last shot, and so far, he was shooting a perfect game. The Middleton Man missed one of the four Skeets, so, if Chocolate could make all his last four shots, he would win. And that's just what happened. He beat the Middleton Man with a perfect score.

After the contest was over a man named Nation came over to him to give him his prize. Nation asked if he could pay Chocolate a call at his suite later that evening, and he said that would be fine. Nation then held up Chocolate's arm and told the crowd he was the winner.

After getting the key to the suite, Chocolate turned and there was Sam standing not far from him. As he walked over toward him, Sam said, "That was some powerful shooting, Chocolate, powerful shooting. I tell you what, I'm gonna let you buy me a steak dinner at the Collieville Grand Hotel, how's that?"

"After getting a secret like that and winning, the least I can do is give you a nice big steak dinner," replied Chocolate.

While they sat enjoying their steak dinners folks were coming up to Chocolate almost the whole time they were eating, telling him that was some fine shooting. Some even said it was the finest they'd ever seen. After dinner, Chocolate showed Sam to his suite. They sat and talked some, and Chocolate offered Sam some of the Brandy that was on the table. Sam had two drinks then said good night. The maid came and asked Chocolate if he would like her to draw him a bath. He told her yes, please. Before she left, he gave her two bits, then took his bath. Once he was all cleaned up, he poured himself a glass of sarsaparilla. As he was relaxing there was a knock on the door. He asked who it was, even though he was sure it was Nation, the president of the Middletons.

"Please come in," he told Mr. Middleton. "Would you like a drink, sir?"

"Yes, thank you, and please call me Nation, Mr. Nagol. Now that's a name for the books."

"What is it you find so unusual about my name, Nation?" Chocolate asked.

"Well, if you were to spell it backwards, that would make it Logan, wouldn't it? And that would make you Chocolate Logan, is that right?" Nation replied, as he took a sip from his glass.

"Okay, so you've done your homework," Chocolate aggressively replied.

"Oh, I always do my homework, Mr. Logan. For instance, I know you have three other brothers and a sister, and I know your Pa was killed before any of you were even born. You see, Chocolate, my Pa is Jonah Middleton, the founder of the Middleton Detective Agency. Mr. Logan . . . . . ."

"Oh, please, call me Chocolate," he told Mr. Middleton.

"Ok, Chocolate, it's like this, my Pa and your Grandpa Logan were the best of friends, and your Grandpa came to my Pa for protection for his son. So, you see at your grandpa's request the Middleton Detectives has kept a close eye on the Logan family since right after your grandpa stopped being the Marshal of Pittsville. And right now, I know that your brother Buff is either in Cockapoo City or almost there, and your brother Gray was heading to Poodle Town. And I knew you were heading here, but what I don't know is why. Would you like to tell me your reason for coming to my town?"

"Certainty," Chocolate replied. "I came here because I wanted to join the Middleton Detectives, so I could go places more freely than my brothers could just being town Lawmen, so I could bring in outlaws and families like that no good for nothing family called the Morgans. You must know that they're out to kill the first Logan they come across."

"Yes, we know all about the Morgans. They've been nothing but trouble. It seems like they've been around since before time and their roots go deep. Rumor has it, they were once tied in with a man in Cockapoo named Bobcat Cobb before he died. But tell me something, did your grandpa ever tell any of you how your Pa died?" Nation asked.

"We know enough," Chocolate replied. "Why do you ask?"

"Well, then you must know when I heard of your Pa's disappearance during the stampede, I had my detectives search that whole area and beyond for several days after that stampede and they didn't find much of anything - not even a body. And it was reported to me that the herd hadn't travelled too far before the men gained control of it and finished the drive to Cockapoo City."

"No, I wasn't aware of that. So, are you trying to tell me that my Pa could still be alive?" Chocolate asked.

"Well, there is that possibility, but I'm only saying that we found no body. What you choose to believe is up to you, but if I were you, I would only tell my brothers for now. I mean, for all we know your Pa could have drowned in the Pyrenees River. The herd was camped right next to it. You see what I'm saying, Chocolate?"

"I do now, Nation, and I'll only tell my brothers for now, until I have more to go on. But tell me somethin' Nation, how is it that you know so much about my family?" Chocolate asked, with a curious look on his face.

"I'm sure you remember Mr. Jonas?" Nation asked.

"Sure, Mr. Jonas owns and runs the General Store in Pittsville, why?"

"We'll, Chocolate, Mr. Jonas is my uncle. He and my Pa, Jonah, started the Middleton Detective Agency. So, when your grandpa went to my uncle Jonas for help, what your grandpa didn't know was that Jonas is my Pa's brother and a Middleton man."

"Well, I can say this for sure, Nation, you've definitely got my attention," Chocolate said with a little laugh.

"Chocolate, with those quick paws of yours you would be a good man to have around. You say yes, and I'll answer any questions you may have," Nation replied.

"Well, I came to Collieville to join up with the Middletons, but I've been thinking all the way here that maybe my place is in Cockapoo City with my brother. You know what I mean?" Chocolate replied.

"I can promise you this, Chocolate, if you accept my offer and join us, I can put you in Cockapoo with Buff. You see, Chocolate, I need someone with your assets, capability, and the determination you seem to have. C'mon, let's take a walk around town and I'll show you our headquarters while I fill you in on how you could be of use to me, your brother and Cockapoo City.

Chocolate grabbed his hat and strapped on his pistols, and out the door of his hotel room they went. As they began making their way towards the Middleton Detectives headquarters, Nation began filling him in on the undercover assignment.

"Now, Chocolate, the Marshal of Cockapoo City is a man named Ben Colby, and we know Ben's Pa, Lance Colby, was the Marshal before Ben. Now it's on record that Lance Colby died from liver damage due to his heavy drinking, but we believe Lance Colby committed suicide. What we don't know yet, is why. Now Holiday, Jr. paid me a visit a few years back.

He told me he suspected his Pa might have been murdered. He said he remembered before his Pa died, that his Pa mentioned to him the possibility of a plan to swindle his Pa and the miners, and that his Pa left his entire fortune to him, apart from a mansion in Shepherdsville which he left to his two grandchildren, Ashley and Thurston Holiday. What I've learned so far is that the Holiday Mansion was sold."

"So, the son sold the Mansion?" Chocolate asked.

"No, the Mansion was sold illegally and without anyone's knowledge, except the crooks who thought they could get away with it," Nation replied laughingly.

"Now, an agent who I planted in Cockapoo a while back tells me that there's a possibility Richard's Pa, Holiday, Sr was murdered at around the same time an ol' prospector named Miner Binder just up and disappeared. I also know that someone filed on the claim, but no one in Cockapoo recognizes the name. Here's where things get interesting - a fellow by the name of Hollister Bobcat Cobb suddenly comes into a fortune, a large fortune. But now he's dead. I have a few key players which you'll be looking into, and I hope by the time you get there, Buff will have more to add."

"Bobcat has a nephew named Napoleon Calico Fatcat Cobb, and he seems to have taken over things. He Changed the name of the saloon from the Bobcat Saloon to the Fatcat Saloon, and Fatcat thinks he's the owner of the Bar X Ranch, which was originally called the Holiday Mansion. And we believe that whoever killed the prospector most likely killed Mr. Holiday, Sr."

"Do we know why anyone would want these two killed?" Chocolate asked

"No, but if I had to take a guess, I'd say gold, land, or both," Nation replied. "And there are two companies the Holiday families own that someone tried to take over - two pet companies. One is called 4 Leggs & Me, and the other is Dillon's Doggie Creations. I believe the takeover of these two companies was used as a distraction from the murders. Interesting, isn't it?"

"Well, I'm in. So, when do you want me to leave for Cockapoo City?" Chocolate asked.

"I'd like for you to leave tomorrow evening on the night stage. I think it would be better if you just eased your way into town. We have a pretty good organization set up in Cockapoo. It was put in place during the Gold Rush. So, Chocolate if you need help, contact a Mr. Thaddeus Clayton or his son, Thad Clayton, Jr., or either of his sons two friends - Dean Moorhead, a fellow who owns the newspaper, and a guy who owns the livery stable who goes by the name Dollar Five. I already told you about the Telegraph office; Chet Basenji. Get word to him but only if you need help. And Chocolate, if anything goes wrong, get out fast because those boys play for keeps. Oh, and one last thing, Chocolate, don't bother sending word to Jonas. As of now you are an Undercover Agent for the Middleton Detectives. I'll take care of that for you. And your horse will be waiting for you at that Livery Stable. And remember, walk easy, Chocolate," Nation said.

"You know somethin', Nation?" Chocolate replied.

"What's that, Chocolate?" Nation asked.

"I sure as heck hope brother Buff trusts his gut and fesses up and takes those guys into his confidence," Chocolate said to Nation.

"No need worrying on that, Chocolate. Mr. Clayton knows your brother is coming. He may be a little put off by the name change, but I assure you, he's been informed of Buff coming to Cockapoo City," Nation assured him.

"Well, Nation, I must say, I got a lot of respect for you and the Middleton Detective Agency," Chocolate replied, laughingly.

So, for the next day Chocolate took in the sites, because that night he would be joining his brother in Cockapoo City.

Confession

HE WAS BORN Benjamin Lance Akita Colby, Jr., but he favored Ben Colby, Jr., or just plain Ben. Most folks around town just called him Marshal Ben Colby. Ben was the only son of the now departed Mr. & Mrs. Benjamin Lance Akita Colby, Sr., of Cockapoo City. Devoted and loyal to her family, Betty Louise Maltese Colby was just like any other western frontier woman. She was raised real proper like and she saw to it that her son, Ben, was raised the same way.

Ben's Pa, Lance Colby, was a family man and farmer and proud owner of the Lazy Z ranch with the same devotion and loyalty to his family as Betty Louise. Lance Colby ended up becoming the first Marshal of Cockapoo City. Years later after Ben's Ma and Pa died, the town's leading citizens came to Ben Colby, Jr. and asked him if he would accept the appointment as the new Marshal of Cockapoo City. Ben remembered it like it was yesterday.

The way Ben had it figured, being the Marshal might help bring back the integrity to the Colby name that it once had when his folks were alive. He was a married man himself now, and living with his wife, Hope, on the Lazy Z and trying to make it livable again. Ben was sitting out on the porch one day with letters he'd found in a box belonging to his Pa, and on the outside of the envelope he was holding was written the word 'Confession'. But before reading the letter Ben closed his eyes just for a minute and drifted off into a deep sleep. His memory started to take him back to when the Lazy Z was one of the biggest working farm ranches for miles around.

With the help of the Greenwood and Sons Freight Company, Ben's Pa shipped Colby crops nearly all over the Nokota and Appaloosa Territory. They were some of the best crops ever grown. Lance Colby knew how to work the land. Every season come harvest time Ben remembered his Pa having to hire some folks from town to help with the harvesting. Ben remembered how his Ma once rubbed elbows with the Claytons, the Greenwoods and the Holidays, some of the wealthiest families in Cockapoo City.

But that all changed when some nasty little rumor started clawing and making its way around town. Rumor had it that Ben's Pa, Lance Colby, had taken up drinking and gambling and fast-talking floozies, and became a regular at the Bobcat saloon. Betty Lou noticed a change in Lance, but she didn't give it much thought. Ben remembered his Ma telling him not to take on so over gossip. She told Ben that gossip was nothing more than chinwag chatter and made up lies by folks with nothing better to do with their own measly little lives.

But Lance Colby was just like any other ordinary man. Ben sadly watched his Pa take to drinking and gambling like a dry rag sucking up water. Ben recalled his Ma asking his Pa one evening while they were having supper, "Lance, honey, some nasty talk is going around town about you."

"Betty Lou, since when did you start listening to loose talk? You always called it chinwag chatter. Now you wanna go and start nagging," Lance replied.

"So, you say I'm nagging. Well Lance Colby you hear me and hear me good. You gonna regret the day you ever heard of Hollister Bobcat Cobb and that Bobcat saloon, mark my words," Betty Lou warned her husband.

Ben recalled that as being the first real argument his folks ever had. But his Ma had called it right straight, because every word told about Lance Colby was true. Lance Colby's gambling nearly lost every cent he had saved in the Cattlemen's Bank and Trust, to Bobcat. If it had not been for his Ma, his Pa would have lost the Lazy Z to Bobcat, too. Seeing how badly his Ma needed money, Ben took a hotel room in town and got a job hauling Freight for Greenwood and Son's Freight Company and gave most of the money he made to his Ma.

Betty Lou saved just about every bit of that money and left it to Ben along with the deed to the Lazy Z, after she died from consumption. Lance Colby lived out the rest of his life on the Lazy Z in shame and guilt. It was told Lance Colby died from liver damage a year after his wife. Lance didn't leave much to show for a man who once had as much wealth as he'd had. Ben began rolling his head from side to side and suddenly he woke up, realizing he was still sitting on his front porch and still holding the letter.

As Ben opened the letter, he began reading it and the first line read, "I, Lance Colby, hereby confess . . ." Ben could not believe it was a confession letter from his Pa that he'd found. Deeply engrossed in the letter Ben began to understand the behavior in his Pa that his Ma, Betty Lou, felt wasn't becoming of her husband, Lance Colby. The letter explained how Bobcat had called in Ben's Pa's gambling debts, and made Ben's Pa, Marshal Lance Colby, Bobcat's ready-made lawman, collared and chained.

Lance Colby's confession letter went on to tell how Bobcat ordered the killing of a prospector that was mining his claim in the little, now-abandoned mining town of Chow-Chow. Lance's letter also spoke of another killing that Bobcat orchestrated, only he didn't mention a name. Shortly thereafter Bobcat came into a great deal of money and gold, but the letter didn't say how Bobcat acquired it all. Lance Colby wrote how Bobcat used his crooked gambling tables to cheat owners out of their land, and in many cases their ranches, too.

It also mentioned how Bobcat and his henchmen rustled cattle and changed their brands. Ben knew that if Bobcat was alive today, this letter would surely hang him high. Lance ended his confession letter by saying, "The Bobcat saloon was my ruination, and Hollister Bobcat Cobb was nothing but a killer and a thief. Son, if you are reading this letter, please find it in your heart to forgive your old Pa. And forgive Bobcat, too, for what he done to me. Your Pa, Lance Colby."

As Ben finished reading his Pa's confession letter, he couldn't believe the things his Pa had kept secret. He wished that his Pa had taken the letter to the grave with him. With Fatcat threatening to tell the good people of Cockapoo that his wife was once a saloon girl at the Hide Out saloon over to Beagle Town if he didn't follow Fatcat's orders, his Pa's confession was the icing on the cake for sure, especially if Bobcat left a similar letter to Fatcat. Now instead of Marshal Ben Colby having one monkey on his back, he now had two, and their names were Fatcat and Bobcat Cobb, and that was a mountain of trouble for any man, and Marshal Ben Colby made sure he walked real easy like.

Ben put his Pa's confession letter in his back pocket then put the box away. Ben knew he couldn't go on being Marshal of Cockapoo City and be a ready-made lawman of Fatcat's as his Pa was to Bobcat, dressed, collared and chained.

Feeling very low, Ben went to Hope and said, "Hope, why now?"

"What is it, Ben?" Hope asked.

Ben gave the letter to his wife and when she finished reading it, all she could say to Ben was, "It'll work itself out, Ben, you'll see."

"But with no deputy, and this being my three-year anniversary as Marshal of Cockapoo City, Hope, you know the town is going to have its usual celebration for me. If I had a deputy at least I could just quietly step out of the picture," Ben replied.

"I'm so sorry, Ben. This is all my fault. If you'd never married me, none of this would be happening."

"Now, Hope, don't go blaming yourself for this. It's not your fault any more than it's mine. It's just that folks like Fatcat and his uncle Bobcat, God rest his ugly soul, are greedy men and only want to control everything and everyone. Anyway, they don't care who they destroy, hurt or kill," Ben replied to his wife.

Marshal Ben Colby could already feel the same collar and chain around his neck that Bobcat had had around his Pa's. In some ways Fatcat was nastier than his uncle Bobcat, and with the money Bobcat left Fatcat, it just made him a more powerful outlaw. The only problem was Fatcat wasn't wanted for any crimes, yet. Ben knew there was no way he or Hope could be a part of this year's anniversary celebrations. So, Ben told Hope to pack some things and have one of the boys bring her to the stage depot in town. He said they were going away for a little while. Ben left for town to meet with the president of the council, Mr. Clayton, to ask if he could appoint someone to watch the town because he and Hope needed some time to take care of a private matter.

Mr. Clayton replied, "Sure, Ben, whatever you and your lovely wife need. I can appoint one of my top hands while you're away. But tell me, Ben, do you know how much time you'll need, or even where you're going?"

Ben replied, "I don't know, a week, maybe two. Hope and I will be heading to Collie City, Mr. Clayton."

Mr. Clayton was a very smart man himself and although he didn't know what was on Marshal Colby's mind, he knew in his heart from the way Ben answered him, that this wasn't good. Ben had one more stop to make before meeting Hope. He needed to pick up something at the Marshal's office. While he was there, he remembered having the letter in his back pocket. Not wanting to bring it with him on their trip, Ben thought to lock it up in the bottom draw of his desk. Then he left to meet Hope at the stage depot. The two of them were looking forward to this much needed trip.

It wasn't a long trip, but it would be one layover at a small stage stop. As the stagecoach pulled out of the stage depot in Cockapoo City, Ben already felt the collar and chain Fatcat had around his neck loosening up. When they arrived in Collie City, he got a room at a hotel for him and his wife. After they unpacked Ben and Hope decided to go and get a bite to eat. After a great meal Hope asked, "Ben, honey, can we walk around town some? It's such a lovely evening and some of the shops look to be still open."

"Why, sure, darling, we can have a look-see in a dress shop or two," Ben replied.

"How did you know I wanted to a look at some dress shops, Ben?" Hope asked, smiling at Ben.

"I know the woman I married, and I know you ain't leaving Collie City or any town without a new dress and hat," Ben said to his wife.

They went into three different ladies' dress shops before Hope found a dress and hat that she liked and wanted to buy, then headed back to the hotel. For the next several days Ben relaxed in the hotel room, and often sat out front of the hotel taking in the sights while Hope shopped her little heart out. By the time their little vacation was nearing an end, Hope had far more things to take back home than she'd come with.

On the night before they were to leave for Cockapoo City, Ben said to Hope, "My God, woman, what did you do, buy everything in town?"

"They're just a few new things I needed Ben. We got some Sunday socials coming up, and I don't want to wear those same old clothes and hat's with different ribbons on them," Hope replied, convincing Ben that she needed everything she'd bought.

On their last night they took in a singing show at one of the gambling and theater houses. Hope could tell that Ben wasn't looking forward to going back to Cockapoo City, but he didn't really have much choice in the matter. The next morning, they took the first stage from Collie City home. Ben felt like a new man, and one of the first things he had on his mind to do was find him a good deputy, maybe even a few. Mr. Clayton always had Ben's back, but he never told Ben about the Middleton Detective Agency being in Cockapoo City, either. It wasn't because Mr. Clayton didn't trust Ben, it was more because of what Ben didn't say. Mr. Clayton was a man who followed his gut, and his gut told him that there was much more going on in the Marshal's office. Like other folks in Cockapoo, Mr. Clayton knew of the rumors that were told back when he was a little tyke about Marshal Lance Colby, but there just wasn't any proof. But his Pa told him all about Lance Colby, Bobcat and his henchmen. And when Mr. Clayton, Jr., took over his Pa's seat on the town council, he had a pretty good idea of who was who in Cockapoo.

When Ben and Hope arrived back in Cockapoo one of the men from the Lazy Z was waiting at the stage depot with the buggy. "I see you got my wire," Ben said. "I was thinking you might not get it in time to meet us."

His ranch hand replied, "I was in town picking up some stuff for the barn. Chet saw me and told me he had a wire for me, and it said you were coming in on the morning stage, so I just hung around town till you and Mrs. Colby got in, sir. It didn't make sense to go all the way back to the ranch, then come back here. I hope you didn't mind me being off the ranch, sir." As he was putting the bags in the buggy he asked, "Is this everything Mr. Colby?"

"Yes, and no, I didn't mind you waiting in town for us. It was the right thing to do. Now let's head on home. That was one dusty ride and we can't wait to get home and freshen up," Ben replied.

The next morning things were back to normal. Hope had fried chicken, potato salad and blackberry pie packed for Ben's lunch, so he wouldn't have to eat at the café in town. Ben slept in just a little longer than he usually did, but the smell of hot coffee and biscuits woke him up. Ben got washed up, dressed, and pinned on his badge. When he walked into the kitchen Hope had his breakfast waiting for him.

"You know, a man could get used to this and never want to leave home," Ben said. He kissed Hope on the lips and sat down to eat.

"Well, now, you just sit down here and enjoy your breakfast, darling."

Ben took one bite of his eggs and a bite of the bacon and said jokingly, "Hope, you gonna get the fellas around here fat and lazy, including me."

"Oh, Ben, eat your food and get to town," Hope replied. "I'll have a nice supper waiting for you when you get home."

"Oh, honey, I may be a little late," Ben said. "If I don't run into Mr. Clayton in town I may need to ride out to his ranch and let him know we're back."

"Understand, darling, and I'll keep your supper warm," Hope replied.

Once he was finished with his breakfast, he kissed his wife. All Ben could think about on his way to the barn to saddle his horse, was getting to the Marshal's office and getting his Pa's confession letter from the bottom drawer of his desk. Ben rode out of the barn and waved goodbye to Hope until they were out of each other's sight.

But what Ben was unaware of was that while he and Hope were away on vacation, a young man rode into Cockapoo City who Mr. Clayton became fond of right from the start.

16

The Buff Logan Story

WAKING UP TO the fresh morning smell of the prairie, Buff knew he did the right thing when he decided to make camp last night. Reaching in his saddle bags Buff pulled out an 18th century time piece. It was a gold and enamel casing, set with diamonds and pearls. His Ma had given each of the boys a special timepiece for Christmas one year. Now having an idea of the time, Buff washed up in the little creek he camped near.

He got a fire going and made himself some bacon and beans for breakfast and a pot of coffee. He knew he would be in Cockapoo City before night fall, which would give him plenty of time to send a wire to Mr. Jonas letting the family know he'd arrived in Cockapoo City and that all is well.

He was as happy as anyone who had been on horseback for two days could be, because he knew he'd be sleeping in a warm bed in some one's hotel tonight. Buff knew if he felt this good, then Nugget must feel even better. After giving Nugget her cubes of sugar, as he did every morning, Buff cleaned up everything and started getting ready to ride. He put out the fire and threw his saddle over Nugget and off they went, next stop Cockapoo City.

It was just getting along evening time and Buff knew he was in the home stretch. According to his map, Cockapoo City should be just over the next rise. As he came over the rise, he could see a sign up ahead that said: "Welcome to Cockapoo City, Population 500. Ben Colby, Town Marshal."

Buff thought to himself, "Not a moment too soon." He still had plenty of food and water, but he was tired and dusty from the ride. It was the farthest he'd ever been away from home in his young life.

The first thing on Buff's mind was to get his horse, Nugget, comfortable as soon as he hit town. As he followed the winding road into Cockapoo, he looked up at the street sign. It read: "Front Street." Having never ever seen the inside of a town before, Buff was filled with excitement, and as he came around the corner, he saw a big red barn with white trimming.

It was the stable. The sign above it read: "Stable your horse here twenty-five cents a day or one dollar a week. Dollar Five, Proprietor." Buff rode up so he could see inside. It was a sizeable place with plenty of stalls. It had several horses already, but room for a few more. Buff called out, "Hello, anyone here?"

From behind him a voice answered, "Hello, sir, I'm Dollar Five. What can I do for you?"

When Buff looked behind him, he saw a little guy. Buff was sure he was Welsh, no doubt a Terrier. He had tan hair and seemed to be well mannered and very business-like. "Hello, Dollar Five, my name is Buff Nagol, but my friends call me Buff."

"Nice to meet you, Buff," Dollar Five said.

"Nice to meet you, too, Dollar Five," Buff replied. "Tell me, can you stable my horse?"

"For sure, Buff," Dollar Five answered him. "I have plenty of room, and just in case you didn't see the price list, my rates are twenty-five cents a day or one dollar a week. Which would you like, Buff?"

Buff thought a minute, and then said, "Let's make it a week." Buff grabbed his saddle bags and bedroll and asked, "Tell me, Dollar Five, is there a nice clean place to eat and sleep in town, and somewhere I can send a telegram?"

"Yeah, two doors down you'll find the Telegraph office," Dollar Five answered. "The fella who runs it is named Chet Basenji, and you can try my Aunt Bea's place for lodgings. She has nice big rooms and you'll get the best hot meals in all of Cockapoo City. She's a little bold and a little stubborn. In fact, some have called her a tough old goat, but she's the best for miles around."

Buff looked at Dollar Five and said, "Tough old goat you say? Okay, little buddy, I'm sold. Now how do I get to your Aunt Bea's place?"

"Follow me to the door, I'll show you. Now, soon as you leave here, make a right. That will lead you back to Front Street. Continue walking down Front Street for about three short blocks and you'll see Bea's Place on the left. It's at the other end of Front Street. You can't miss it."

Buff turned and said, "You take good care of Nugget for me, now, ok? She's a good horse."

"Don't worry, Buff, I will. Hey, maybe I'll see you there," Dollar Five said waving goodbye.

"Thanks, Dollar Five," Buff replied. Buff lifted his cowboy hat, ran his paws through his soft, wavy blonde hair, and put his hat back on. Then he threw his saddle bags and bedroll over his shoulders and headed out towards Front Street, but the first stop was the Telegraph office. After Buff sent his wire, he asked the clerk, Chet, to bring any answer wire to Aunt Bea's Place.

Buff was a bit tuckered out from the ride but filled with excitement seeing his first town. Buff thought he would walk around a bit. As soon as he turned onto Front Street his eyes bugged wide open. "Wow, what a town!" he said to himself. He saw lots of horses tied up to the hitching posts on both sides of Front Street. Buff was amazed by Cockapoo; it looked like a rich town. He saw at least two saloons so far. One was called Stella's Place. Buff walked up so he could get a look inside and it was some place. The outside was painted dark blue with white trimming and there were two big windows, one on each side. And right on the windowpanes it said "Stella's Place" in big white letters.

Inside there was a large brown bar to the left, and in the middle of it hung a portrait. Underneath it said: "Ms. Stella Siamese." Buff stood there looking in the window trying to get a look-see at Stella. There were lots of tables and chairs centered around the room, and from the ceiling hung three chandeliers. There were thick red drapes with the name Stella written across them, hanging in front of what appeared to be a stage. Then as if like magic the drapes opened, and this beautiful woman walked slowly out and on to the stage.

She was somethin' to look at, too, Buff just knew it had to be her, Stella. She was wearing a beautiful long red and black dress with black high heel shoes. Buff walked inside just for a minute. He heard the woman say, "Welcome to Stella's. This is my house, and these are my ladies." Then six ladies walked on to the stage, wearing colorful red short skirts and black stockings, real costume like. As Buff continued to listen Stella said, "Fellas have won lots of treats in here, so, pick a chair, any chair, to lose your money in. We play Poker, Three Card Monte, Faro and Twenty-One in here, so get your money ready boys, cause ol' Stella's gonna clean you out!"

Laughing as hard as he could, Buff got up and walked out of Stella's. As he continued his stroll around the town, he came across a place called the Fatcat Saloon. The sign above the saloon said, Calico Napoleon Fatcat Cobb proprietor. It wasn't as nice looking as Stella's Place. And what Buff didn't know, but would later learn, is that it was once called the Bobcat saloon, owned by Fatcat's uncle, the late Hollister Bobcat Cobb, and this was where his Uncle Chad shot and killed Pace Morgan, the man who cowardly shot and killed his Pa on the cattle drive.

Fatcat was a big guy. He had marble and brown hair with a shade of black, and short legs. Fatcat ran his saloon just like his uncle Hollister Bobcat ran the Bobcat saloon, with watered down chicken and beef broth, crooked Faro dealers, and stoolies who played Poker for the house. Fatcat cut costs wherever he could. He was a greedy man who could not be trusted, and he ran the only crooked gambling house in Cockapoo. Fatcat had no love nor respect for Lawmen, who he referred to as Johnny Law, and hated every lawman he encountered.

The Fatcat saloon was just down the street from Stella's. The outside of the saloon was painted brown and at the very top hung a sign that read 'Fatcat Saloon', with a picture of a cat in the center. Inside the saloon were wood floors, tables and chairs, with a chandelier hanging smack dead in the middle of the ceiling. There were some cowboys sitting around drinking broth and getting drunk. When Fatcat found out his pigeons had money, he would serve them the best whiskey in the house, then wait until they were good and drunk, and just right for plucking. Then Fatcat would tell his stoolies to get them into a crooked Poker game and clean them out of all their money.

Having seen enough of Fatcat Saloon and Cockapoo City for now, Buff made his way to Bea's Place, tired and ready for a soft bed. Opening the door to Bea's Place Buff walked in. The woman standing behind the registration desk was a Lhasa Apso with white hair. She had a slight under bite and was getting along in years. "Well, hi there, short, light, and handsome," she said. "You stand real tall. What can I do for you?"

"That little fellow over at the stable, name of Dollar Five, said I could get the best meals for miles around and a nice clean room here. Do you have a nice room I can rent, ma'am?" Buff asked, standing there with a smile on his face.

"Why, sure, darlin.' Will you be staying with us a spell or just for the night?" Aunt Bea asked.

"Time will tell ma'am. You see, I'm looking for work, Ms. Bea," Buff answered.

Aunt Bea looked at Buff and said, "So you're new around here I see. I didn't catch your name."

"Yes, I just rode in tonight, and my name is Buff, ma'am. Buff Nagol," He replied.

"Folks around here just call me Aunt Bea, so why don't you, too? And that little fellow over to the livery stable, Dollar Five, is my nephew. So, what kind of work you lookin' for, Buff?" Aunt Bea asked.

Buff replied, "Well, ma'am, I can do ranch work and I'm pretty handy with this pistol."

"Well, I'm sure Dollar Five and his friends can help you find work. As for now you just make yourself right at home, Buff Nagol, for as long as you want. Me and my nephew will be here if'n you need anything."

"Thank you, Aunt Bea, that's right neighborly of you. And I almost forgot, the little fellow at the livery stable told me to tell you he sent me," Buff replied.

"And anyone sent here by my nephew gets the twenty dollars a month special—room and board, because he's a mighty fine judge of character," Aunt Bea replied. She gave Buff the key to room fifteen and he went upstairs. He was in for the night. When Buff opened the door, he saw two big windows overlooking Front Street with white lace curtains, a bed big enough for three, and a dresser with mirror and washstand. The room had a very large closet. The flooring was Oak wood with scatter rugs on some parts of the floor.

Buff liked the room and for ten dollars a month, it wasn't bad. Buff got settled in his room then went back downstairs to sit out on the porch and wait for Chet. It wasn't a long wait, and soon he saw Chet coming down Front Street with his reply. Buff read the wire and learned that everyone was fine, and that Gray made it to Poodle Town all right, and Chocolate arrived in Collieville in one piece. 'Will forward', Mr. Jonas had added, and Buff knew just want he meant. He then went up to his room and went to bed.

The next morning Buff was awakened by the smell of eggs, bacon, ham, and fresh baked bread. He got out of bed, washed up, got dressed, and ran down the stairs. When Buff walked into the dining room he said, "Good morning, Aunt Bea."

"Mornin', Buff," she replied. "Did you sleep alright?"

"Just fine, Aunt Bea, just fine. That is some bed. And Dollar Five was right, you do have a nice place," Buff replied, then asked, "Am I the only one having breakfast this morning?"

"Oh, heavens no, child. My regulars will be coming in any minute now, and the four of you are gonna get along just fine, you wait and see," Aunt Bea replied. Dean was the first of her so-called boarders to walk in.

Dean looked at Buff and said, "Good morning. I'm Dean Moorhead and I'm half owner of the town's newspaper, The Cockapoo Eagle News."

"Nice to meet you, Dean. I'm Buff Nagol," he replied.

Dean's family was the Dalmatians. He had white hair with brown markings. He was intelligent, tall, and wearing black framed glasses.

"Thaddeus Clayton, III at your service, Buff. But my friends call me Thad," he told Buff, walking in right on Dean's tail.

Thad was like his Pa, from the Beagle side of the family, and very sociable. He had black and brown hair and was a little on the short side. Thad was part owner with Dean in the town's newspaper.

"Nice to meet you, too, Thad," Buff replied.

Dollar Five looked at Buff and said, "Buff, that's one sweet horse you got there,"

"Thanks, Dollar Five," Buff said.

Dean looked at him and asked. "Where are you from, Buff?"

"Oh, I'm from Pittsville," Buff replied.

Dean asked, "You looking to stay in Cockapoo City, Buff?"

"Well, it's like I told Aunt Bea last night. That depends on me finding work," Buff replied.

"Marshal Colby needs a deputy," Thad said. "You any good with a pistol, Buff?"

"About as good as the next fellow, you might say," Buff answered.

"Well, then, after we eat, let's all go see Marshal Colby and see about getting our new friend here some work," Thad suggested.

"You know, Thad, I believe Marshal Colby and his wife are still out of town." Dean replied.

"Oh, yeah, I forgot. Well, we can stop by my place and see my Pa, he would know. And besides, I want Buff to meet him anyway," Thad replied.

They all sat down and began eating breakfast. After the first bite Buff said, "Very good indeed, Aunt Bea,"

"Well, help yourself, darlin, there's plenty more," Aunt Bea said.

Once they finished eating Thad got up from the table and said, "Let's move, men."

Buff thought it must be fate. Things couldn't have worked out any better if he had planned it himself. So, when they arrived at Clayton Manor, Buff was impressed. It was a beautiful two-story, gray stone mansion with white trim, and was indeed worthy of its name. Thad asked the boys to wait in the parlor until he got his Pa.

Thad's sister, Rebecca Clayton, walked into the parlor. Rebecca looked more like her Ma's side of the family. They were Basset. She was smart, friendly, and she worked as the bank manager for her Pa's Bank, the Cattlemen's Bank of Cockapoo City.

"Hi, Dean, who's your new sidekick?" Rebecca said real smart like.

He replied, "If you must know, Rebecca, his name is Buff."

"Hello, Buff, my name's Rebecca."

"It's nice to meet you, Rebecca," Buff said to a very pretty Rebecca Clayton.

"See you boys later," Rebecca replied.

Thad came back in with his Pa and said, "Pa, I want you to meet our new friend, Buff Nagol. He just rode into town last night, and he's staying at Aunt Bea's with us. He's gonna try for the deputy Marshal job with Marshal Colby."

"It's nice to meet you, son, but Marshal Colby is still out of town. He'll be back in a few days," Mr. Clayton said. "But, tell me, where you from, Buff Nagol?"

"I'm from Pittsville, sir," Buff replied.

"Son, are you sure your name ain't Buff Logan?" Mr. Clayton asked.

A bit surprised Buff replied, "What makes you ask a question like that, sir?"

"Because if it is, I've been waiting for you to get here, that's why. You see, Buff Logan, I'm an associate of the Middleton Detective Agency. It's like this, son, you see, my Pa, Thad's grandpa, Mr. Clayton, Sr., helped Nation's Pa, Jonah Middleton, to get set up here in Cockapoo during the Gold Rush. Cockapoo was nothing but a Tent City full of miners and new homesteaders. With Cockapoo City being the first major town in Komondor County, the Middletons planted an agent to run our Telegraph office but he was suddenly killed. Which is why I was praying that you didn't meet up with any rough play out on the prairie. You see, Buff, my son, Thad, and his friends, Dean and Dollar Five, well, you might say they're my associates, and Nation contacts me through Dean's and my son's newspaper. That's how I knew about your family, and that Chocolate and Gray arrived safely at their destination, as did you," Mr. Clayton told Buff.

"Well, maybe I'll get to know all of you and Cockapoo City as well as you all know me," Buff replied laughingly.

"Did you know Buff's Pa, too, Mr. Clayton?" Dean asked.

"Well, I wouldn't say I knew Buff's Pa, but I did have the pleasure of meeting Roy Logan. I don't think Buff was born when his Pa was murdered trying to bring his herd of long horns to Cockapoo, isn't that right, Buff?" Mr. Clayton asked.

"Yes, sir, we were born shortly after my Pa was murdered. So, we're around the same age as Thad, Dean and Dollar Five, give or take a day or two," Buff replied.

"Do they know who killed your Pa, Buff?" Dean asked.

"My Pa was murdered, Dean. Murdered. And, yes, we know. They didn't make a secret of it," Buff replied.

Mr. Clayton said, "You're right about that, son. In fact, it was the Morgan brothers, Dean."

Mr. Clayton got up and fixed himself a glass of brandy broth and said, "I will never forget that night I met Roy Logan. It was right here in this very room when we closed the deal. It was Mr. Holiday, Mr. Greenwood, and your Grandpa, Thad. In fact, it was the biggest sale of Hereford Cattle in these parts. They went back and forth but Roy Logan knew just what his Hereford Cattle was worth. And he would have gotten just what he was asking for his herd any place he took it. Yeah, Buff, your Pa knew his beef."

"I don't know if anyone ever told you, Buff," Mr. Clayton continued, "but your Pa's foreman, Chad, walked out of here that night with a six-hundred-thousand-dollar check in his pocket for that beef. Mr. Greenwood was holding out trying to get your Pa to come down in price. But when he realized it wasn't going to happen, he came on board with us. There was some shooting afterward and your uncle got arrested. But once things were all cleared up, Marshal Lance Colby had to let your uncle Chad go and the rest is history, as you know."

"I knew some of it, Mr. Clayton. You see my brother, Chocolate, overheard Grandpa Logan talking about it one night to the family, and Chocolate told us. But hearing you tell it makes me feel even better that my brothers and I followed in Grandpa Logan's paw print and became lawmen."

"Well, I'm glad to hear you feel that way, young man.," Mr. Clayton said. "Listen Buff, I'm not sure if the Marshal is back yet but I'll pick you up in the morning and we'll go together and see. And, Buff, I want you to know something. If you or your brothers ever need anything, and I mean anything, you come to me, son. You understand me?"

"That's right kind of you, sir, and I'll do just that. Thank you, sir," Buff replied.

"I got to run now, boys, so you fellows let me know how things turn out," Mr. Clayton replied.

Dollar Five looked at Buff and said, "Gosh, Buff, I'm powerful sorry." Dean and Thad said so, too. Buff was thankful for this moment and now he knew he wasn't alone. They all put their paws together and swore that what was talked about in this room, stayed here. Come morning, Cockapoo would have a new Deputy Marshal, and the four boys had become a pack.

17

The Deputy

MARSHAL COLBY RODE hard and fast to town but as soon as he turned his horse onto front street, he saw Mr. Clayton. Ben noticed that Mr. Clayton wasn't alone. There was a young man in the surrey with him. Ben looked at the young man but couldn't recall ever seeing him in Cockapoo before. Ben rode up in front of the Marshal's office at the same time as Mr. Clayton and got a closer look at the young man. Ben was sure he had never seen the young man before, but Ben somehow knew at that moment that retrieving the letter he so desperately rode so hard and fast to town for, would have to wait.

Marshal Colby looked at Mr. Clayton and said, "I thought you had one of the men from your ranch watch over the town till Hope and I got back, is this fellow any good?"

"No, no, Ben," Mr. Clayton answered. "Buff didn't watch the town, and I did get one of my ranch hands to deputy the town. And he did a good job, too. But I'm glad you decided to only stay away a week, which is why I came to town this morning. You see Ben, Buff here came to town while you and Hope were away. And Ben, I know this young man's family and believe me when I say, he really is the right man for this job. You got my word on that, Ben."

"That's all I need to know," Marshal Colby replied.

Buff extended a paw to Ben and said, "Good morning, Marshal Colby, it's good to meet you, sir."

"It's good to meet you, too, young fellow," the Marshal replied. Before taking Buff inside the Marshal's office, Ben turned to Mr. Clayton and said, "Oh, Thaddeus, Hope and I are right sorry about spoiling my three-year anniversary celebration party the town had planned, but we just had to get away for a while."

"Ben, we all need to get a way sometimes and it was just your turn," Mr. Clayton replied. "I hope you know, Ben, that if you need help with anything, you can come to me."

"I do, Thaddeus, and thanks for understanding," Ben Replied.

"Don't forget now, Ben, that invitation to supper is still open so you and Hope come by the ranch real soon. Well, I'll leave you lawmen the town and be on my way back to the ranch. I'm sure the two of you will get along just fine," Mr. Clayton replied as he rode off in his surrey.

Marshal Colby looked over at Buff and said, "Let's go inside and have a seat. We'll jaw a bit then I'll show you around the town. Sound good to you?"

"Yes, sir," Buff eagerly replied.

Once they were inside the Marshal's office, Marshal Colby started telling Buff about the different folks he will be meeting when he starts to show him around. The marshal said, "First I'll tell you about ol' Red, the rooster. You see Buff, ol' Red and his hen belong to the three winos, Dingo, Dunker and Ned. They have a little shack just on the edge of Front Street and we trade with them for some of the hen's eggs to have at the Marshal's office, for the price of one bottle between the three of them, that is."

"But they're some good ol' boys," Marshall Colby continued. "They just drink a little too much broth, but they're harmless. Now let me see, you already know the Claytons, one of the families that founded our little town, so I guess I'll tell you about the other two founders."

Ben started by telling Buff all about the Holiday family, one of the richest families to ever live in Cockapoo. Ben said, "Now, Richard C. Holiday, God rest his soul, was a very wealthy man. He owned gold mines and land. You know, Buff, that man's ranch was so big that he owned land clear into Appaloosa Territory. They've got a sweet little wine vineyard and cultivated orchards with rows of plum and peach trees that just filled the valley, and some of the sweetest grapes from off a vine you ever tasted. It's told he'd had that mansion built from the ground up for his first wife. His only son, Richard Holiday, Jr., married a saloon girl, who gave him a set of twins, Ashley and Thurston, two of the cutest Tibetan Terriers with tan and cream hair. After his first wife died, he married a woman named Martha Shar-Pei, who had a daughter named Victoria, who hated those twins more than anything."

"I tell you, Buff," Ben continued, "Mr. Holiday was a good man, and even though he didn't trust his son's wife, he made that saloon girl feel like part of the family, too. But she played Holiday, Jr., is what she done."

"Where is she now?" Buff asked.

"Dead. They tried to hang Richard, Jr. for her murder, but the family had too much money to let that happen. Buff, I tell you, they brought in a high-powered lawyer and he proved, dead to right, that Richard, Jr. was innocent," Marshal Colby told his new deputy.

"Do you believe he was innocent?" Buff asked, Marshal Colby.

"Yes, I do, and I believe justice was fair that day. He got off and that was the end of it," Marshal Colby explained.

Buff said, "Well, I'm glad to hear that because I would hate to think that a clever lawyer and money could buy murder on any day, Marshal Colby."

"Yeah, you're so right, Buff," Marshal Colby replied.

"So, what happened to Richard, Jr?" Buff asked.

"He just up and left one day, no one knows where. But that Holiday mansion was something to see. There were two tall stone statues, one on each side of the road, with a cast iron gate with the Holiday name smack dead center. Nothing but money, Buff," Ben said. "If you ride by sometime and look up, you can see it sitting there on top of the hillside; three stories with tall, white columns in a row, lined up from left to right along the front of the mansion. I couldn't talk about the inside because I was never invited in, but when Holiday and his wife passed it was said that he left everything to his two grandkids, Ashley and Thurston. Victoria was not pleased and planned to get even."

Ben continued, "The Mansion was put up for sale and the twins left town shortly after that. Now the ranch is called the Bar X Ranch. I don't know who owns it now, but, Buff, they've been causing some trouble around here. I can't prove it, but it's just got to be them. C'mon, let's take a little walk over and meet the Greenwood brothers. Their Pa, Thomas Greenwood, was the other founder of our little town, and when my Pa was Marshal, I worked hauling freight for these boys."

As they walked, Ben said, "They got some money, too, not as much as the Claytons or the Holidays, but they do alright - Charlie and Matt, two English Sheep twins that look just alike, can't even tell em' apart. They say Matt had a thing for Ashley Holiday. There it is, Greenwood Freight Company. Come on, Buff, let me introduce you to some nice fellows."

As they walked up to the building Charlie and Matt were outside loading up one of their freight wagons. Marshal Colby said, "Got a lot of freight today, I see."

Matt replied and said, "Hey, Marshal. Yeah, business been right good lately. We miss you around here."

Marshal Colby replied, "Hey, fellas, I want you to meet my new Deputy Marshal, Buff. Buff, say hello to Charlie and Matt."

"Afternoon, fellas, nice to meet you," Buff replied.

"Back at ya," Charlie and Matt replied in unison.

"Well, be seeing you, fellas. Got to be pushing on," Marshal Colby replied.

As Marshal Ben Colby and Buff headed down the street, Ben said, "Buff, my boy, next on our list is the lovely Ms. Stella Siamese Rollins. Ms. Stella runs the only honest saloon in the whole town, and she's something to look at for sure."

As they were walking along, Fatcat came up behind them and said, "Some people just have all the time in the world."

Neither Marshal Colby nor Buff said a word as Fatcat raced past them. Once Fatcat was down the street, Marshal Colby said, "Now, there goes Calico Napoleon Fatcat Cobb. You know, Buff, that man owns and runs the only crooked saloon in Cockapoo City, with his watered-down chicken and beef broth. I can't tell you how many times I've tried to shut him down, but I can't seem to catch him. Now that there are two of us, maybe we'll have a better chance. He's a deck of cards, Buff, and he knows how to play every trick in the book just like his uncle Hollister Bobcat Cobb."

"Well, maybe we'll throw in a few tricks of our own," Buff replied.

When they walked into Stella's, Buff got to see her up close. He thought Stella was even more beautiful than he did the first time he saw her his first night in town. You could tell she had class. Stella said, "New deputy I see. Well, now, deputy... if I need help you gonna come a-runnin'?"

Buff was grinning from ear to ear as he said, "I'll do my best, Ms. Stella."

"Well, now, that's all a lady can ask for, isn't it, Marshal?" Stella replied, looking over at Marshal Colby.

"Come on, Buff, we got things to do," Marshal Colby said, smiling.

As they left, Stella called out, "Y'all come back real soon, now, ya hear."

Marshal Colby said, "Next up, Buff, I'll show you the Eastern Brothers' bank. Now these brothers are kind of new to Cockapoo City. They've only been in town a few years, but, Buff, they've been buying up open land outside the town for a while now. Matt Greenwood believes they're up to no good. He wondered why a banker would need so much land. Matt thinks their trying to take over Cockapoo City in some way."

Buff said, "Matt just might be right."

Marshal Colby told Buff that they were almost done with their walk around town, and they only needed to pay a few more visits. Next on the list was the town barber, Dakota Bernard Saint. "We just call him Dakota," Marshal Colby told Buff. "Now, Buff, everybody gets to meet Dakota. He came to town a few years after my Pa passed on. He's a real easygoing, sociable fellow. He's big with black and brown hair. And he can cut his own hair, too."

As they walked in Dakota was grooming some fellow but stopped for a minute to meet the new deputy. He said to Buff, "Your 'bout due ain't ya?"

"'Bout due for what, sir?" Buff asked.

Dakota said, "For a grooming, son. Come see me 'bout Tuesday week. First one's on the house."

Buff said thanks and chuckled. Once they were out of the shop Buff turned to Marshal Colby and asked, "Tuesday week, Marshal, what does it mean?"

The Marshal replied, "Dakota was telling you to come see him, Tuesday of next week. You'll get used to him."

"Well, I'll be," Buff said laughingly.

As they continued their walk, Marshal Colby said, "Now, Buff, we have a Judge here, too. His name is Judge Affenpinscher Tuesday. Because of his long and strange name, folks around here just call him Judge Tuesday. He's a nice enough fellow, a bit on the quiet side. Just don't you go gettin him riled up, but he likes getting other folks riled. He's a smart little fellow, too. When he's in town holding court it's usually at the Cattlemen's Association Bank building. That's it over there," pointing across Front Street.

Buff replied, "So, he's a traveling Judge?"

"Yep, he goes from town to town, but just in the Komondor County Territory. He spends most of his time here though. Nice ol' fellow, that Judge Tuesday. He intimidates ya' just lookin' at ya," Marshal Colby said.

"Next up is the Honorable Mayor, Lakeland Terrier Todd. Just address him as Mayor Todd unless we're having a social or somethin' formal. Then he likes to be called the Honorable Mayor Todd. He's a bit standoffish when you first meet him, but he warms up to you right good. Some town folks don't trust him much, though," Marshal Colby told Buff.

"Has he given them reason to not trust him?" Buff asked.

"I don't really know, Buff, but there is talk. You know how town folks can be once they hear somethin', it's gets around real fast, true or not."

Buff replied, "Well, I guess that's something I'll need to pay attention to."

When they arrived at the Mayor's office the sign in the window read "Out for the Day."

Marshal Colby said, "We'll, come back later, maybe the Mayor will be in by then. Now last on our list is someone I hope neither you nor I will ever need anytime soon. Doc Joshua Cavalier King Charles Stone, the 3rd. You can just call him Doc Stone. His family ran a traveling circus a while back and they put on a show here once. Joshua wanted to be a doctor, so he quit the family circus and started studying medicine. I'd say he came to Cockapoo bout' three years back. He's smart and he's usually cheerful most of the time. Let's see how he's doing today."

When Buff and Marshal Colby got to the Doc's office the sign in his window said, "Out on a call. Back soon."

"Well, Buff, I guess the next stop is to drop you off at home."

"Yeah, it's been a big morning," Buff replied. "What time schedule would you like me to have, Marshal?"

"About eight will be fine," replied the Marshal. "Oh, look there, Buff, the Doc's back, and it looks like he's waving for us to come over. Let's have a look see."

Marshal Colby and Buff started walking over to Doc Stone's as he was walking toward them. They met up in the middle of Front Street. When they were face to face Doc Stone said. "I think you'd better high tail it over to Fatcat's saloon Marshal. I'm sure I heard shooting when I passed there on my way into town."

Marshal Colby looked at Buff and said, "Aren't you the lucky one?"

"How's that, Marshal?" Buff asked.

"Action, son, first day on the job," the Marshall answered.

"Oh, I see," Buff replied. "Well, I was enjoying the peace and quiet myself."

When Marshal Colby walked in Buff was right on his tail with his pistols still holstered. The Marshal said, "Now, let us all just settle down and cool off."

Suddenly a shot came from outside the window and Marshal Colby fell to the floor. Buff ran out the saloon door and around the side of Fatcat's saloon just in time to see a man blowing the smoke from his pistol. The man looked up and aimed his other pistol when Buff said, "Don't even think about it, fella, you're not good enough - no brag, just take my word for it. Now drop em,' and get those paws in the air."

The man dropped his pistol's and raised his paws in the air. Buff took him inside Fatcat's with a pistol pointed in the man's back. The Marshal was still on the floor. With both pistols now drawn, Buff said. "Now I want everyone to move over to one side of the bar, please, and Mr. Barkeep, I want you out in the open where I can see your paws. And while you're at it, collect everyone's pistol. You, cowboy, with the rolled cigarette."

"Who me?" The cowboy asked.

"Yeah, you. Go fetch Doc Stone for me." When Buff had things in Fatcat's saloon under control, he knelt on one knee and saw that the Marshal had been hit in the shoulder, and there was a good amount of blood coming from his arm. Doc Stone came running through the doors and said, "Oh, no, Ben! Some of you men get him to my office and go easy on him," the Doc commanded.

Buff asked, "What you think, Doc?"

"I don't know, yet, and who are you?" Doc Stone asked.

"I'm the new deputy," Buff answered. "We stopped by your office earlier, but you weren't in."

"Well, why aren't you out looking for the fella who did this?" the Doc said in anger.

Buff replied. "I already got him right here, Doc. I'll be back soon as I lock him up."

Doc Stone said, "What's your name deputy?"

"Buff Nagol, sir."

"Nice work, Buff," Doc Stone replied.

On the way to Jail Buff said, "So, what's your name fella?"

The pistol toting slinger answered, "Lucky. Lucky Tessel."

Buff asked, "Is that supposed to mean something to me, Lucky Tessel?"

"You'll find out in due time, Johnny law."

"Good," Buff said. "I'll be here."

Buff locked Lucky up in the jail and said with a smile, "Now don't you go nowhere." Then he headed back to Doc Stone's office where he found Marshal Colby sitting up in bed with his shoulder wrapped. The Doc was telling Marshal Colby that his days as a lawman were over. He told Marshal Colby that he had broken paws, and that they would only be good for walking, and using a rifle from time to time for doing a little bit of hunting. Doc Stone told Ben that if he was younger, it might be different.

Buff said, "I can't believe this is happening. He was just showing me around town. I can't believe it, Doc."

The Doc said, "I'm sorry, too, but there's nothing else I can do."

"Now what, Marshal?" Buff asked.

"Well, Buff, it's up to the town now, but with the Clayton's backing you, it's my guess you'll be the new Marshal," Ben replied.

"What? But . . . but . . . I don't know anything about this town. I don't even know the folks in it," Buff stammered.

"Marshal Nagol, you're ready," the Marshal said. "The way you handled Lucky Tessel, you're ready, son."

"Can I help you home, Marshal?" Buff asked.

Marshal Colby replied, "No, Buff. Doc Stone will see that I make it home alright, won't you Doc?"

"You know I will, Ben." Doc Stone replied.

Looking at Buff Marshal Colby said, "You know, Buff, it might be a good idea if you slept at the jail tonight, and with one eye open for Sandy - that's Lucky's brother. He might try to brake him out. Make sure you get one of the boys to keep you company. Dollar Five, Dean or Thad would love to pitch in and help. Those boys are good to have on your side, and Doc will let Mr. Clayton know what happened. I don't think he'll come by tonight, but I'll make sure he does first thing in the morning. I'm sure they'll want to have a meeting and I'll do my best to be in town for that. And, Buff, it's your town now. Clean it up, starting with Fatcat's Saloon."

Buff walked outside and down Front Street, heading back to the jail. All the way there he was saying to himself, "Gray and Chocolate, where are you guys? I need you."

Murder Rap

B UFF WAS UP the next morning making coffee and going over some ideas in his mind, just in case Ben Colby was right and the board does appoint him the new Marshal of Cockapoo City. Aunt Bea walked into the Marshal's office with a big smile on her face and sadness in her heart at the news of Ben Colby's shooting, "Good morning, short, light and handsome," she said.

With a surprised look on his face Buff replied, "Good morning, Aunt Bea, how did you know where to find me?"

"Well, I had shopping to do this morning and when I got to town Cyrus over at the general store called me over. From the way that man was jumping up and down, a body would think Cyrus had a hot paw. So, I thought I'd better go see what he wanted. Well, when I got there Cyrus was like a bag of nerves and that's not good for Cyrus. Once I calmed him down, he told me Ben had been shot at Fatcat's saloon yesterday afternoon. He said he heard that Ben might have broken paws. He told me that you and Dollar Five were holding down the jail. Is this all true, Buff?" Aunt Bea asked.

"Yes, Aunt Bea, every word of it. Ben will never have full use of his paw's again, thanks to Lucky Tessel," Buff answered Aunt Bea.

"Well, I believe I'll make Ben a nice supper and have one of the boys take it by there this evening," Aunt Bea said.

"That's right neighborly of you, Aunt Bea. You be careful while you're in town now, ok?" Buff replied.

"I'm planning on it. See you later, sugar," Aunt Bea said, as she was leaving the Marshal's office.

As soon as Aunt Bea closed the door to the Marshal's office, it opened again and this time it was Mayor Todd's messenger boy, Tobias Bombay, with a note from the Mayor asking Buff if he would come see him at once.

After reading the note Buff said, "Thanks, Tobias. Tell the Mayor I'll be right there." Buff got up, grabbed his hat and headed straight for the Mayor's office.

When Buff arrived at the Mayor's office, Mr. Clayton and Judge Tuesday were there, too. Mayor Todd invited Buff in and offered him a seat, and started explaining to Buff that Mr. Clayton, Judge Tuesday, and Ben Colby all agreed that he would be a great Marshal for Komondor County, and the town of Cockapoo. Mayor Todd said that considering everything that had happened, the town would be beholding to him if he would accept the badge and be the new Marshal of Cockapoo City.

"I would be right honored to accept the badge," Buff said.

Mayor Todd said, "Buff, will you please stand and raise your right paw, place your left one on the Bible and repeat the Oath after me."

Buff repeated the Oath word for word: "I, Buff Nagol, promise to do my best to uphold the laws of the town of Cockapoo City and the Marshal's office. I promise to protect the town folk and keep the peace in Cockapoo City and Komondor County to the best of my ability, so help me God."

Mayor Todd pinned the badge on Buff's red denim shirt. Just as Buff had finished, Dean arrived at the Mayor's office to take pictures of the town councilmen and the new Marshal for the paper. After pinning the badge on the new Marshal, Mayor Todd walked over to Mr. Clayton and asked, "Thaddeus, you seem to know this young man, who, by the way, I've never seen before. Tell me, do you think he's the right one for our town?"

Thaddeus Clayton replied, "Yes, Mayor, indeed I do. In fact, you might even say he's the prefect one. You look like you're not pleased, Mayor. Is there something you disagree with?"

"Don't be ridiculous, Thaddeus. Cockapoo City is getting a new young Marshal, something we've been needing for a long time now. I just wish I knew more about him, that's all," Mayor Todd replied.

"Well don't you worry your sweet little head Mayor," Mr. Clayton answered, "because you can rest assured that I know all we need to know about this young man."

Mr. Clayton and the Middletons didn't believe a word that came out of Mayor Todd's mouth. Mr. Clayton believed for a long time that Mayor Todd was either behind all the corruption in Cockapoo or he allowed himself to be bought off by the corruption, but he had no proof. He also believed that Fatcat and his late uncle, Bobcat, were smack dead in the middle of it all. Mr. Clayton thought that if Buff turned out to be the kind of Lawman his grandpa once was, they might just get to the bottom of it all.

"So, Marshal, I understand you have a prisoner for me in the Colby shooting?" Judge Tuesday said.

"Yes, I do," the Marshal replied.

"Good work, Marshal. Say, can you have the young man in my court in about an hour or two? I have a little time before I need to be getting over to Poodle Town. No sense in waiting a week for me to get back here."

"Yes, sir, I can have him there, Judge," replied the Marshal.

Mayor Todd asked the new Marshal, "Say, Marshal, do you have anyone in mind for a deputy? Because if you don't, I have a few fellas in mind who will be right proud to wear the star."

"You know, Mayor Todd, I do have some ideas," the Marshal replied. Then he got up and went around the room, shaking hands and thanking each one of the town councilmen. When he got to Mr. Clayton he said, "Mr. Clayton, I want to thank you most of all for having enough faith in a stranger to ask him to be your town Marshal. I will do my very best."

Buff walked out of the Mayor's office and went with Dean to the newspaper office to send a telegram to his brother, Gray, in Poodle Town. He wanted to let Gray know about Marshal Ben Colby's shooting, and that he is now the new Marshal of Komondor County. Buff explained to Gray without coming right out and telling him much of anything, and for good reason, just that he needed him in Cockapoo and with any luck, on the next stage. He signed it Marshal Nagol, Cockapoo City.

Buff told Dean that he needed to get the prisoner, Lucky, to the Judge in a little while and asked him if he would like to sit in on the hearing.

"Without a doubt," Dean spoke up. "I'd be happy to, Marshal. This would be a great story for the paper, front page at best."

Excited by having a big story for the town's paper, Dean said, "You know, Marshal, Lucky and his brother, Sandy, have always been trouble makers, but I never figured either one to be a killer. It just doesn't fit. This all seemed strange to me, and now that we have a new Marshal, I can share this. I don't believe Mayor Todd can be trusted, either. I haven't told anyone except Mr. Clayton, and he believes as I do. Oh, and Marshal, I'd love to do a story on you for the paper."

"I'd love to do a story for the town's paper, Dean, but let's sit on it for a while. I have a feeling there's more going on here than you or Mr. Clayton may know, and I want to hear more of your thoughts and his about Mayor Todd," The Marshal responded.

On his way out of the newspaper office the marshal saw Dollar Five Crossing Main Street and he called out, "Dollar Five, I need to speak with you."

"Okay, Buff, I'm just heading to pick up breakfast for Lucky. I'll meet you back at the jail," Dollar turned and replied.

When Buff arrived back at the marshal's office, he took a seat behind his desk and waited for Dollar Five. When Dollar Five returned to the jail, he saw the Marshal badge pinned on Buff's shirt.

"Well, now," Dollar Five said. "I'm mighty pleased to see that you accepted the job, Marshal. You do it proud, and it looks like it was made just for you."

"It feels right, Dollar Five. I think once I get to know the town and the people, things will settle into place," Marshal

Nagol replied. "Dollar Five, do you have about an hour or two free? I need some help getting our star border to court."

"Be happy to help you with Lucky, Marshal, but I think we should also be on the lookout for his brother, Sandy, because he might try to do something stupid like try and free Lucky," Dollar Five told the Marshal as they left the jail on their way to deliver Lucky to the courthouse.

When they arrived before Judge Tuesday, the Judge greeted them both as they walked into the courthouse with Lucky. Sandy was sitting in the courthouse with both ears opened wide. Judge Tuesday asked Buff to present his case. Buff stood and began to plead his case to the Judge.

"Judge Tuesday, a few days ago I entered Fatcat's saloon with Marshal Colby. I was his new deputy then and I am a witness to this shooting. I saw a man, who I know now to be Lucky Tessel, standing on the outside of the saloon, looking in. While this fellow, Sandy, who I now know is Lucky's brother, was trying to start a ruckus with another cowboy. When Marshal Colby and I walked in he asked everyone to settle down," Marshall Buff testified. "Right then Lucky shot through the windowpane and Marshal Colby fell. At this time, I'd also like to present the pistol which we believe fired the shot injuring Marshal Colby."

The Marshal expressed to Judge Tuesday that he believed the whole thing was part of a larger plan, and that he'd like to look further into the case.

"Well, Mr. Tessel," the Judge said, "since the town has no one to represent you, do you have anything you wish the court the hear?"

"Judge, all I can say is that I was set up to take this fall and that I didn't shoot Marshal Colby. Someone else must have done it. I had planned to shoot over the Marshal's head. So, someone must have heard me and my brother planning to put a scare into Marshal Colby, and used us to try and kill him," Lucky said, pleading his case to the Judge.

"After hearing the testimony of Marshal Nagol here, and the defendant, Lucky Tessel, and weighing the evidence, I have made my decision. Will the prisoner please stand?" the Judge said. "Lucky Tessel, with the Marshal being an eyewitness to this shooting, I am left with no other choice but to sentence you to three years in the Canine Territory Prison for the attempted murder of Marshal Benjamin Colby."

Judge Tuesday instructed the Marshal to wire Sheriff Jack Russell of Gordon Setter County and make the necessary arrangements for Lucky. Judge Tuesday also granted the Marshal the right to start his own investigation into the Colby shooting, and adjourned the court. Buff and Dollar Five started heading back to the jail with Lucky. Lucky yelled out to Sandy, who was just leaving the courthouse, "Sandy, tell Ma what happened here and ride fast."

"Okay, Lucky, I'm on my way."

Buff asked, "Dollar Five, when is the stage due in?"

"Today the stage comes early morning and early evening. It should be here come supper time. Why, Buff?"

"For one thing, my brother just might be on that stage. I sent a wire off to him this morning when I left the Mayor's office to take the next stage. I'm hoping he will be on it when it comes in," Buff replied.

Once they arrived back at the jail, Buff asked Dollar Five if he knew what Lucky meant when he told his brother to tell his Ma what happened there today. Dollar Five looked at the Marshal and said, "How much time do you have?"

"What do you mean?" The Marshal asked.

"Just kidding, Marshal," Dollar Five said. "I'd be happy to tell you all about Ma Tessel."

He told the Marshal that the Tessel family is scattered all over Komondor County. They have a little ranch deep in the heart of the Mastiff mountains. "They call themselves mountain folk," he said. "They have very little manners, at least not the kind folks around here are used to. Ma Tessel is a pistol totin', rifle carryin' son of a polecat, and that rifle she's always totin' stays loaded with buckshot."

Dollar Five continued, "Ma Tessel has jet black hair, and she's big and strong as an ox, too. Some even say she loves cold weather and that was one reason why she loves living up in the Mastiff Mountains. She has three boys and one girl, and she's extremely loyal to every one of them, Marshal. Their Pa's name is Zachariah and she named one of her boys after him. Zack is his name. But Zack left home soon as he was old enough. They're all pure-bred Bernard, even the Pa. I believe her maiden name was Saint. Then she married Zachariah Bernard Tessel. Marshal, they can cause a lot of problems for us," he said with a stern voice.

"Are you telling me that they're a rough family, like coming into town and tree Cockapoo City?" Buff asked Dollar Five.

Laughing, Dollar Five replied, "No Marshal, I don't think Ma Tessel and her boys would do anything that bad, but they're pretty darn close."

"And, Dollar Five, that's one of the reasons I sent that wire off this morning to my brother, Gray. Because he's just as fast with a pistol as I or my brother, Chocolate," Buff replied.

"Well, it's getting along evening time, Marshal. You want to go check on the stage?" Dollar Five asked.

Just then the door to the Marshal's office opened. It was Gray. Buff looked up with a smile on his face and said, "Hey, Gray, how're you doing? Oh, man, it's so good to see you."

"Well your wire said to come as soon as I could," Gray replied, "and when it's kin folk, you just drop everything, right brother?"

"Right," Buff agreed with his brother. Then he turned to Dollar Five and said, "Gray, this is Dollar Five. He's one of my deputies. You'll meet the others tonight."

"Good to meet you, Dollar Five," Gray said.

"It's good to meet you too, Gray,"

"So, Buff, from your wire it sounds like there's a lot goin' on around here. What's this all about?" Gray asked his Buff.

"Look, first let's get you settled with a room at Aunt Bea's place. It should be around supper time when we get there so you'll get to meet Dean and Thad. Then we'll fill you in on everything," Buff told his brother. Then he turned to Dollar Five and asked. "Dollar Five, will you stay here with Lucky, while I get Gray settled at Aunt Bea's?"

"Sure thing, Marshal," Dollar Five replied.

"I'll send Thad over with some supper for you, okay? I'm sure he's eaten by now. Then Gray and I will come by and stay the night and meet Marshal Russell in the morning," Buff said to Dollar Five. So, Buff helped Gray gather up his things, and went to get him settled in and introduce him to everyone. When they arrived at Aunt Bea's, as always, she had supper ready and waiting. When Buff and Gray walked in, Dean and Thad had just finished having there supper.

Aunt Bea said, "Well, now, who do we have here?"

Buff replied. "I'm sorry I didn't tell you about my brother coming in on the evening stage, Aunt Bea, but there wasn't enough time. Gray, meet Dollar Fives', Aunt Bea."

"Hi, Aunt Bea, it's so good to meet you," replied Gray.

"Aunt Bea, I would love to have my brother stay here with us. Do you think you have a room left for him?"

"Now, you know I do," Aunt Bea replied. "There's always room in my house for you boys."

Gray said, "Aunt Bea, yeah, that's right. Hey, Buff, you know when I was in Poodle Town, I had a room at Aunt Bea's sister's place, Ms. Mollie."

"We'll, did you, now? And how is dear ol' Mollie?" Aunt Bea asked.

"She's just fine, Aunt Bea," Gray replied.

"You know, I been trying to get Mollie to come and live here with me and sell that house of hers, but she a stubborn old goat. Well, don't ya just stand there, sit down and eat," Aunt Bea told Buff and Gray.

After dinner the boys took Gray on a walk around Cockapoo City and took a plate of supper for Dollar Five and one for Lucky, too. While they were showing Gray around town, they each took turns telling Gray about the Middleton Detective Agency having a set up in Cockapoo, and they filled him in on the Colby shooting as well. When they arrived at the Marshal's office Buff said, "Gray, how about paying a call on Fatcat with me in the morning?"

Gray replied, "It sounds good, Buff, but don't you think it might be better if one of the other fellas go? I mean, you boys got a lot going on here that I still don't know enough about, so I might not ask the right questions."

"Okay, Gray, maybe you're right. Say, Dollar Five, do you have anyone who can keep an eye on the livery stable for you?

That way you can babysit Gray and Dean can hang out with me," Buff said jokingly.

"Alright, now, Buff, we'll have none of that," Gray replied.

Dollar Five said, "Yeah, Marshal, I do have someone. His name is Beauceron Ransom."

"Beauceron Ransom? Dollar Five, ain't he that little fella who's always hanging around town looking for a handout?" Thad asked.

"One and the same. But he's one hard worker, let me tell you. He even brought me some business. He helps out Ms. Stella and her girls by giving them rides from time to time, and other folks, too, and that makes me money," Dollar Five replied.

"Well, at least by working for you he doesn't have to go around town begging for handouts. I think that's right friendly of you, Dollar Five," Thad replied.

"I think that's right friendly of you, too, Dollar Five. It's always good to help a body in need, right, Buff?" Gray said, jokingly, referring to himself coming to Buff's aid.

"Right, Gray, just so long as a body can be trusted. So, Dean, it looks like you or Thad. Which one will it be?" Buff asked.

"Well, I've got some work around the ranch Pa wants me to do, so I can't do much of anything tomorrow, fellas," Thad said.

"Okay, Buff, I have some things I need to finish up, so how 'bout I be here, say, around 11-ish? That way we'll be sure Ms. Stella will be up," Dean replied.

"It's a date. See you in the morning, and thanks, Dean," Buff replied.

Once they had the plans set for tomorrow, Dollar Five, Dean and Thad left Buff and Gray at the marshal's office. The two of them sat up for a long time talking. Gray told Buff all about his trip to Poodle Town, and Buff told him what sleeping under the moon and a starlit sky with your horse and a hot fire was like. Before going to bed, Buff turned to his brother and said, "Oh, Chocolate made it Collieville just fine, too, Gray. I forgot to tell you."

"I'm very happy to hear that," Gray replied.

19

Blackmail

"COCK-A-POODLE-DOO...COCK-A-POODLE-DOO." LIKE A clock on the wall Ol' Red the Rooster kept good time. Even though the three winos who owned Ol' Red lived on the other side of town, from time to time he sounded so near. At the first sound of Ol' Red's crowing, Gray bolted upright with a start, and said, "What in the world, Buff, did you forget to tell me something before we went to sleep last night?" Gray rolled over and asked his brother.

"That's just Ol' Red, the Rooster, Gray. He wakes us up every morning around this time. I'm sorry I didn't tell you Gray, I really did mean to. Guess it must have slipped my mind...... darn it," Buff replied with a sneaky laugh.

"Well, now that Ol' Red has my attention, why don't you tell me about him?" Gray replied.

Buff told Gray about the three winos outside of town, and their arrangement of trading eggs for drinks. Explaining Ol' Red to Gray Buff couldn't help but laugh. "It's a win-win all around," Buff chuckled.

"So, should I go fetch us some eggs?" Gray asked.

"I tell you what, I'll go with you."

Buff and Gray headed out of the marshal's office to see the town drunks and make a trade for some double yolk eggs. On the way Buff told Gray how nice it was having him in Cockapoo and that they needed to get Chocolate there, too. It was a nice little walk there and back but well worth it, because now they had eggs for breakfast and eggshells for the coffee. The two of them spending time together like that seemed to do some good for both brothers. It seemed to give them the confidence they needed to take on the responsibilities of bringing law to a territory that had very little.

The coffee and the eggs were ready, and just in time. "Morning, Marshal," Dollar Five said, checking in for duty. "Morning, Gray. Looks like you two slept good."

"In fact, Dollar Five, I did. I only wish someone had been nice enough to tell me about Ol' Red," Gray replied laughingly. Sipping on a cup of coffee, Buff just sat behind his big old marshal desk trying to decide on the best place to start the investigation.

"Good morning, Buff," Dean said as he walked into the marshal's office.

"There's a fresh pot of coffee with eggs shells on the stove if you want a cup, Dean." Buff replied.

"Where to first, Buff?" Dean asked as he poured himself a cup of coffee.

Buff replied, "First, I want to thank you guys for offering to be my deputies. It really means a lot to me. I been sittin' here this morning thinking on where to start, Dean, and I believe the best place to start is Fatcat's saloon, because that's where it all started."

Dean replied, "Just let me have a cup of coffee and I'll be right with you."

Soon after their coffee Buff and Dean left the jail together and started walking down Front Street and into Fatcat's saloon.

"Good morning. I'm Buff Nagol, your new town marshal. And I'm sure you know Dean, one of my deputies. And you are?" The marshal asked.

Looking like he was about to jump right out of his skin, the barkeep stuttered, "M-my - n-name's - bartender, Marshal."

The Marshal looked at Dean and smiled, then said, "Let's try this again. My name is Marshal Nagol, the new Marshal. What's your name bartender?"

"Oh . . . My name. Oh! I'm sorry, sir, Marshal. It's Harrier, sir, and it's nice to meet you," Harrier stammered.

"That's better. Now, Harrier, is Fatcat in? We'd like a word with him," Marshal Logan replied.

"Mr. Fatcat is in his office, Mr. Marshal, sir, but he ain't receiving callers just now. I was instructed to tell all callers looking to do business with Mr. Fatcat to come back mid-afternoon."

Buff asked Harrier, "Is that a fact? Well, we didn't come here to do any business with him. I tell you what, Harrier, why don't you just point me in the direction of Fatcat's office and let me tell him my reason for calling on him this morning."

"It's upstairs, first door on the right," Harrier replied all jumpy like.

Buff and Dean walked upstairs and knocked on the door, but no one answered. The Marshal kicked in the door and the first thing he looked for was Fatcat's paws. The Marshal wanted to make sure they were empty and in his sight. But to their surprise, Fatcat was sitting behind his oak desk counting last night's take from his gambling tables. When Dean and the Marshal entered his office, Fatcat looked up as the door slammed open, saying, "Hey, what is this?"

"I did knock," the Marshal answered Fatcat in a strong stern voice.

"Well, I didn't hear you knock, Johnny law," Fatcat replied.

"The name is Nagol, Marshal Buff Nagol. You'd do well to remember that. I'm sure you know my deputy, Dean Moorhead."

"Marshals, Sheriffs, Middleton Detectives, badge-totin' John laws, or Johnny laws all the same to me. I hate the lot of ya. Now, what do you want with me, Marshal?" Fatcat asked.

"Do you have any idea why Lucky would want to shoot Ben Colby?" The Marshal asked.

"Because he's Johnny-law, and all of you are going down in time, you'll see," Fatcat answered.

Buff walked over to Fatcat's desk, leaned over, and slapped him across the face with his paw and said. "Don't threaten me, Fatcat. I eat scumbag saloon owners like you for breakfast. You see, Fatcat, I'm not Marshal Colby, and I can be your worst nightmare if you want me to be. Now, thank you for taking the time to see us. I'll be saying Good Morning to you," the Marshal said. As he walked out of Fatcat's office he turned and said, "And by the way, get this door fixed and charge it to the Marshal's Office."

They walked out of Fatcat's office and Dean said to Buff, "Nice fellow, but he's gonna start some trouble, Buff, and that you can bet on."

Buff turned to Dean and said with a smile, "You're probably right Dean, but it won't be blackmail, once he realizes who I am. From the look on his face just now I believe Fatcat doesn't have a clue. Next on our list is Ms. Stella Siamese Rollins."

When the Marshal and Dean arrived at Stella's they noticed how quiet the saloon was, but there were a few cowhands sitting about drinking broth. The Marshal and Dean walked over to Sam, the barkeep. "Sam," Dean called out. "Will you let Ms. Stella know our new Marshal would like to have a word with her, please?"

Sam did as he was asked. Before long Stella came walking downstairs shaking her head from side to side. She rolled her eyes over in the direction of the Marshal and said, "Marshal, I know why you're here, and I got nothing to say. Nothing, I tell ya."

But Marshal Nagol knew better. "Stella, can you tell me anything that might help?" he asked.

Stella said, "Seriously, Marshal, you're gonna get me killed."

"I promise you, Ms. Stella, that won't happen," The Marshal replied with a big smile on his face.

"And I second that, Ms. Stella," Dean said.

"Well, now, a lady just can't refuse protection like that, and from two gorgeous men to boot," Stella replied, and threw them both a kiss."

"Now, what can you tell me about Ben's shooting?" The Marshal asked.

"Well, I know for a fact that Ben Colby had something to do with that ranch, the Bar X, I believe it's called. Surely he must have told you about that when he showed you around the town?" Stella asked.

"Yes, but he told me very little, and he never mentioned that he had anything to do with it," the marshal replied.

"Well, the day before the shooting, Payton, he's the foreman of the Bar X, and Fatcat came walking into my place and took a seat. Well, now, I thought that was strange since everybody knows Fatcat's been trying to run me and my girls out of Cockapoo City for the longest time. Anyway, I walked over to their table, it being my place and all, and I said, 'order a drink or start them paw's moving.'"

"Those two low-down, dirt-rotten cheapskates ordered one beer between the two of them, just one lousy beer. Now I ask you, how's a girl supposed to make a living like that Marshal?" Ms. Stella asked.

"I'm sure I don't know, Stella," replied the Marshal. "But if you can, would you please continue on and tell me what else you saw?"

"Well, Marshal, I saw Ol' Ned sitting by himself, so I took a seat at Ned's table." Stella said.

"I see. Go on, Ms. Stella." The Marshal said.

"Well, I heard them say something like take Colby out, something about him not having thick skin and he might talk. With all the noise I wasn't too sure, though. Then one day I saw Lucky Tessel with Fatcat. But everybody knows Lucky and his brother, Sandy, worked at that ranch. Now Marshal, that's all I can tell you. I suggest you question Ben Colby," Stella told the Marshal.

"Why didn't you say something to Colby about all this?" Marshal Nagol asked Stella.

Stella threw her head back and laughed as she said, "Honey, sugar pie, darlin', when you work in this business the first rule of tongue is mind your own business. And Ben wasn't hurt too bad. He can still walk, can't he? Besides, Ben could well be up to his ears in something with Fatcat and Payton. Now I got no more to say, Marshal," Stella said, nervously.

Marshal Nagol said, "Thank you, Ms. Stella, for taking the time to speak with us, and as I told you, someone will be keeping a close eye on your place as promised."

"Do me one favor will you, Marshal?"

"If, I can, Ms. Stella," the marshal replied.

"Will you please stop calling me Ms. Stella?" she said, smiling.

"You got it, Stella. And will you please just call me Buff?" the Marshal replied.

Leaving Stella's Saloon, heading back to the Marshal's office, Buff said to Dean, "If Colby has anything to do with the Bar X, someone was pointing a pistol at his head or blackmailing him. I just can't believe the man that stood up for me to be Marshal could have anything to do with Payton, let alone Fatcat."

"Maybe you're wrong about Marshal Colby, Buff," Dean replied.

"You've known him longer then I have," Buff said, "but when I get a feel for someone, I'm usually right, Dean, although I can be wrong from time to time. But I don't think so this time. C'mon, let's get back to the jail and look the office over really good."

Dean asked, "Haven't you done that yet, Buff?"

"No, I haven't had the chance 'til now," Buff replied.

"Well, let's get back there and get it over with," Dean replied.

When Buff and Dean arrived back at the jail, Dollar Five and Gray were laid back, one on the chaise longue reading the paper, and the other one in a chair reading the paper. Buff came in and said, "Come on, Dollar Five, you and Gray get up. We need to search this office."

"What are we looking for, Marshal?" Dollar Five asked.

"Clues, my boy," Buff replied. "Clues, or anything that looks interesting."

The four of them took the office apart and still found nothing. Buff took a seat behind his desk scratching his head. He reached down with his right paw and opened the bottom drawer. It was locked, so he had to force it open, and to his surprise there was a white envelope. "Wait a minute," he said. "I think I found something, but it appears to be stuck on something. Oh, wait, I've got it." Buff pulled until the envelope was in his paw. "It's a letter for Ben."

"Open it Marshal," Dollar Five replied.

"You're not supposed to open folk's mail, Dollar Five, unless they're no longer living," the marshal replied.

"Oh, Marshal, you're the new Law around Cockapoo. Open it up and read the letter already," Dean replied.

Just as Buff was about to open the letter, the Sheriff from Canine Territorial Prison, Jack Russell, walked in with two of his deputies and said. "I was sent to pick up a prisoner named Lucky Tessel. Is the Marshal here?" The Sheriff asked.

"That would be me," Buff replied, offering his paw. "Nice to meet you, Sheriff. Hang on and I'll get him."

Buff went upstairs to bring Lucky down. He signed the release papers and Lucky was now on his way to Parsonville to serve his three-year sentence at Canine Territorial Prison. Dollar Five asked, "So, Marshal, what about Ma Tessel and Sandy?"

The Marshal just said, "Well, we'll just have to deal with them when, and if, the time comes. Don't go borrowing trouble, Dollar Five."

"Oh, it's gonna happen, Marshal. You can bet your boots on it," Dollar Five replied.

"Now that Lucky is taken care of, I'm heading out to the Lazy Z and have a talk with Ben about this letter." Buff asked Dean, Dollar Five and Gray to sit tight and wait until he got back from the Lazy Z, and out the door the Marshal went.

When he arrived at the Lazy Z, Ben was sitting outside. He saw Buff ride up.

"Get off your horse, Marshal, and have a seat," Ben hollered out.

Buff tied his horse to the hitching post and walked over to have a seat alongside Ben. "Nice day," Buff replied.

"I know you didn't come way out here to tell me how nice a day it is, now, did you, marshal?" Ben asked.

Buff replied in a serious tone, "No, Ben, I didn't. In fact, it's about this letter that was found in your desk."

As the two new friends sat under the shaded tree, Ben said, "I see you found the blackmail letter. You know, if Hope and I had just not have taken that trip, you wouldn't have ever found out about that letter. You see, I forgot that letter was in the desk. I had it in my pocket and didn't want to bring it with me, and with all that has happened I somehow forgot it was there, and now you have it."

"Is that what this letter is, Ben, a blackmail letter?" Buff asked.

"You're telling me you haven't read it, Marshal?" Ben asked.

"No, Ben, I haven't read it, and why would I? I found it in your desk, it belongs to you. But why don't you tell me about it?" Buff asked his new friend.

"I think I'll do that," Ben Colby, replied.

Ben started by telling the Marshal how he met his wife, Hope, in a saloon called the Hide Out, in Beagle Town, and how she ended up in Cockapoo, the wife of a lawman. Ben told the marshal that one day Payton and Fatcat came through the door of the Marshal's office and began telling him the story of how he met and married a saloon girl. "They intended to tell the town if I didn't see things their way," Ben said. "And, Buff, that's not even the half of it. You see, Hope and I didn't go through my folks' things right away, but Hope was doing some cleaning one day and found a box of papers, and among those papers is that letter you're holding. It's my Pa's Confession letter. It paints a story how Fatcat's uncle, Bobcat, had his own ready-made lawman in my Pa, Buff. And with everything else Fatcat had hanging over my head, they had control of me. You know, in a funny way, I'm kinda grateful to Lucky for shooting me. You see, Buff, it's now your job to expose them, and me along with them."

"Now, I did do some of what they instructed me to do," Ben continued, "which was to destroy all the papers that the Land Office had on the two ranches, and anything to do with an old mining town. Then I was told to keep my mouth shut or they would spread the story of Hope's background. Well, not knowing the possibility that Bobcat didn't leave a similar letter to Fatcat when he died, I couldn't take that risk. I didn't care about me, but Hope was trying so hard to put her past behind her and start a new life as my wife."

Ben told Buff that he started receiving wires from the Middleton Detectives but that out of fear for his wife, he didn't dare send any replies. And that was when Chet Basenji, a Middleton agent, showed up in Cockapoo City.

Buff said, "Ben, you let them blackmail you and now you've left this up to me to solve when I don't know my left paw from my right?"

"I'm sorry, Buff, I really am," Ben replied.

"Tell me, Ben, is this why Lucky was hired to kill you?"

"If it was ordered by Fatcat, yes, maybe," Ben answered. "Maybe they thought that I talked, and they wanted to plug me up. They knew everything that went on in my office, Buff, but what I couldn't figure out was how they knew."

"I'll do my best to get to the bottom of this Ben, and the sooner I get started, the sooner I'll have my answers. Thank you for telling me the truth, Ben, I know it couldn't have been easy, and I promise you that nothing will get in the papers about Hope. You're due at least that much," Buff replied.

Buff walked over to his horse, then turned and asked, "So, Ben, is there any point in my checking with the Land Office?"

Ben replied, "I would, Buff, because the clerk, Bentfoot, runs a really tight office, and he keeps good books. There's no telling what he might have kept. But, Buff, make sure you and your deputies watch each other's backs, because these guys shoot first and ask questions later."

"We will, Ben. Be good to yourself and Hope. And if I need you, I know where to find you," Buff said. Then he threw a leg over his saddle and turned his horse Nugget back towards Cockapoo.

Let Us Pray

O N HIS WAY back to town Buff thought of nothing else except his conversation with Ben Colby. Buff decided to take Ben's advice and stop by the Land Office to have a talk with the clerk, Bentfoot Pumi. When Buff got back to town he stopped by the jail. Gray, Dollar Five and Dean were still sitting there waiting patiently for his return. He asked Dean to stay and watch the jail and told Dollar Five and Gray to come with him to the Land office.

On the way there Buff said, "Boys, we've got us one big mess of trouble. Get this, Ben told me that he was being black-mailed by Fatcat and Payton and was made to do whatever they told him to do."

"If it's like you say, then what do you expect to find at the land office?" Gray asked his brother.

"Yeah, Buff, it's got to be a waste of time," Dollar Five said, agreeing with Gray.

Buff replied, "Well, for one thing Ben told me to. And I happen to trust Ben Colby, so just humor me fellas."

When they walked into the Land Office, Bentfoot, the clerk, said, "Good afternoon. What can I do for you? Oh, hello, Dollar Five, I didn't see you back there."

"Hello, Bentfoot. Look here, Bent," Dollar Five replied.

"Dollar Five, please, I didn't like being called Bent when we were little, and I like it even less now that I'm full grown. My name is Bentfoot. Please use it," Bentfoot replied.

"Oh, alright, already. Listen up, Bentfoot. This here is Buff, the new Marshal, and this is Gray. We're his deputies. We came here to have a look see at any records you might have on the Bar X Ranch or the Holidays," Dollar Five said.

"Let me do this, Dollar Five," the Marshall cut in. "Bentfoot, I'd like to see any records you might still have on the sale of the Holiday Mansion or the Bar X ranch."

"Marshal, most of those files were pretty much destroyed when the old land office caught fire," Bentfoot said. "Then the town council voted on building this brand new one, and I must say I love it, don't you?"

"Sure, Bentfoot, sure," the Marshal said, placatingly. "So, Bentfoot, nothing was kept or saved from that fire?" the marshal asked.

"There was a box of scorched papers that we found during the cleanup, I guess they could have been from the fire. Someone might have been saving them. I remember a letter was found with those papers that didn't get burnt. But the clerk before me mailed it a long time ago. I remember the letter was made out to someone name Kaleb, something or other, and I believe it was addressed to Shepherdsville," Bentfoot said.

The Marshal asked, "How can you remember all that, Bentfoot?"

"Marshal, some things you just don't forget, like during the gold rush. I wasn't too young then that I can't remember some of those times. It was rough. Folks were getting robbed and killed by claim jumpers. I remember there was this ol' prospector who got himself killed back then. I don't know his name but it's a safe bet that someone still living in Cockapoo remembers that ol' prospector," Bentfoot told the Marshal.

"His name was Miner Binder, Buff," Dollar Five said. "And the way I heard it was, soon as he made his big strike, he left the Big Top Saloon with two men, and was never seen or heard from again, according to the way Aunt Bea heard it."

"Okay, I don't know nothing about folks disappearing or gone missing and maybe it's all tied together," the Marshal said. "All I know is that Ben told to me to start with the Land Office."

"Buff," Dollar Five replied, "all those things that happened back then are true in fact. Most town folks back then felt, and still do, that Miner Binder was murdered."

"Then we'll solve it one way or the other," the Marshal replied. "But for now, Bentfoot, can you show me that box of scorched papers, please?"

"Nope, I can't, Marshal. The papers were thrown out a long time ago, but I did manage to keep a file on the Holidays. You think that might be of use to you?" Bentfoot asked.

"Bentfoot, Ben Colby was right about you, and I could kiss you, my boy. Yes, that file could help us a great deal, I hope," Marshal Buff replied.

"Then I'll get it for you, Marshal, just give me a minute. But I think you should be kissing Dollar Five. Had it not been his mentioning the Holiday family when you all came in, I might not have thought of it," Bentfoot replied

While Bentfoot was in the back room going through old and current files, Buff turned to his deputies and said, "You know, when I was at Ben's he told me some things that didn't make sense. He said that Fatcat and Payton knew everything that went on in the marshal's office, but that he never could figure out how they were gettin' their information. He also mentioned something about receiving wires from the Middleton Detective Agency. Dollar Five, you're from here, do you know anything about this?"

"Very little, Buff, but Dean and Thad hung around some with that crowd," Dollar Five said. "What's going on here, Marshal?" Dollar Five asked.

"I'm not sure yet, but before I left, Ben told me that the Bar X Ranch and the Holiday Mansion are one in the same, and that Holiday, Jr. asked the Middleton Detective agency to look into the possibility of some illegal stuff going on," Marshal Buff answered him.

"That's not news. Everyone in Cockapoo knows they're the same Mansion. But that could be why he was asking for help," Dollar Five replied.

Gray said, "Buff, there's more going on here then we know."

"Yeah, I know, and the sooner we know what they know the better," Buff replied.

Bentfoot returned from the back room with some maps and newspapers. After giving the documents to the Marshal, the Marshal noticed the heading on one of the papers. It said: 'Holiday leaves Fortune to son.' The Marshal asked, "Do you have a room that we could use, Bentfoot, so we can look things over and won't be in your space?"

"Sure, anything for the law. First door down the hall on your left. And take your time, there hasn't been any action around this office in a long while," Bentfoot said with a smile.

So, they each grabbed some papers and went to the room and started looking them over. After about an hour or so Gray said, "Well, I can say one thing for sure, there are two companies listed here: 'Dillon's Doggie Creations' and '4 Leggs & Me.' And Holiday, Jr. is to receive the entire estate lock, stock and barrel, should anything happen to Holiday, Sr. Wow!"

"Buff, I found some land deeds and a map. Have a look at these, you know I don't read maps too good," Dollar Five said to Buff.

"Let me have them, Dollar Five," Buff replied. Buff looked over the land deeds carefully because they were complicated and confusing at first. But after reading the documents, he knew that all the land was still owned by Holiday Jr., as well as the two companies.

After Buff explained things to the boys, Dollar Five asked, "I hear what you're saying, but what does it all mean, Buff?"

"It means that if Fatcat did buy the mansion, he must have unknowingly bought it illegally, because it was sold with forged documents. You see, the Holiday twins didn't own the mansion, their Pa did, and he didn't sell it. That's what this means, Dollar Five," Buff explained.

"So, there really is a good chance ol' Fatcat got taken. Now that's music to my tender little ears, Buff," Dollar Five replied.

"My ears too, Dollar Five," Buff replied. "You see, right now we don't need to know who sold the mansion or who the owner is, even though it all points to Fatcat and Victoria. We'll prove that later. Right now, we just need to find out who's trying to take what Mr. Holiday, Sr. worked so hard to build and leave to his family. And we might just uncover a murderer to boot."

Buff was looking over the maps, then asked Gray to come and look them over. "Gray, what do these markings look like to you?" he asked.

Gray looked at the maps and said, "They look just like the markings grandpa Potts made after he staked out a claim."

Now knowing the possibility of there being two claims and that the Holiday Mansion could be sitting smack dead on top of one of the richest gold strikes ever recorded in Cockapoo City, Buff asked Bentfoot to look and see if anyone had filed a claim on them. And sure enough, one of the claims had been registered by Holiday Sr., and a second claim had been registered in the name of Hollister Bobcat Cobb, Fatcat's uncle. But the whereabouts of the second strike wasn't clear enough to make out. But they now knew it was somewhere near the Holiday mine. Which meant on Holiday land. Buff now had a pretty good feeling about it all.

Buff said, "Now, if it's as you say, Dollar Five, and Fatcat was suckered into believing that he actually bought the Holiday Mansion, then his uncle Bobcat must have left him proof of the stolen claim. And this could tell us that ol' prospector was murdered for his claim, and what's left of the body could be buried there."

"If we only knew who sold the Holiday mansion it might explain a lot more, even the murder of the prospector," Dollar Five replied.

"That doesn't matter right now, Dollar Five, because these papers are forgeries, which means it was sold illegally, remember," the marshal replied.

Bentfoot walked in to see if the fellows needed anything and he overheard what the Marshal said, so he answered, "Marshal, Victoria told me the twins gave it to her and left Cockapoo City. You know, Marshal, Victoria carried a kind of hatred for the Holiday family that just wasn't measurable. Victoria's Ma, Martha, married Richard Holiday, Sr., and he moved them into that big mansion on the hill. You see, Marshal, Martha wanted Richard to adopt Victoria after they were married, but Richard saw right through Victoria. His son, Richard, Jr., didn't like her and he didn't trust her either. So, ol' man Holiday never adopted her and that was what started the hatred Victoria has for the twins, Thurston and Ashley," Bentfoot replied.

"How do you know all this, Bentfoot?" the Marshal asked.

"Well, if you rub paws with the right folks like my Ma did in Cockapoo City, you'd know," Bentfoot answered.

"You mean the gossiping ladies' group of Cockapoo City?" Dollar Five asked with a laugh.

"Yes, Dollar Five," Bentfoot sarcastically replied. "Now, where was I? Oh, yeah. You see, Marshal, Victoria was very clear and honest about her feelings for the Holiday family. Victoria hated that family so much that I believe she would have done just about anything to make the twins' life miserable."

"Well what about outside the law?" Gray questioned.

Bentfoot replied, "I can't speak to that, but Victoria wasn't nothing to play around with either, that's for sure."

"Well, that would explain the reason for those wires Ben was getting from the Middleton Detectives. Apparently, Holiday, Jr. was checking up on the villains of Cockapoo City, you might say. But that's not what you're feeling, is it Buff?" Gray asked.

"Yes, Gray, in a way it is. But from what I'm learning about Victoria," Buff answered, "It doesn't sound to me like she's clever enough to be a villain or villainess. It's my guess though that she's jealous enough of Ashley and Thurston to forge papers to sell that mansion and cheat Fatcat out of his money if she knew he was looking to buy it. Victoria's a thief and liar, and I'm going to put her and her husband just where they belong, behind bars. Bentfoot, thank you for all your help," Buff told him as they were leaving the land office.

When they got back to the jail Thad was there waiting with Dean. Dollar Five started telling them about everything they found over at the Land Office. Buff knew with everything Ben Colby had told him, along with what he learned from Bentfoot's excellent bookkeeping. He had enough to at least arrest Fatcat and Payton on blackmail charges, but he wanted them for murder too. Buff said, "Dollar Five, do something for me."

"Sure, Marshal, what is it?" Dollar Five asked.

"Send a telegram to Nation Middleton. Ask him if he has anything more he can give me on this case, and please wait for his reply," Buff said.

Buff knew he'd find Payton at the Bar X, so he figured he and his deputies would just go out to the Bar X and arrest him. He didn't think Payton would put up a fight, because he'd know it would only make matters worse for him if he did. And if Buff got lucky, he might just catch Fatcat out at the ranch, too. For now, Victoria had to wait, because without the deed of sale to make sure it was her signature and Fatcat's on the forged sale papers the land office had on the Holiday Mansion, all they can prove is that it was sold. It was too bad the signature page was missing.

When Dollar Five returned with Nation's reply, he handed the wire to Buff. It confirmed what Ben Colby had told him, that the wires had been requested by Richard Holiday, Jr., but all that he could add was that Victoria and her husband, Mike Eastern, had, in fact, set up a dummy company called "The Cesky Corporation," in an attempt take over the Holiday Estate. Nation's wire also said that he'd sent another agent, Buff's brother, Chocolate, to assist Chet Basenji, and his job was to get hired on the Bar X Ranch as an outlaw named Kid Chocolate.

Buff couldn't believe what he was reading. "Chocolate," he yelled out.

Nation said that he wished he could do more, but that it was their baby now, and to walk like they were on eggshells.

Gray looked at Buff and asked, "Buff, what about brother Chocolate?"

"Hold on to your shirt, brother. Nation planted Chocolate on the Bar X Ranch as an outlaw, Kid Chocolate."

"What's our next move, marshal?" Dollar Five asked.

"I know what our next move is, Dollar Five. What I don't know just yet is how. But I know this, with my brother undercover on the Bar X ranch, it's not going to be like walking on eggshells, that's for sure. It's going have to be an all-out surprise attack for sure, and it's going to be them or us," Buff replied.

And Gray replied, "LET US PRAY."

21

Perfect Cover

FACED WITH THE realization of the danger Chocolate was in Buff knew his deputies had to operate like a gang of vicious outlaws with no regard for human life and a thirst for killing, or Chocolate could end up a notch carved in the handle of an outlaw's Forty-Five. Buff knew it was kill or be killed and he did his best to make sure his deputies knew it too. Nevertheless, they were faced with, a ticking clock that wasn't on their side.

Gray could see the concern in Buff's eyes, and the anxiety in his heart was something they both shared. Gray tapped his brother on the shoulder and said, "Buff, look, it's getting along supper time, and believe me, I feel the same as you, but I'm sure we all could do with some food. Why don't we continue this at home?"

"Gray's right, Buff. You know we think better on a full stomach," Dollar Five replied.

"You're so right, fellas. I always did think better on a full stomach," Buff jokingly replied.

The boys got on their horses and headed for home, and as usual, when Buff walked through the door his nose was in the air. "Oh, man, I'm smelling ham hocks, my favorite," he said.

While the boys were washing up for dinner Aunt Bea was setting the table. When they came down to eat Aunt Bea said, "So, I hear you all had a big discovery at the land office this afternoon."

Dollar Five replied, "I see good ol' Bentfoot stopped by for an early supper."

"Yes, he did," Aunt Bea replied. "And he filled me in on everything."

"Now, Aunt Bea, you can't keep mixing in with law work. You might just get hurt one of these days," Buff said.

Aunt Bea put her hands on her hips and said, "Now, listen, I've known Victoria ever since the day that girl was born and there is nothing she wouldn't do inside or outside the law to get even with those twins. And for what? Her own jealousy. You boys have got a big mess coming your way if'n that girl is involved. She been waitin' to get her nasty, grubby little paws on that mansion since the day she laid eyes on it. Buff, you and Gray wouldn't know this, but Thad, Dean, you and Dollar Five should remember that Victoria was the reason Ashley and Thurston left Cockapoo in the first place. I can't stand that little wanna-be rich girl, Buff. You need to jail that hussy."

"Well, Aunt Bea," Buff replied with a laugh, "I see you have no love for Victoria, the wanna-be villainess. But now we know our brother Chocolate is undercover on the Bar X so we must stay within the law. Otherwise, we not only lose our brother but Victoria and those other rotten outlaws as well."

"Maybe the law could stand some new rules from an ol' school," Aunt Bea replied. "Why on earth is it always easy for sinful, evil folks to rob, kill and even murder good law-biding folks, and get clear away sometimes? But the law don't say nothing about fightin' fire with fire."

"Aunt Bea, you should'a been a Marshal. You just gave it all to me right from your silver tongue," Buff replied.

"I did? Well, hallelujah! When do I get my star?" Aunt Bea replied jokingly.

"Wait a minute, Aunt Bea, I might just give you my badge because I have a feeling Buff's plan has somethin' to do with me," Gray replied jokingly.

"And you'd be right, Gray," Buff replied with a smile shaking his head up and down. "Gray, my boy, desperate times calls for desperate measures. Besides, you're the only one in this room who can pull this plan off. Come on, let's eat up and go over me and Aunt Bea's idee."

The boys sat there laughing and joking after finishing the wonderful supper Aunt Bea had made. They each grabbed something from the dinner table to help Aunt Bea clean up when they were done. Buff said, as he patted his brother on his back, "Ok, Gray, here's the plan. No one on the Bar X has gotten a good look at you. So, you see, Gray, this plan was tailor-made for you."

"If it's got to do with getting Chocolate off that ranch," Gray replied, "I'd hold up a bank. Go ahead, Buff, let's hear your plan."

Buff took the map he had of Komondor County from his saddlebags and spread it out across the dining room table. He pointed to the Bar X ranch. "Gray," he said, "At sun up you ride out to the Bar X and get hired. Tell them anything, or better yet, Gray, show them your quick paw draw. That's a sure hire. Once you're inside, find Chocolate. Let him know we're coming in the morning to attack, and you two can cover us from the inside. And remember, Gray, these boys play for keeps so you and Chocolate watch your backs and make sure you leave that badge here."

"Then we're gonna ride out to the Bar X Ranch around noon. Once we get within eyeball of that ranch, boys, we're going to get off the horses and leave them in some bushes and out of sight. Dean, you and Thad have got to make your way up to the gate real quiet like and take out the guards. And try not to fire a shot. And remember, there are some high and low points on the way up to that Mansion, and they're sure to have some guards on lookout. If you run across one, hit him with the butt of your rifle, tie him up and gag him good," Buff carefully explained to his deputies.

"Buff, you got any idea how many guards they might have on the Bar X Ranch?" Thad asked.

"No, I don't, Thad," Buff replied. "We're just gonna have to take them out. That's all there is to it."

"I have any some idee 'bout that, Thad," Dollar Five spoke up.

"Well, speak up man. Tell us what you know," Buff said to Dollar Five.

"Five on the gate, two or three on the grounds in front of the Mansion, and I don't know how many on the inside," Dollar Five replied to Buff.

"And where did you get this information, Dollar Five?" Buff asked.

"Buff, I been up there a few times," Dollar Five said. "They send for me now and then when they have horses needing to be shod. You know, come to think of it, Buff, those boys are hard on horses."

Buff took a sip of water and said, "Now, like I said, that Mansion has some high and low spots on the way up, and they make a good hiding place to post guards. So, before we get anywhere near the grounds or the gate, we need to take out all the guards. We don't want anyone coming up behind us."

"Hey, I got an idee, Buff," Dollar Five said.

"What's your idee, Dollar Five," Buff repeated jokingly after Dollar Five.

"Stop poking fun, Marshal. I know how to say the word," Dollar Five replied. "Look here, since they know me a little, why don't I ride up there and ask to see if they have any horses needing shoes? I could tell them that I was on my way back from Poodle Town and I just thought I'd stop on my way back to see if I could make some money. That way I could see how many, and where, the guards on lookout point might be hiding. I might get lucky and even take one or two out," Dollar Five offered.

"Dollar Five, you keep on thinking like that and you're gonna make me take a drink and salute you," Buff said. "Why, that's the best idee you've come up with yet."

"I second that," Gray replied. And so did the others.

"I believe it'll work, Buff. Just remember to allow me time to find Chocolate, so it's got to be perfect timing," Gray replied.

The boys sat there and listened as Buff continued with his plan of how they would rush the Bar X Ranch from the outside, and it was a spectacular plan indeed. The fellas didn't know that Aunt Bea was still in the kitchen cleaning up - and listening.

As she walked into the dining room clapping her paws, Aunt Bea said, "Now, Buff, that's a mighty fine idee you got there. I hope ya go there and bring down the house and drag 'em all out by their tails, kickin' and screamin'."

"Why, thank you, Aunt Bea, but the word is idea, not idee," Buff replied with a grin.

"Well, I'm too old to start changing now, so take it like it is, boys," Aunt Bea said laughing out loud.

"You know something, Aunt Bea?"

"What's that, Buff?" Aunt Bea asked.

"Well, we know there's a gold mine or two somewhere on that property and one belongs to the Holidays," Buff said. "If we could speak with Ashley or Thurston, they might be able to tell us something. And what I'd like to know is whose been mining the gold mines?"

"Well, I can't help you with that, but I can get Ashley and Thurston here, even maybe by tomorrow, and you can bet on that," Aunt Bea replied.

"You know how to reach the Holiday twins, Aunt Bea?" Buff asked.

"Why, sure, darlin. Their grandpa left them a mansion in Shepherdsville and it's just as nice as the one he built here. I've only spoken to them once since they left Cockapoo, but I'll send them a wire in the morning and let them know they're needed in Cockapoo City," Aunt Bea said.

The fellas agreed with Buff's plan for getting Chocolate off the Bar X Ranch.

"Well, now that we have a game plan, whatta you boys wanna do?" Buff asked.

"Well, seeing as its past my bed time, I'm going to bed," Dean replied.

"I second that, Dean," Thad said.

"Gray, what about you?" Buff asked.

"Oh, I don't know. I'll be around," Gray replied as he walked out the door closing it behind him. Even as a child Gray loved play acting, and this was right on time. With his own idea in his head Gray walked over to Dollar Five's stable, saddled up his horse, Lady, and rode nice and slow like up to Fatcat's saloon, but not before taking a hotel room at the Cockapoo House. It was all part of his plan.

Aunt Bea said, "Well, I'm going to stay up for a bit and finish putting a hem on a dress I promised Ms. Stella, and then go to bed too."

Buff looked over at Dollar Five and said, "Well, Five, it's you and me making the rounds tonight, buddy."

Reaching for his cowboy hat Dollar Five said, "Well, let's roll," and out the door they went.

Buff took the left side of Front Street and Dollar Five took the right. They slowly made their way down the street checking door knobs and windows, making sure the businesses were locked up nice and tight. Buff came up on Fatcat's saloon. He beckoned to Dollar Five to come over to his side of the street. While standing on the outside of Fatcat's saloon they watched as a ruckus was starting. Buff walked into Fatcat's saloon with Dollar Five behind him. Buff said, "Ok, Fatcat, can you keep the noise down so decent folks can get some sleep?"

"But all the decent folk are in here, Marshal," Fatcat replied real snooty like.

"Just keep it down. If I need to come back in here again, I'm closing you down for the night. Maybe a night in jail will improve your manners some," the Marshal replied.

Looking around the saloon Buff saw his brother, Gray, sitting at a table near the back of the saloon playing poker. He looked at Dollar Five and asked him, "Hey, Dollar Five, do you see what I see?" nodding his head towards the back of the saloon.

Dollar Five looked around then said, "That's Gray."

"It ain't Santa Claus," Buff replied.

"Well, he did say he'd be around, didn't he?" Dollar Five said.

"That he did, my boy, that he did. And there's no time like the present to get things rolling, I always say," Buff replied. But before they left Gray looked up and smiled as Buff and Dollar Five walked by him and out of Fatcat's saloon.

Buff and Dollar Five headed back towards the jail, and when they got there, they each took a couch to rest their bones. With no prisoners to look after, it was indeed a night just right for sleeping. Suddenly there was a knock on the door. "Marshal! Hey, Marshal! Let me in, Marshal!" It was Ned, one of Cockapoo's three wino's and he was lit.

Dollar Five opened the door when he saw who it was. He looked over at Buff and asked, "Put him in a cell for tonight, Marshal?"

"Yeah, let him sleep it off. Man is he lit," the Marshal replied. "Dollar Five, put him all the way in the back just in case he's in a singing mood tonight."

"Come on, Ned, I got your cell all ready and waitin' for you," Dollar Five said.

He took ol' Ned upstairs and put him in a cell leaving the door open, as usual. After getting Ned settled down for the night, things got real peaceful like, and before long Buff and Dollar Five were both asleep, dreaming they were smelling coffee. Only it wasn't a dream. In fact, it was Ned.

Ned was up and had made a fresh pot of coffee. Buff woke up just as Ned was handing him a cup of coffee. Buff said, "Ned, why don't you get yourself a job and stop all this drinking and become a respectable man?"

"Oh, Marshal, ain't nobody gonna give me no work," Ned replied.

"I don't know about that, Ned," the Marshall said. "I just might put you to work sweeping out the jail if you stop that drinking and get cleaned up. But tell me, Ned, why do you drink so much anyway?"

"I can't tell you, Marshal, I just can't tell you. Would you really give me a job though? I wanna leave this town." Ned asked.

"Where would you go, Ned?" The Marshal asked ol' Ned, the wino.

"I got kin folk, Marshal. They ain't laid eyes on me near thirty years or better, but they be kin, just the same," Ned replied.

"Tell you what, Ned, why don't you start cleaning up the cells? Everything you need is in the hall closet. If you work hard, I'll give you enough money to leave this town." The Marshal liked ol' Ned and he was pulling for him, but only time would tell.

Taking a sip of the coffee Ned had made for him, Buff looked out the window just in time to see Gray coming out of the Cockapoo Hotel where he had taken a room last night. Gray got on his horse and rode past the jail and saw Buff looking out the window. Gray took off his Stetson hat, looked up toward the sky, then at Buff still looking out the window of the jail. Gray muttered as he rode out of town, "I'm heading for the Bar X ranch," and Buff understood every word. He stood there and watched as Gray rode out of town.

Gray took his time getting to the ranch as it wasn't that far out of town. When Gray arrived at the ranch he rode up to the gate and asked, "Who's in charge here?"

One of the cowboys sitting on the gate jumped down and said, "That depends on what business brings you here, cowboy."

"I could see as I rode up that this was a mighty big spread, so I was wondering if the boss man was taking on any extra ranch hands."

The guard opened the gate and said, "Hey, didn't I see you in Fatcat's saloon last night?"

"You may have. I was there," Gray replied.

"C'mon in, I'll take you to him. What's your name?"

"Most folks just call me Gray," he replied.

As they got closer to the house Gray asked the cowhand, "So, what's your name?"

"They call me Luke. You know, I was watching you last night and you play a fair hand of poker, and you handle yourself real professional like too. The boss man just might like you. He sure couldn't do no worse," Luke said, making conversation with Gray.

Gray was looking around and thinking to himself how big the ranch was and how many hands they might have. Once he was inside Gray counted seven so far and with the three men he saw on lookout that made ten. To Gray, the inside of the mansion looked like one of the army forts. Luke showed Gray to an office with two more guards standing outside the door. This made twelve, Gray thought to himself. Luke knocked on the door and a voice from inside said, "Come in."

Luke opened the door and as they walked in, he said, "Gray, this is Payton, the foreman. Payton, this is Gray, and he wants to have a word with you." Then he left the room and waited just outside the door.

"What's your business here, cowboy?" Payton asked.

"My name is Gray, not cowboy, and my business is I'm looking for work. You see, I like to eat, and it takes money to do that, so I need work."

Payton replied, "I like your style, cowboy. Now don't get yourself all bent out of shape. I call everyone cowboy at one time or another, so be cool, Gray. You came at the right time. We could use another hand. You any good with that pistol?"

"Yeah, I'm good with it. In fact, I'm right good with it, only I'm not hiring out my pistol," Gray replied.

"Well, I'm not hiring you for your pistol," Payton said. "I just want to know how good you are, just in case we need it, is all. C'mon, follow me. I'll show you the bunkhouse and introduce you to the men."

Everything was going according to plan. Payton took to showing Gray where he would be sleeping, and suddenly he was looking at his brother, Chocolate, right dead in the face. "Gray, this is Chocolate. He's good with his pistol, too, so I don't want no trouble from you two," Payton said.

Gray took Chocolate's paw to shake and said, "Nice to meet you, Chocolate."

"Nice to meet you, too, Gray. Say, Payton, if you got work to do, I can show this cowboy around," Chocolate replied.

"Watch it, Chocolate, now this one here, he doesn't like being called cowboy," Payton responded with a laugh.

"Thanks for letting me know. I'd hate to get off on the wrong foot," Chocolate replied.

Payton left Gray and Chocolate standing outside the bunkhouse. Chocolate turned to his brother and asked, "Gray, what are you doing in Cockapoo City?"

"Well, right now I'm following through on an idea brother Buff put together to get you out. You see, we know all about what's been going on here, and Nation Middleton told Buff how you got here. Long story short, Chocolate, brother Buff is getting ready to bring down the house, but we had to get you out of here first," Gray told his brother.

"And just how is he going to do that? Have you taken a good look at this place? It's set up like an army post, and they run it like one, Gray. Buff couldn't possible know that," Chocolate said to Gray.

"Now, Chocolate, you know Buff. When he puts a plan together it's done. He's coming tomorrow morning to get us out of here. I'm here to warn you and see to it that we both walk out of here alive and well in the morning," Gray told his brother.

"Gray, I'd feel a lot better if you had told me it was your plan," Chocolate replied laughingly.

"No worries, Chocolate. Buff will have a posse of several deputies with him. You'll see, it'll work. It has to," Gray replied.

For the rest of the day Chocolate filled Gray in on what little he had found out about Fatcat, Payton, Victoria, and the gold they were looking for. Chocolate and Gray just laid low doing chores around the ranch and trying not to look like lawmen. Time went by so fast the cook was outside banging the triangle letting the hands know it was time for supper. Chocolate turned to Gray and mumbled, "They eat really good around here, and the cook is excellent."

"That's good to know," Gray replied, "because I'm starved. All that work we did this afternoon gave me a big appetite."

"What work?" Chocolate said to his brother. "I think that cushy deputy job you got is making a light weight out of you."

As the sun began to set and the moon started to turn a bright orange, Gray and Chocolate got up from the table and walked outside with the other men. Luke walked over to where the two unbeknown brothers were standing and asked. "So, how do you like the Bar X so far, Gray?" Rolling a cigarette, he offered one to Gray.

Gray said to Luke, "No, thanks, man, that cigarette's a death sentence for sure. But as for the Bar X, I think I'm going to like working here, at least for the moment. It's really a nice spread. Who owns it, though? Payton?"

Luke replied, "No, some big shot in Cockapoo is all we know. Well, boys, that's enough questions for tonight. I'm heading for the bunkhouse and get some shut-eye, and if you boys know what's good for you, you'll do the same. Sun up comes mighty early around here. And any other questions, take them to Mr. Payton."

As Luke headed for the bunkhouse, so did Gray and Chocolate, with Payton following right behind.

Payton came into the bunkhouse and said, "Ok, fellas, tomorrow the boss will be stopping by, so let's be sharp," Payton said, then turned and walked out of the bunkhouse.

Gray thought to himself, "Lord, if you can hear me, please be with us tomorrow, Good night."

Bringing Down The House

EANWHILE, BUFF WAS back at the jail eating the fried chicken and greens Aunt Bea brought over for the boys' supper and going over the plan with his deputies for good measure. No one was going home tonight. Buff wanted everyone together, on time, and up at the crack of dawn. And he prayed, unknowingly just as his brother did, asking the good Lord to be with them and see to it that everything goes like clockwork, because now he had two of his brothers on the Bar X ranch with their lives in danger and there was no room for any mistakes.

In the morning Buff told his deputies one last time that he wanted no mistakes, then Buff and his deputies rode hard and fast out of town and were soon within sight of the Bar X. Buff looked at Dollar Five and said, "Ok, Dollar Five, you're on."

Dollar Five rode on ahead and up to the gate. As far as he could see, there were three men well hidden in the hills surrounding the ranch, but he couldn't be sure there weren't others. When he was close enough, he saw at least two men guarding the gate and one of them said, "Hey, don't I know you?"

Dollar Five replied, "You should, I shod enough horses for you. Man, you guys can run a good horse into the ground."

"That's right. Dollar Five. Man, you sure do good work. So, what brings you up this way, you miss us or something? We didn't send for you," the man guarding the gate said standing next to his buddy.

"Yeah, I know, but a guy from Poodle Town was in Cockapoo last night and asked me to come out there this morning and shoe some horses for him. So, I thought on my way back to Cockapoo I'd stop by and see if you fellows needed some work done since ya'll boys so rough on horses," Dollar Five replied.

"Man, what's in Poodle Town? That town's so small it can't be much work there," one of the guards replied.

"I go wherever there's money, and there's plenty work out that way. Poodle Town is up and coming. It'll be on the map soon enough, you'll see," Dollar Five replied. As he started to turn his horse and ride away, the guard that knew him said, "Hey, Dollar Five, where ya goin'? I thought you came out here looking for work."

"You mean you fellows got work for me?" Dollar Five asked with an unexpected look on his face. And to his surprise the man answered, "We sure do, man. Come on in," and the man opened the gate to let him in.

Dollar Five thought to himself, "This couldn't have worked out any better."

From where Buff was sitting things were looking mighty fine. It was even better than he had planned. Having three of his deputies inside was just what he wanted.

"Once Buff saw Dollar Five go in Buff said, "Ok boys, we're going to leave the horses here and split up. We're going the rest of the way on foot. Dean, you take the right, and Thad you take the left. I'm going straight down their throat."

They each went their separate ways on foot, walking slowly, carefully, and mindful of the noise the ground can make, especially when stepping on branches. Dean noticed a flickering light a few feet ahead of him. He waved his paws at Buff and pointed. Buff took out his pair of binoculars and saw the guard with a rifle sitting on a big rock. He looked back at Dean with his paws crossed, letting Dean know to take him out. Dean started crawling his way towards the guard sitting on the rock smoking a rolled cigarette. When he was within reach of the man on guard, Dean hesitated, but only for a minute. Reaching slowly for his pistol as he eased up behind the man, Dean knocked the man's hat off and hit him hard on the head with the butt of his pistol. The man fell backwards into Dean's arms. With his bandana, Dean gagged the captured outlook man, cuffed him, and laid him nicely behind the rock the man had been sitting on.

Buff took out his target without any problem, but Thad had a bit of trouble trying to take out his target. When Thad hit the man over his head the man's pistol went off, letting Payton and the others down below know that something was up. Payton noticed that Fatcat was riding in from the other direction, so he waited until Fatcat rode up in his buggy. Jumping out of the buggy and walking over toward Payton, Fatcat asked, "Payton, was that a shot I just heard?"

"Yeah, it was, boss," Payton replied.

"Well, don't just stand there, man. Send someone out to look over the grounds," Fatcat commanded.

Fatcat turned and went into the mansion. Payton went out to the bunkhouse and told the men to get their pistols and cover the grounds and shoot whoever they saw that didn't belong on the ranch.

Gray looked at Chocolate and said, "I think something just went wrong,"

"You said it, brother," Chocolate replied.

"So, what're we gonna do? You know this place better than I do," Gray said to Chocolate.

"Not, really. But look here, let's try and make our way to the barn and get a couple of horses and shoot our way out of here," Chocolate told Gray.

"Sounds like a good plan to me, brother," Gray replied.

But when they entered the barn, they heard someone moving around in one of the back stalls. They couldn't see if the man had a pistol or not, so Chocolate said, "Ok, fella, toss that pistol out, butt first, and you follow after, real slow like."

The man did as he was told. When they saw who it was, Gray just stood there laughing. "Dollar Five, what the heck are you doing here?" Gray asked.

"Shoeing horses, what else?" he replied laughingly.

"We can see that, but that wasn't part of Buff's plan," Gray said to him.

"I know, but it sure worked out ok for you two, didn't it? Now tell the truth," Dollar Five told Gray and Chocolate.

"Let's get out of here first, then we'll decide that, ok, boys?" Chocolate said.

Payton saw the barn door open and the three men trying to make their way out of the barn. He shot his gun in the air and called out, "Hey, where you boys off to?"

Not having one good answer between the three of them that made sense, they walked over to Payton and grabbed him by his arm and started dragging him into the barn. "Come with us, Mr. Foreman, we got some use for you," Gray said. "You're gonna help the three of us get off this ranch"

"I smell Johnny law," Payton replied.

"That we are," Gray told Payton.

Then from out of nowhere a shot was fired hitting Gray and he fell to the ground, taking Payton with him. Chocolate and Dollar Five ran into a stall for cover. They each tried to locate the shooter.

Then Gray called out, "Hey, boys, I'm hit."

"We know, Gray, we saw it. Where are you hit?" Chocolate called out.

"I'm not sure. It feels like all over my body, but I think it's my shoulder, and it's hurtin' somethin' awful," Gray said.

Chocolate called out, "Just hang on, Gray, we can't locate the shooter, but Dollar Five's got a good eye on you. And Buff's out there and I got a feelin' he's gonna take this ranch pretty soon."

"Anytime would be soon enough for me," Gray replied as he held on to Payton.

"You three are crazy if you think you're gonna get off this ranch alive," Payton said.

"Payton, you say one more word and I'm going to put my good arm right down your throat," Gray replied in pain.

Chocolate said, "That's right, brother, hold on to our ticket off this ranch."

Back out in front of the ranch Thad was making his way over toward the Marshal. When he was close enough to the Marshal, he said, "I'm sorry, Buff, but when I hit him over the head, his pistol fell to the ground and fired."

"Don't worry about it, Thad," Buff said. "At least we're closer to the ranch now, but I think something's wrong."

Just then a voice called out from behind the gate, "Hey, who's that out there? What do you want here and why're you shootin' at us?"

"I'm Marshal Buff Nagol from Cockapoo City, and I want all of you to put down those rifles and pistols and come out with your paws high, or we're coming in," Buff called out.

"Well, my name's Luke. I work here, and you must be one crazy lawman if you're figuring on coming in here."

Buff motioned to his deputies to move out. He knew they would likely hit what they aimed at since he'd taught them all to shoot. Then he yelled out to Dean and Thad, "Take the ranch, boys," and they did. They took out the two men that were guarding the main gate first. Soon after, shots were coming from every direction. The men that were on the grounds of the ranch ran back into the mansion.

Back inside the barn Chocolate told Gray that he and Dollar Five were going out to help Buff, and to keep his pistol on Payton. Chocolate and Dollar Five came running out of the barn, ducking pellets that were coming from the Mansion.

Dean made his way across the ranch hiding behind some brush, and the first place he checked out was the barn. He thought if he ran off the horses no one could get away. Dean kicked the barn door in and found Gray laying on his back in a pool of blood with a hole in his shoulder. Gray was still holding his pistol on Payton. Dean ran over to him and asked, "Gray, you alright?"

"No, Dean, I'm not. I'm lying here in pool of blood, with a hole in me and bleeding to death. Will you do something already, please?" Gray replied.

Dean looked at Gray's wound and said, "Oh, you'll be alright, but I can see someone is dead in that stall over there."

"He must have been the one who shot me. So, Chocolate did get him out after all. Hey Dean, look around outside and see if you can find a pump or a trough with some clean water in it, and fix me up until we get back to town. Then Doc Stone can take this pullet out my shoulder," Gray said to Dean.

"Sure, Gray, I'll get you cleaned up."

Dean finally got Gray cleaned up and found some clean rags to wrap his shoulder. Then they headed out the barn with Payton in tow. But from where they were, with all the shooting still going on, they couldn't tell if Buff and the boys had taken the Mansion yet. So, the two of them walked real careful with Payton grinning from ear to ear, his paws cuffed behind his back.

Payton, said. "Man, if your Marshal tries to take down that mansion, he's gonna get shot up somethin' bad. We got some fire power in there."

But what Payton didn't know was that the Marshal had already taken out most of the hands on the ranch. That's what all the shooting was about. Things were looking to be a bit under control except for a few men still inside the mansion. Marshal Buff saw Chocolate and Dollar run around to the back of the mansion. He signaled for them to come in from the back while he and Thad took the front. With shots still being fired from inside the mansion, the Marshal started shooting at the front door until it was weak enough for him and Thad to kick it in. Once they were inside the shooting stopped and the Marshal said, as loud as he could, "Alright, boys, let's drop those pistols, and come on out." Soon a door opened halfway down the hall, as if by magic. Then out from behind the door stepped a long-haired Javanese.

She was beautiful. She must have been one of Fatcat's saloon girls. She had vivid blue eyes, painted red lips, wearing a pink skirt and a white T-shirt, with writing on it that said, 'Fatcat's Kitty Kats.' Standing bold and proud in her white leather, knee high boots and pink Stetson cowboy hat, she wore a white pearl two-paw pistol holster around her waist and was carrying a rifle.

She walked up to the Marshal and looked him straight in the eyes and said. "How y'all boys, doin'? My name is Peggy Waggy. May I help you?"

The Marshal and Thad just looked at one another, then the Marshal said, "I'm Marshal Nagol, and I've got some warrants here to serve."

Ms. Peggy Waggy said, "Surely you don't have one of those warrants for little ol' me, now, do you, Mr. Marshal Man?" blinking her seal-colored eye lashes.

As he came walking out of the same room, Fatcat said, "No, Peggy, the Marshal is here to arrest me and my boys."

"Does that mean the fun is over?" Ms. Peggy asked. "Now, don't be a spoil sport and go spoiling the fun, Mr. Marshal Man. We ain't hurtin' nobody."

"Ok, Marshal, what is it this time? I don't know why badge toters keep coming for me. I've done nothing wrong," Fatcat told the Marshal.

"Like I told you that day I kicked down the door of your office, Fatcat. My name ain't Ben Colby and I didn't bring my deputies out here to admire this place. You and Payton are under arrest for attempted murder, and blackmailing Marshal Colby. And I promise you'll have your day in court," Buff told Fatcat.

Chocolate walked up behind Fatcat and tapped him on the shoulder. Fatcat turned around and rolling his eyes said, "Another badge-toting lawman?"

"You look out that window, Mr. Fatcat, you'll see two more badge-toting lawmen coming this way with Payton in tow. I'm sure Lucky will be happy to see you two fellas," Chocolate replied laughingly.

"This may not be the time or place, but Chocolate, we been worried about you ever since Nation told us you were out here undercover. You like living dangerously, don't you? Where's Gray?"

"Buff, Gray took one in the right shoulder," Chocolate replied.

"What? Is he alright?" Buff asked.

"Yep, but the sooner we get him to Doc, the better I'll feel. We made a soft spot for him in a wagon out there," Chocolate replied.

Just then Dollar Five and Dean walked in with Payton in cuffs. "Buff, you boys got things wrapped up in here or what?" Dollar Five asked.

"Yep, it's a rap, now let's get Gray back to town," Buff replied.

With Gray lying wounded in the back of Fatcat's wagon, Buff tried to make the trip to town slow and steady. As soon as they hit town, Buff, Thad and Dollar Five headed straight for the jail to lock up the prisoners. "I'll be right over." Buff said, as Chocolate and Dean carried Gray to Doc Stone.

"What do we have here?" Doc Stone said as he opened his front door.

"It's one of the Marshal's brothers, Doc," Dean answered.

"Bring him in and take him to the back room and lay him down easy, boys. It looks like he's lost a lot of blood. How long ago did this happen, Dean?" Doc Stone asked.

"Like an hour or so, Doc," Dean replied.

"And who's this fellow?" The Doc asked.

"I'm Buff's younger brother. My name is Chocolate. Tell me, sir, is my brother going to be alright?" Chocolate asked.

"It would have been better if you had gotten here sooner, but I'll do the best I can. Like I said, he's lost a lot of blood from the way things look. I'll know more once I get the pellet out. You boys go get a drink or something. I'll send for you," Doc told them.

"If it's ok with you, Doc, I'll just sit outside in the night air. You let me know as soon as you know something," Chocolate told Doc Stone with a look of concern.

It was nearly a half hour later when Buff had arrived. Doc Stone came out and said, "I got the pellet out and the bleeding stopped, and I gave him some laudanum for pain. Now you deputies get off my porch and go back to watching your prisoners or somethin'. You can come for him first thing in the morning. G'night, fellas."

When they got back to the jail Fatcat was yelling, "Marshal! Marshal! I want my lawyer! I want my lawyer!"

The Marshal walked in and said, "Come on, now, fellas, cool it. Judge Tuesday is due back in Cockapoo in two days. He'll hear your case then."

It was the longest two-days Fatcat, Payton and the others had ever seen, but their day in court finally arrived. Both Fatcat and Payton pleaded not guilty, but after hearing the Marshal's evidence, Judge Tuesday found them guilty and gave them both three-years hard labor at Canine Territorial Prison for blackmailing and attempted murder of a peace officer.

The Marshal tried to tie Fatcat and Payton to the murder of the ol' prospector, but he didn't have enough evidence. Luke and three other surviving Bar X ranch hands pleaded not guilty to having knowledge of any illegal doings at the ranch claiming they just worked there. And with a lack of proof, Judge Tuesday did the only thing he could do. He fined Luke and the others $200 dollars and 10 days in jail for resisting arrest and shooting at peace officers and ordered them to stay out of Cockapoo City.

When Judge Tuesday tried Ms. Peggy Waggy he said, "Tell me, Ms. Waggy, how does a sweet innocent looking young lady like you get hooked up with jokers like these?"

"Well, judge, your honor, sir, I really don't know, sir. It musta been one of those things called bad judgment," she said to the judge.

"To say the least," Judge Tuesday replied laughingly. "Well, young lady, I'm ordering you to stay clear of Cockapoo City, too, with an exception by the Marshal, if he wants, and a $200 dollar fine. And if it's not paid, I'm ordering the Marshal to lock you up and throw away the key. You got that, young lady? Now got out of my court."

"I'm going, your honor," Ms. Peggy Waggy said as she turned and wiggled her way out of the courthouse.

"Oh, Marshal, about your search warrant a while back, I'm placing the Bar X and all its properties in the custody of the Cockapoo City Marshal's Office, to search and seize all evidence. This court stands adjourned," were the last words the judge said before leaving the bench.

Walking the Judge to the stagecoach Marshal Buff said, "So, I guess we'll see you back here in two weeks, Judge."

"I'd say in about a week. See you then, Marshal. You know, you're doing a fine job out here. Keep up the good work," Judge Tuesday told the Marshal.

"I'm so glad that's over, and thanks, Judge Tuesday," Marshal Nagol said as he helped the judge into the stagecoach.

Tumbleweed Wagon

AFTER A HARD fought battle with the Bar X Ranch, Calico Napoleon Fatcat Cobb and Payton Leonberger were now nicely tucked away in the Cockapoo City jail awaiting the tumbleweed wagon to take them to Collie City. They would take a train to Parsonville and then on to Canine Territory Prison where they would begin serving out the three-year sentence, they'd been given a few days ago by the Honorable Judge Affenpinscher Tuesday. The Tumbleweed Wagon, also known as The Jail On Wheels, was to pick up prisoners throughout the territory sentenced to do hard time at Canine Territory Prison, but Luke Chinook and the three other surviving ranch hands would just be doing 10 days in the Cockapoo jail, then kicked out of town with Ms. Peggy Waggy.

Sheriff Jack Russell, Jr. sent Buff a wire a week before the trial even started informing him that the Tumbleweed Wagon would be making its way through Cockapoo City, giving the Marshal enough time to have the prisoners ready should they be found guilty, which they were, and they were all ready and waiting. This would make this the second time the Tumbleweed Wagon came through Cockapoo City. The first time was a year or so back when the Sheriff came to pick up Lucky Tessel. With the Tumbleweed Wagon due sometime today, ol' Red was right on target with his crowing. Buff was used to it, but he could only imagine what it was doing to Fatcat and Payton who, to his knowledge, didn't even know ol' Red. With his saloon clear on the other side of town, they might have never heard ol' red's beautiful vocals. Buff had most of the paperwork in the office completed. It was getting close to noon. Buff was sitting behind his desk waiting for Sheriff Russell and thinking, if Lady Luck was on their side, they might just come up with enough evidence to tack on a few murder charges to Fatcat and Payton.

Buff figured with the three year sentence Judge Tuesday had given them, and with the possibility of getting out in two years for good behaver, it may give him enough time to sink his teeth into gathering enough evidence to charge Fatcat and Payton with murder while they're still doing time, if he only had something, anything, that would tie them to the killing of the old miner. But at least for now, Gray's shoulder would have time to heal from the pellet he took during the deadly raid staged on the Bar X.

"Hey Marshal, Marshal, the Tumbleweed Wagon, here she comes. And it looks bigger than the one that came for Lucky," Dollar Five said as he ran into the jail.

The Tumbleweed Wagon was something to see. It looked like a small metal house on wheels with three metal barred windows, one on each side and on the locked door in the rear of the wagon. Stepping down off the tall wagon was Sheriff Jack Russell, Jr. himself. The sheriff had ten deputies on horseback travelling with him. Sheriff Russell, Sr. had started transporting prisoners many years ago, and the wagon had been attacked several times. They hadn't lost a prisoner then, and they weren't about to lose one now.

"It's mighty good to see you again, Buff. Say, I hear you got Mr. Calico Napoleon Fatcat Cobb himself for me this time, is it true?" Sheriff Russell, Jr. asked with a smile.

"It's true Sheriff. We got his sidekick, too," Buff replied.

"No! Not Payton Chinook?" The Sheriff asked.

"One and the same," Buff told Sheriff Russell, Jr.

"I don't know how you and your deputies do it, Marshal, but all I gotta say is keep up the good work, cause me and my deputies don't mind at all comin' to pick up outlaws like those no-do-gooders. But I gotta tell ya that I'll sure be happy as heck when that railroad makes its way out here. Ya know, it's gonna save us a lot of time and money, Buff," the Sheriff said.

"Whatever happened to the railroad coming out this way, Sheriff? It seems like the talk started and then stopped, just like that," Buff replied.

"The way I hear tell it, Buff, the man who owned the railroad needed money bad so he auctioned it off. But the good news is that the new owner has plans of takin' it all the way into the Appaloosa Territory. It might take a minute, but I sure won't mind it at all. That would sure put this ol' Tumbleweed Wagon to rest. Say, Buff, you ever been inside one of these things?" the sheriff asked.

"Sheriff, I've never even heard tell of a Tumbleweed Wagon until I became a lawman," Buff replied laughingly.

"Well, I'll give you and your deputies a look see inside before we leave in the morning, if you like. But for now, you got a place right cheap that me and my deputies can sleep tonight?" the sheriff asked.

Buff said, "Dollar Five, take Sheriff Russell and his deputies to the hotel. Tell Mr. Shar-Pei that Sheriff Russell and company are my guests. Tell him that they're staying the night, and make sure they get the best rooms he's got. And tell him I said to service them in the hotel dining room, and make sure their bellies get nice and tight. And, Dollar Five, tell him I said to send the bill to the Mayor."

"To Mayor Todd, Marshal?" Dollar Five asked.

"You heard me right, Dollar Five," Buff told him.

Sheriff Russell said, "Well, that's right neighborly of you, Buff. And if you ever come to Parsonville, expect the same thing."

Buff felt the least Mayor Todd could do was put the lawmen up for the night. Since the time he had lived in Cockapoo City, Buff began to feel as Mr. Clayton and some of the other town folk, who remained nameless, that Mayor Todd's office was corrupt, dating back to the gold strikes. But, like Mr. Clayton, Buff couldn't prove his suspicions either. But being the town Marshal, Buff knew it was his job to bring in lawbreakers to stand trial no matter who they were. It was Marshal Buff Nagol's intention not to rest until Mayor Todd's butt was firmly tucked away on a Tumbleweed Wagon, or train, heading to Canine Territory Prison.

For the last two days Buff had been pulling night duty at the jail, and thanks to Aunt Bea, he didn't get stuck eating that free food offered by the café to the Marshal and his deputies. It wasn't because they didn't appreciate it, it was just that the cook wasn't a very good cook. But tonight it would be different. It was Dollar Five's and Dean's turn to pull night duty. Judging by the time, both his deputies were about due and, as usual, they were right on time. The door to the marshal's office opened, and Dean walked in with Dollar Five trailing right behind. "Hey, Marshal, Aunt Bea said come on home and eat your supper," Dean said.

"Like music to my tender little ears, and I'm on my way, boys. Look, Fatcat and Payton have had their supper. I'm sure you saw the Tumbleweed Wagon when it came through town. In the morning Sheriff Russell said if you'd like to see it, he'll give you a look inside before they leave," Buff told his deputies.

"I know I would," Dean replied. "I'd love to have some pictures for the paper. I missed it the last time."

"Well, fellas, I'm outta here. Listen, if Sheriff Russell or any of his deputies should come by and need anything, see to it that they get it, and charge it to the Mayor's office," Buff said as he closed the door to the jail behind him.

It was such a warm night Buff decided to leave his horse at the stable and walk home. He passed the Cockapoo Hotel on the way and saw Mr. Shar-Pei standing outside the Hotel rolling a cigarette. "Marshal, can I see you for a minute?" Shar-Pei called out.

Buff walked over to see what was on his mind. "Marshal, did you really tell Dollar Five for me to send the bill to Mayor Todd's office for payment?" Shar-Pei asked the Marshal.

"Yep, Shar-Pei, I most surely did. I don't see it being a problem, do you?" the Marshal asked.

"No, sir, marshal, it'll be a pleasure. And I'll make sure those lawmen leave my hotel tomorrow with a story to tell," Shar-Pei replied.

With Bea's place in view Buff was one happy but tired Marshal. He could see Gray, Chocolate and Aunt Bea sitting out front. "You look beat, brother dear," Gray yelled out to him.

Buff just threw up his paw, shook his head and kept walking. Once he was through the gate of Bea's Place he said, "It's been a long day, boys, but my biggest mistake was giving you two the day off. Gray, now that I can see you're able to feed yourself you can go in with me. Oh, never mind. A one paw deputy ain't no good to me. Chocolate, you go with me tomorrow."

"I see that metal house on wheels made it to town," Aunt Bea replied.

"It's called a Tumbleweed Wagon, Aunt Bea," Gray replied.

"You can call it what you want but it still looks like a metal house on wheels to me. At least, all around town you can see and feel folks being right happy with the Judge's ruling. Well, I'll go inside and get out a plate of food for you, Buff. You wanna eat inside, or out here?" Aunt Bea asked.

"Be nice to eat out here, Aunt Bea. I'll go inside and get cleaned up," Buff replied.

Once Buff got cleaned up, he got a sarsaparilla and walked back out to the porch and joined Chocolate and Gray. He looked over at Chocolate and said, "Chocolate, you look like a man with a heavy mind."

"It shows that much?" Chocolate asked.

"Yep, just like that day you came into the den after hearing Grandpa tell the family about the cold rainy night," Buff replied.

"It's funny you should mention that right now, Buff, because I do have something might heavy on my mind, something Nation told me just before I left to come here. Ya know, boys, he told me that after those outlaws stampeded Pa's herd, he sent some detectives out a few days after to look over the area where it happened. He told me that they found not one single trace of a body. He did say there were plenty of pawprints and tracks made by the cattle. He said that for all they knew, Pa could've floated right down the Pyrenees River," Chocolate told his brother.

"Are you saying what we think you're saying, Chocolate?" His brothers asked.

"Well, boys, yes and no. You see, Nation didn't come right out and say Pa was alive, but he gave me the impression that he believed Pa could be. But he told me to believe what I felt. And I believe somewhere out there our Pa is alive," Chocolate replied.

"Well, then why hasn't he come home after all this time, answer me that?" Gray asked.

"There are a number of reasons for that, Gray, and the one I'd like to think is that Pa must have lost his memory, you know, and he don't know who he is," Buff answered Gray.

"So, just how are we supposed to find a man neither of us have ever laid eyes on before? He's just not gonna fall right into our laps ya know, boys," Gray replied.

"I don't know, Gray, but I got a feeling Chocolate is right," Buff replied. "I believe Pa is out there somewhere, and believe me, we'll find him. And it won't take a life time either. First off, we need to let the family know."

"That's no good, Buff," Chocolate said. "Nation said it might be better if just the three of us know for now. And I believe he's right. Remember, the Morgans are still looking to kill us. But I know something that we might want to keep in mind. Remember the gold-plated belt buckles grandpa Logan gave the five of us?" Buff and Gray sat there listening to their brother, both nodding that they remembered them. Chocolate said, "Remember grandpa said that now we have one just like the one he gave Pa? Well, now we just need to ask Ma to send us a picture of Pa," Chocolate told his brothers.

Buff replied, "Okay, Chocolate, you have a point, and for now we'll do it your way."

Aunt Bea was coming outside with Buff's supper when she noticed the sadness in their faces. "What happened, boys? Why so sad?"

"We're not sad, Aunt Bea. Just thinking over things, that's all," Buff replied.

Aunt Bea sat the plate of food down on a table next to Buff and he went for it. "Well, by the way you're going after the food, Buff, everything must be fine," Aunt Bea said with a little laugh. "Well, I'll leave you boys to your law work. I got some things to put away in the kitchen before I go to bed. Call me if you need anything." Aunt Bea knew this was one of those times the boys needed to be left alone with their law work, which she always respected and understood. They said good night to Aunt Bea and each one kissed her on the cheek.

Trying not to talk with his mouth full, Buff said to Chocolate, "Say, Chocolate, why don't you bring me and Gray up to date with everything you and your big secret agent boys, the Middleton Detectives, know. This is just as good a time as any," Buff said laughingly to Chocolate while kicking Gray on the leg getting him to laugh with him.

"Well, Buff, the information we've been able to gather checks out with what I got from Payton during the time I was on the ranch," Chocolate said. "You see, it looks like ol' man Holiday could have been murdered, and this could possibly tie in with the disappearance of the ol' prospector in that abandoned mining town called Chow-Chow during the Gold and Silver strikes. Payton told me they found silver on the Bar X and that they also owned land in the Great Mastiff Mountain area, and that's where they struck gold. Now, if we can prove that ol' man Holiday was in fact murdered, and the prospector's claim was on Holiday's land, which by the way, was jumped by Fatcat's uncle Bobcat . . . . . ."

Buff interrupted Chocolate and said, "I'm beginning to see the picture. Well, we know about Chow-Chow and the gold, but no one ever mentioned anything to me about a silver strike or the possibility of ol' man Holiday begin murdered, Chocolate. But the prospectors name was Binder. And he disappeared sometime after his big strike from what I been hearing around town. You see, after I was sworn in as Marshal, we searched Ben's office and found what turned out to be a confession letter Ben's Pa left him. Ben told me his Pa was up to his neck in gambling debt to Bobcat, and Bobcat called it in putting a collar and chain around his Pa's neck. Then after he married

Hope, Fatcat and Payton used her past as a saloon girl to blackmail him into destroying everything the land office had on the Bar X Ranch. But you mean to tell me you got all this from Payton while on the ranch?" Buff asked his brother.

"Yes," replied Chocolate. "Now here's where my own theory comes in. Buff, if Fatcat's uncle Bobcat left him word somehow of what he discovered, it would explain why he needed the Holiday Mansion. I also know that Mr. Clayton and Mr. Greenwood discovered gold, too. But ol' man Holiday bought up a good part of the Great Mastiff Mountain area with his gold, then hired men to mine the property and his fortune was born. So, it would have been easy for someone to jump Holiday's claim. Especially if that someone couldn't read or write, such could have been the case of Binder."

"But what about Victoria?" Buff asked.

"Well, the way I see it, Buff, Victoria was just out for revenge on ol' man Holiday for not adopting her after he married her Ma. So, all she had to do was attack the ol' man's grandkids, and she knew just how to do that," Chocolate explained.

"Which gives her a good reason to forge the papers to sell the mansion, using the takeover of the companies as nothing but a big front?" Buff asked.

"That would make sense. And so she sold the mansion to the one person she knew was looking to buy it, namely, Fatcat Cobb. Which means that Bobcat most likely did leave Fatcat knowledge of what he discovered," Chocolate added.

"So, Victoria's nothing but a tiny little fish in a great big pond, waiting to be eaten by a big fish, Fatcat." Buff and Gray just sat there laughing their tails off and clapping their paws.

"Let's not get too excited fellas and put the cart before the horse because as we know, being peace officers, without proof to back this up, it's only a theory. And we know theories don't hold up in a court of law. And all we've got is theory," Chocolate replied laughingly.

"Chocolate, ever since we were little tykes, you was always a kill joy," Gray replied laughingly. "Now I know we got to get permission from the Judge, Chocolate, so we can search that mansion."

"And on that note boys, I'm going to bed," Buff replied.

"Hey, Buff, whose got night duty tonight?" Gray asked.

"Dollar Five and Dean. Thad said that he'd stop by and see if anyone wanted to be relieved," Buff said.

By the time Buff woke up and got to the jail, Sheriff Jack Russell, Jr. was standing out front waiting for him. "I just thought you might want to have that look-see inside."

Chocolate and Gray were right behind him. Now that all the boys were standing out in front of the Marshal's office, Sheriff Jack Russell, Jr. called out to one of his deputies to bring the wagon around. Man, it was something to see.

Dollar Five said, "It's nothing but a metal jail on wheels, just like Aunt Bea said."

Inside there were benches on each side, enough space to hold at least eight prisoners.

Thad and Dean already having had a look at the wagon, were coming out of the jail with Fatcat and Payton in tow, both of them putting up a ruckus all the way to the wagon.

"I'm coming back for you, Marshal, and all your deputies, too," Fatcat said, shaking his fist at them from between the bars of the wagon. "Wait and see, you no-good-for-nothing, badge totin' Johnny Law."

"Man, I never thought I'd see the day, Fatcat and Payton locked up in a Tumbleweed Wagon and on their way to Canine Territorial Prison. This is going to be one heck of a front-page story, Thad. We're gonna be busy as bees," Dean said.

"Now, boys, who wants to take a trip with me to Shepherdsville?" Buff asked.

No one said a word as they stood there looking at each other. Dean spoke up and said, "Well, Marshal, you just heard me tell Thad that we got work to do if we're going to make the morning headline. Better look someplace else, Buff."

"That's ok, Dean, I'll need someone to stay behind and walk that badge around town, and it might as well be you and Thad," Buff replied.

"I'm in, Marshal, I'll go. You can depend on me," Dollar Five said. "I'm sure I can get Bentfoot and Beauceron to look after the Livery Stable."

"What's going on, Marshal?" Chet asked as he was walking by the Marshal's office.

"Making plans, Chet. Heading to Shepherdsville for a spell," Buff replied, trying not to appear too friendly like toward the undercover Middleton Agent.

"Well, have a nice trip, Marshal. See you when you get back," Chet Basenji replied.

"You know, Buff, I know someone who would sure love to go on that little trip with you fellas," Dean said. "Matt."

"You know, I was gonna stop by the freight office on my way to send this wire to the Holidays that Aunt Bea forgot to send and ask Matt if he wanted to take a little trip," Buff replied.

"What made you decide to take a trip to Shepherdsville?" Thad asked.

"Well, Thad, with the mansion in our custody now we have the right to search it when we get ready. I'm thinking that now is a good time to have a talk with Ms. Ashley and Mr. Thurston, and I think it might be better if we go to see them in Shepherdsville, rather than asking them to come here. And besides, Aunt Bea could use a little get away time," Buff replied.

24

Shepherdsville

B UFF KNEW HIS office needed to work fast finding answers to some of the still unanswered questions since before he and his brothers came to town. So, Buff went along with Dean and Thad to the newspaper office so he could send the wire to the twins. But first they stopped by the Greenwood Freight and Stage office. When they arrived Matt said, "Hey, Marshal, Dean, Thad, what brings you fellas on this side of town?"

"Well, Matt," Buff said, "I'm planning a little trip to Shepherdsville and gonna have me a talk with Ms. Ashley and Mr. Thurston. I hear tell you're still sweet on Ms. Ashley, so, I was wondering if you might wanna come with us and say a word or two. She'd be right happy to see you from what I hear."

"Oh, Marshal, I would love nothing more than to lay these eyes upon her sweet, lovely face again, but I'm afraid Ms. Ashley don't want anything to do with me. If she did then she would have written me at least once. But, yeah, I'll go along, Marshal. Hey, I have a good idea. Why don't we just drive one of our stage coaches? It would be a lot easier and more comfortable, especially if Aunt Bea comes along. And we'll have room to put all that food I know you're gonna ask Aunt Bea to fix," Matt said laughlying to Buff.

"You know, Matt, you're right on both counts so we'll be leaving come sun-up. Be ready, Matt, and you can bet we'll have plenty to eat," Buff told Matt as he headed toward the newspaper office with Dean. By the time Buff left the newspaper office and got to Bea's place, Dollar Five, Chocolate and Gray had just about finished filling Aunt Bea in on their plans. Soon as Buff walked in the house he walked into the kitchen and Aunt Bea turned and looked at him.

"I hear tell you're going to see my babies," she said.

"You heard right, Aunt Bea. Say, why don't you come with us?" Buff asked.

"I can just see me on horseback," Aunt Bea replied laughingly.

Buff said, "Oh, yeah, I forgot to mention. I asked Matt to come along with us and he suggested we all ride in one of his stagecoaches, although I still feel at least two or three of us should ride horses."

"You see there, Aunt Bea? You can ride in style to Shepherdsville," Dollar Five replied.

"I'll think on it a piece," she replied.

"Well, you want to think fast, Aunt Bea, because we're leaving come sun up. Gotta get an early start," Buff replied.

"What's the rush?" She asked.

"Well, now that I got the right to search that Mansion anytime I want, I wanna have a talk with the Holidays first, then get back here and do it. No telling what we might find out, and we all could use some time away from Cockapoo, and now is just the right time. So, think away Aunt Bea," Buff told her with a laugh.

"Well, it would be nice to see my sister Mollie," she said. "Dollar Five, if'n I'm going in the morning, somebody better be going over to the general store and get Cyrus to fill my regular order for me, as it's gonna be a night of cooking. I'm going to need a nap by the time we hit Poodle Town," Aunt Bea laughingly said.

And off to the store Chocolate and Dollar Five went. When they returned with everything she needed, Aunt Bea started cooking and the house began to smell like fried chicken, ham hocks and apple pie. With Buff's help tasting everything, he and Aunt Bea finally closed their eyes after packing the food around 10 o'clock.

Come sunup Matt was on his way to Bea's place but decided to check with the newspaper office first to see if Ms. Ashley had responded to the Marshal's wire, and there was a reply. And to Matt's surprise, there was a wire waiting for him, too, from Ms. Ashley. Matt smiled when he saw the wire. He hopped on the stage and slapped leather to Bea's place. When he arrived, Matt knocked on the front door and called out, "Marshal, hey Marshal! Marshal!"

Matt's hard knocking and loud voice caused Buff to fall off the couch where he'd slept last night. Buff said, "I'm comin', Matt, I'm comin'! Man, what is it?" Buff asked standing in the doorway in jeans and bare paws."

"She wrote me, Marshal! She wrote me," Matt said with a smile.

"What does she have to say, Matt?" Buff asked.

"I don't know. Been afraid to open and read it," Matt replied.

"Come on in, Matt," Buff said. "We're going in the dining room and you're gonna open it and read it out loud to me, and then we're gonna pack that stage and be ready to go when Aunt Bea gets ready," Buff replied.

When Buff and Matt got to the dining room, they took a seat at the table. Matt opened the wire and started reading. "Dear Matt, I would like to apologize for not writing to you. The only explanation I can offer is that with everything that had happened, all I wanted to do was forget. Somehow during the process I forgot you, and I am so sorry for letting that happen. When I received the wire from the new Marshal coming here to talk with us, my prayer was that you would come with him. So, I wanted to make sure, just in case you have some doubt, that I still love you very much and I hope you still love me. I do hope you make the trip as seeing you would be the best thing to happen to me since leaving Cockapoo City. All my love, Ashley."

Matt was beaming from ear to ear. "Come on, Marshal, let's get that stage packed so we can go," he impatiently replied to the Marshal.

"No, Matt, we need to eat breakfast first," Buff said. "So let's just wait till Aunt Bea gets up and fixes it."

Just then Buff heard the eggs hit the hot waiting pan and said, "She's up. Let's go have some breakfast, Matt, and then everyone else will be up and ready to eat, too. We'll leave by 10 or so. It's supposed to be right good weather today. Should be able to make Poodle Town by early evening. We'll stay the night in Poodle Town," Buff replied.

"No, no Marshal, we could be in Shepherdsville come night fall driving straight through," Matt explained.

"No good, Matt. Aunt Bea's coming along with us and she wants to see her sister, Mollie, in Poodle Town, then go on to Shepherdsville to see Ms. Ashley and Thurston," Buff told him.

"Oh, I'm sorry, Marshal, I didn't know she'd decided to come along," Matt replied.

Everyone was up and getting ready and the house was filled with excitement. Aunt Bea called everyone to breakfast and once they were done Chocolate and Dollar Five started loading the stage. Dollar Five said to Aunt Bea, "Three carpetbags Aunt Bea? How long're you plannin' to stay?"

"A lady can never have too many clothes, Dollar Five," She replied.

Buff came out of the house and said, "Listen up, everybody. I'm going to read Ms. Ashley's wire. She says here that they're all happy to hear we're coming for a visit and to make sure we bring along Aunt Bea, and to be safe." Aunt Bea chuckled as Buff put the wire in his pocket.

Once everything was packed on board the stage, they were on their way, with Matt in the driver's seat and brother Charlie right beside him. The Greenwood Brothers Stage Line were top of the line Concord Coaches. With four large painted yellow and white wheels, the coach itself was all brown with yellow writing that said Greenwood Brothers Stage Line in big letters along each side of it, and yellow paw prints in several places. When Matt gave those leather reins a good hard and stern jerk, those six black horses started moving the stage on its way. Buff and Chocolate were on horseback, while Gray and Dollar Five were seated inside with Aunt Bea.

Once they got going Gray turned to Dollar Five and said, "Look at Aunt Bea, Dollar Five, she's smiling from ear to ear."

"Enjoying the ride, Aunt Bea?" Dollar Five asked.

"I sure am, and I just love these smooth leather seats. And you know, these curtains at the windows have zippers along the side of them. A body don't need to worry about dust once you zip them up. I never seen anything like that before," Aunt Bea replied.

"When I helped Matt put them on the stage, Matt told me that their Pa came up with the idee, and they put them on all four of their coaches," Dollar Five said to Aunt Bea.

From the driver's seat of the stagecoach Matt swung his head over and asked, "How you gettin' along in there, Aunt Bea?"

"I'm doin' just fine, Matt, darling," She replied.

Buff rode his horse, Nugget, up beside the coach and said, "You know, Matt, we been makin' good time," Buff said.

"I figure we should be pulling into Dogwood Relay Station in a bit. You know, Buff, I like the closeness you three boys have. Ma and Pa saw to it me and Charlie had that same closeness, but I gotta tell ya, boy, I wasn't too sure after our Pa passed, though."

"Oh, why was that, Matt?" Buff asked.

"Brother Charlie had a thing for saloon girls, and, Buff, once in a while Marshal Colby would bring him home drunk after hanging out at Fatcat's Saloon and being cheated at those poker tables. Sometime the Marshal would have to send a boy to have me come fetch my Charlie. But then Mr. Clayton hired us to move all his freight and boy, we got so busy ol' Charlie didn't even have time to eat, let alone drink or hang out with saloon girls," Matt said as he laughed out loud. "I guess you can say, Buff, that the good Lord works in mysterious ways, cause he surely pulled one on ol' Charlie. You know, I always figured Ma asked the good Lord for that favor," Matt said with a smile.

"You just might have a point there, Matt," Buff replied with a knowing smile.

"Well, Dogwood Relay Station is just up ahead. We'll get somethin' to eat and a fresh team of horses there, then we should be pulling into Poodle Town in another hour or so. Say, I forgot. This is your first time out this way, isn't it?" Matt asked. "You know, Buff, so far this Dogwood Relay Station and the Pyrenees Relay Station on route to Collieville, have been rebuilt, and get this, Buff, both have sleeping quarters and washrooms, too. Yeah, me and ol' Charlie have done alright. I think Ma and Pa would be proud."

Matt swung his head over the side of the stagecoach and said, "We're more than halfway to your sister Mollie's, now, Aunt Bea."

Aunt Bea waved her paw out the window of the stagecoach letting Matt know she'd heard him. Looking at Aunt Bea Dollar Five noticed a familiar look on his aunt's face and asked, "Your trick knee's acting up again, ain't it?"

"Dollar Five, I nearly forgot about this ol trick knee of mine till I sit for a long time. But I'm afraid so, and if'n it don't get to feeling better soon, you boys will be going on to Shepherdsville without me. And I just might be taking an unplanned vacation with Mollie for the next week," Aunt Bea told Dollar Five.

Dogwood Relay Station was run by two brothers Matt and Charlie had known for many years, Jed and Flint Boxer and they were good station masters too. Once that stage pulled in Jed and Flint started helping Aunt Bea with the food, and their mouths started to water. Growing tired of their own cooking, Jed and Flint were real happy to see that there was enough food to feed everyone, and still have plenty left for later. Once they had everything laid out on the table Flint called out, "Come and get it."

Everyone sat down and started eating. Flint began to tell Matt and Charlie how things were going, and that they would be needing to go on a horse buying trip soon, and round up some of the boys to help break them in. Charlie said, "You know, Flint, we got a wire from Mr. Miloh's foreman. He said that Mr. Miloh had some new breeding stock we could look over. Now might be a good time for you to round up some of the boys and head out his way and have a look-see at some of those horses. And also check out the Logan rancher I hear they got some real good stock. Whatta ya think, Matt?"

"Sounds like a good idea to me," Matt replied. Buff, Gray and Chocolate just looked at one another and smiled.

"Then we'll get right to work on it. Say, Matt, you fellas still looking to expand into the Appaloosa region of Nokota Territory?" Flint asked.

"Yeah, in fact, we're hoping to take it clear through to Buckskin County, unless someone decides to expand the railroad from Collie City. That whole area is growing, and those folks are going to need transportation," Matt replied.

Charlie was the first one to get up from the table. He walked around to where Aunt Bea was sitting, put his arms around her shoulders and said, "My, Aunt Bea, I forgot how good of a cook you are, but you out did yourself this time."

"Brother, Charlie, you never spoke a truer word. Mighty fine vittles indeed, Aunt Bea," Matt replied.

Once they were done eating and well rested, it was time to get loaded and back on the trail. And within a few hours of leaving the Dogwood Relay Station, Charlie was pulling the stage into Poodle Town with Gray leading the way to Mollie's rooming house. When they arrived Mollie came running out and said, "Hey, hey, young fella, the stage depot is down the street and this ain't no stage stop."

As Mollie turned to go back inside her house, she heard someone calling, "Mollie, Mollie, bring your butt back here," Aunt Bea called out to her sister at the top of her voice.

"Bea, is that you?" Mollie asked.

"Who else, Mollie? Now you know ain't too many other folks gonna put up with you for too long," Aunt Bea replied as Dollar Five helped his Aunt off the stage so she could greet her sister.

"Y'all better c'mon in this house. Oh, my word, Gray is that you? Ya'll sure took you're own sweet time to come calling on a body," Mollie replied.

"Ma Mollie, it sure is good to see you. Come meet my brothers, Chocolate and Buff," Gray replied.

"Buff? Yeah, you're that new Marshal over there in Cockapoo City. I heard about you jailing Fatcat, something neither Marshal Colby nor his Pa could do. My hat's off to you, young fella. So the three of ya'll is brothers, well now that's right fine," Mollie replied.

Sheriff Tull arrived and was pretty surprised when he walked through the door and saw a room full of folks. And he was very happy to see his one-time deputy, Gray. "Hey, Nagol, it's been a long time. Nice to see you. What brings you fellas out this way?" Sheriff Tull asked.

"Alec, it's mighty good to see you, too. Meet my brother, Chocolate, and my brother, Buff. I believe you know the rest of these fellas," Gray replied.

"Yeah, I know Dollar Five and Matt and Charlie. I kinda feel like I know your brothers, too, at least the Marshal. We get the Cockapoo Newspaper here, too, and Poodle Town ain't that far from Cockapoo City. But I know y'all didn't just drop in. What brings you here, Marshal?" Sheriff Tull asked.

"Well, Sheriff, we're on our way to Shepherdsville to have a talk with Ms. Ashley and her brother Thurston," Buff replied.

"Oh, yeah, I heard they moved out to the Shepherdsville Mansion when they're grandpa passed on. What time are you fellas leaving?" Sheriff Tull asked.

"Well, we thought we'd layover here and let Aunt Bea rest up, and continue on in the morning," Buff replied.

"Buff, darling, I'm afraid I won't be going to Shepherdsville with you boys. My trick knee is acting up again," Aunt Bea said.

Dollar Five said, "Yeah, Marshal, I forgot to tell you when we stopped at the relay station."

"I'm sorry to hear that, Aunt Bea," Buff replied.

"Well, I'm sorry, too, Aunt Bea," Sheriff Tull said, "but if you fellas wanna finish that trip today, we can. Shepherdsville's not that far away and I even know a short cut that will get you there in about 45 minutes or so, providing I go along for the ride. We got plenty of daylight left."

"Now that sounds like a very good idee to me, Marshal," Dollar Five replied.

"It sure does, Dollar Five. Tell you what, why don't we rest up a bit and get a bite of food? I have something I'd like to say first," Buff replied.

Chocolate and Gray knew what Buff was trying to say, and although the three of them never decided on when the right time would be, they each knew in their heart that it was time to let the ones closest to them know who they really were. And there couldn't have been a better time than now.

Once they all sat down at the table Buff took his spoon and gently hit it against his glass. Once he had everyone's attention, he said, "When my brothers and I made the decision to leave Pittsville and follow in our grandpa's path, we had no idea that we'd meet folks like you, nor be taken in and treated like family by you, Aunt Bea, which is why we've come to this moment. We didn't set out to deceive anyone, but it was our family that felt it would be better it we didn't use our real name just yet. Grandpa Logan came up with this idea to spell our last name backward, making it Nagol, because of a vendetta against grandpa Logan when he was Marshal of Pittsville. And the Morgans are out to kill any Logan they find, including grandpa. I don' know how much you already know about the Logan family, but that's who we are."

"What was the reason, again?" Aunt Bea asked.

"It was because of the Morgans, Aunt Bea. You see their Grandpa Logan was Marshal Logan of Pittsville, and he had to shoot and kill both Asa and Gus Morgan, and now the Morgans are out for blood," Dollar Five explained.

"How long have you known about this, Dollar Five?" Aunt asked.

"Me, Dean and the Claytons knew from the first day Buff rode into Cockapoo City. You see Aunt Bea, me, Dean and Thad have been working as associates to the Middleton Detectives, and Chocolate is one, too," Dollar Five explained.

"Well shut my mouth. Mollie, our very own nephew, an agent," Aunt Bea replied.

"I suppose, Alexander, you, Matt and Charlie are going to tell us that you're agents too?" Mollie asked.

"No, Ma Mollie, not me," Alex replied.

Matt and Charlie said, "Don't look at us. We run a Freight and Stage line our Pa left us, but I'm sure it won't get outside this room."

"I knew there was something special about you boys," Aunt Bea replied.

"Well I can tell you, boys, if y'all want to get to Shepherdsville before night fall, we better get going. And I need to stop by the jail and let my deputy know I'll be away for a few days," Alex replied.

"Well, we better get going, fellas. Charlie, are you coming?" Matt asked his brother.

"No, you fellas git, cause I'm staying here and work on the rest of this food. I'll see you boys when you get back," Charlie replied.

Buff looked over his shoulders as he walked out of Mollie's house behind Gray. They each got on their horse and followed Sheriff Tull to the Sheriff's office. Riding beside Gray, Sheriff Tull turned to Gray and said, "I should have known that anyone with those quick paws had to have been some kin to the former Marshal Russell Logan, and his grandson at that. Boy, I didn't see this one coming."

"I'm powerful sorry, Alex, for running a con on you," Gray replied.

"Don't be, Gray. In fact, I'm proud to know you and your brothers," Alex responded.

Alex told the fellas to have a seat while he wrote his deputy a note. While waiting for Alex, Buff casually walked over to look at the wanted posters tacked on the bulletin board in the Sheriff's office, when he noticed a familiar face. Buff couldn't believe his eyes. It wasn't a wanted poster: it was a lost and found poster hanging on the board.

Turning to Alex, Buff said, "Say, Alex, a missing person poster? I've never seen one like this before, they're usually Wanted posters."

"Yeah, Marshal, but that notice has been hanging there for quite a while. Someone comes in from time to time and pins up a new one. A man named Nathaniel Pug ran off a while back and his family been looking for him is all I know. I do know that he's not wanted by the law here, or any place else that I know of," Sheriff Tull replied.

LOST AND FOUND POSTER
MISSING LOVED ONE

To all parts of the Nokota
Territorial Region
knowledge of the whereabouts
of our kin
Nathaniel Peanut Pug...
Please contact
Shih Tzu City Mayor's office

"Come here Dollar Five. Look at this and tell me who it looks like to you?" Buff asked.

"It's our Ned, the wino, Marshal. And at the bottom here it says wire the Shih Tzu City Mayor's office," Dollar Five said.

"Well, now fellas, it would seem like we've got another reason for coming this way. Hey, Sheriff, may I take this poster with me?" Buff asked.

"It's yours, Marshal," Sheriff Tull replied.

"You gonna wire the Mayor, Marshal?"

"No, Dollar Five, we're going to see him in person just as soon as we can," Buff replied.

"You see, just before I offered Ned the job of cleaning up the Marshal's office, I asked him why he drank so much. He gave me the impression he might be hiding something, and now this poster. Let's just say that I believe we just might have stumbled across something worth looking into," Buff replied.

"Well, Marshal, if you fellas are planning to ride to Shih-Tzu City, I guess I better come along to see to it that you don't get yourselves shot dead going through Palomino Canyon," Sheriff Tull said.

"What's Palomino Canyon, Sheriff Tull?" Buff asked.

"Palomino Canyon, Marshal, is the place where all the low-life outlaws hang out now, like the Morgan brothers and the Red Basset Gang. It didn't used to be like that, it was once the best place to find some of the bestselling horses for miles around, and if there's another way to Shih Tzu City, I haven't found it," Sheriff Tull replied.

"Well, maybe today will be our lucky day, and on the way to Shepherdsville you can tell me all about Palomino Canyon and the outlaws," Buff replied.

Recipe For Murder

SHERIFF TULL LEFT the note to his deputy on his deputy's desk, and after making sure they each had enough food and water, they all left the Sheriff's office heading for Shepherdsville. As they rode out of Poodle Town, Sheriff Tull began to tell Buff all about Shih Tzu City by way of Palomino Canyon. "You know, Buff, Palomino Canyon runs all the way through the Palomino Mountains. It's home to some of the most beautiful Palomino horses in the territory, and so they named it Palomino Canyon."

"I can't wait to see this beautiful canyon," Buff replied.

"Well, the beauty is still there, I'm sure of that. But since the outlaws started making it hard for the ranchers to catch horses to sell, they started calling it the Badlands, Marshal, and like I told you, I don't know any other way through it," Sheriff Tull replied.

"Well there's got to be another way in and out of this canyon." Buff looked over at Dollar Five and said, "Dollar Five, what do you know about Palomino Mountains or the Canyon?" Buff asked.

"Well, Marshal, I guess I know them mountains just as good as the outlaws do," Dollar Five replied.

Buff looked over at Sheriff Tull with a big smile on his face and asked, "Dollar Five, how come you know so much about Palomino Canyon?"

"Well Marshall, this here territory is still up and coming, and I reckon I'm about the only real blacksmith in these parts. I've been just about all over these parts shoeing horses. You might say, Marshal, that I know parts of this here territory that even the outlaws don't know, unless they just learned about them," Dollar Five proudly told the Marshal.

"Dollar Five, do you think you can get us through that canyon without getting the five of us shot up?" Buff asked.

"I can't make no promises now, Marshal, but I reckon you boys have as good a chance with me as you would one of them there outlaws," Dollar Five jokingly replied.

"We'll, I guess you fellas know your business," Sheriff Tull said.

"Well, Sheriff, we know our business remains to be proven, and if I have to go where dead men walk to get to the facts, then that's where I'll be going. Either way, Sheriff, we're not going to live forever," Buff replied.

"You are so right, Marshal, but for now will Shepherdsville do? Cause when we get to the top of that ridge up ahead, we'll be looking down on another big and beautiful Holiday Mansion," Sheriff Tull said.

Once they got to the top of the ridge, they were able to look down on the Holiday Mansion, and it was just as beautiful and as big as the mansion they owned in Cockapoo City. Sheriff Tull couldn't have painted a better picture. "We'll just trot on in from here fellas, we don't want to get those boys nervous down there," Sheriff Tull said laughingly as he took his hat off to wipe the sweat from his face.

Once they were within 20 feet of the Mansion a single shot was fired into the air by one of the men watching the gate. The guard called out, "Who are you and what do you want here?"

"I'm the Marshal of Cockapoo City, my three deputies, Sheriff Tull, and Matt Greenwood. Ms. Ashley is expecting us," Buff answered the guard.

"I'm sorry, Marshal, couldn't see you're star from here, sir. Come ahead. We'll let Ms. Ashley know you're here," the guard watching the gate replied.

The ranch hand opened the gate to allow Buff and the others to ride up the long dirt road to the Holiday Mansion. When the Mansion was in view, Ms. Ashley and Thurston were standing out front waiting. Matt jumped off his horse and walked up to her. He put his arms around her, and before he could kiss her, he said, "Darling, I was so happy to get your wire."

"What wire, Matt?" She asked. Looking very upset and saddened Matt turned and walked away.

Thurston walked up behind Matt and said, "Matt, slow down, and where do you think you're going? So, my sister didn't send the wire. So what? I sent it, but only after she wrote and signed it. Then Pa asked her to see about a little matter with one of the servants and when it was all taken care of it was late. And Pa would never allow Ashley off the ranch at night unescorted, so I rode to town and sent it for her. She knew nothing about it. It was my surprise so stop acting like a little boy and ask my sister to marry you so we can get on with business," Thurston replied.

Matt got down off his horse. He walked over to Ms. Ashley and got down on one knee right out on the front lawn and said, "Ashley, darling will you marry me?"

"Yes, Matt, I will marry you," she enthusiastically replied.

Dollar Five said, "Thurston, I have something for you in my saddle bags. A Lemon Pound Cake Aunt Bea asked me to bring to you." Dollar Five and the others all laughed and went inside.

There was plenty to eat and drink and sarsaparilla or coffee for those who wanted some refreshment. Buff wasted no time and he asked, "Is your Pa home, too? I'd like to meet him and ask him some questions."

"It's good to meet you finally, Marshal Logan," Richard Holiday, Jr. said as he entered the room, extending his hand. "And please don't be upset with Nation because I didn't leave him any choice. I insisted on knowing everything about anyone involved with my family, so I hope you and your brothers,

Gray and Chocolate, will understand, but I make no apologies for my action."

After being taken off guard a bit by Mr. Holiday, Jr.'s directness, Buff, Gray and Chocolate laughed right along with Sheriff Tull and the Holiday family. "Well, now that the cat's out the bag, so to speak, may I continue with my questions?" Buff asked.

"Please, go right ahead," Holiday Jr. replied.

Buff said, "I think it'll save time, Mr. Holiday, if you just start by telling us everything."

"Please, just call me Richard. Marshal, I pleaded with Pa not to marry Martha Papillon. He knew so little about her. But I knew of her daughter, Victoria, and if the old saying is true, the apple doesn't fall far from the tree. Victoria wanted nothing but money, and she didn't care much whose it was so long as she had some of it. After Pa married Martha, she and Victoria came to live in the mansion and things changed. The twins didn't like her, and she hated them. But I didn't allow Ashley or Thurston to mistreat Victoria. I overheard Martha one night asking my Pa had he given any more thought to adopting Victoria. His reply was, 'Martha, Victoria is not my child. I will do whatever I can for her, but I cannot give her the Holiday name.' I believe any love Martha had for my Pa was gone after that."

Richard continued, "Before going to Nation Middleton and asking for his help, I had hired another lawman from Dachshund City in Labradoodle County. He reported to me that before marrying my Pa, Martha was involved with Hollister Bobcat Cobb. Now I'm not one for rumors, but it's been told that Bobcat and Martha were once lovers, and some rumors say Martha had his baby. I believe both Martha and Victoria came here for one purpose only - my Pa's money. I believe Martha murdered my Pa, and I believe Victoria plotted with Mike Eastern to have my wife murdered and me framed for it, getting me out the way. And that's the truth of it, Marshal."

When Richard was finished Buff asked, "Richard, did you happen to tell Nation any of what you told me? And one other thing, Richard, why didn't you say something sooner? A lot of time has gone by."

"Good questions there, Marshal, but when you're dealing with crooks and murderers, timing is everything. You're a young marshal, you have much to learn. But from what I know of your grandpa, I believe you boys are going to be some of the best lawmen to wear a badge. But I know people. I've lived here all my life. It's true I married a saloon girl and had twins, but she was a good wife and Ma. Some say she cheated, some say she lied, and I loved her. If you were me, Marshal, what would you have done?" Richard asked Buff.

Without hesitating Buff replied, "I see your point Richard. You see, the Morgan brothers killed our Pa, and now they're waiting for just the right time to try and take us out. So tell me about the gold mine being somewhere on the property. What about it, Richard?"

"You see, Marshal, Pa's mine is behind the south wall of the library of the Holiday Mansion, in what is now called the Bar X Ranch. Look for a book titled, 'Bringing Down The House.' Remove the book from the shelf, and behind it you'll find a little black spot, and I do mean directly behind that book. With one of your claws scratch the spot and the bookcase will start to move, revealing the entrance to my Pa's mine.

On the inside of either wall there are several lanterns. Light as many as you need, then follow the pathway into the mine. It will take your breath away," Richard said. "Marshal, they would have never found it, not in a million years. As for telling all this to Nation, no, I did not. I didn't know then most of what I know now. I believe you'll find all the proof you need, including how they tried to frame me for my wife's murder,"

The fellows just sat there in disbelief. Gray said, "Richard, tell me this; how did your Pa come up with the idea of building a house on top of a gold mine?"

"You see, Gray, when my Pa had the Holiday Mansion built, he didn't know about the mine," Richard answered. "My Pa bought land in the Mastiff Mountains and hired miners to work it. Land was so cheap in those days and Pa had more than enough money so, he invested and that's when he struck gold.

Pa heard talk of a young man over in Labradoodle County, Appaloosa Territory. I don't recall the name, but he shouldn't be much older than me. Anyway, this man came from a family of draftsmen and builders dating back a ways, and Pa paid him to build the Holiday Mansion. I don't care what folks say, my Pa didn't have it built for Martha. Well, when it was finished Pa was so happy with it that he paid him to build the Shepherdsville Mansion. What Pa didn't know until the man showed him, was that he had built these secret passageways and tunnel, behind the wall of the library. He showed Pa this secret button that would open and close the bookshelf. So, naturally as a little boy I played in them a lot."

The secret gold mine on the
Holiday Ranch in Cockapoo City

"One day," Richard said with a laugh, "I found a shiny rock among some yellow glinting stuff. My Pa must have jumped ten feet high when I showed it to him. He said to me, 'Richard Holiday, Jr. you've got the best darn muzzle in the world,' which made no sense to me. But after Pa was finished explaining it, I later understood my Pa's reaction. I had discovered gold while playing in one of the tunnels beneath the Holiday Mansion."

The fellows just started laughing and thought this was one of the best stories they had ever heard. And it showed how folks can take something and tell it over and over and it never ends up being told the way it really happened.

"What an unbelievable story, Richard. When I first came to Cockapoo City and met Mr. Clayton and Marshal Colby, your family history was told to me, and not one of them knew how it all really happened," Buff laughlying replied.

"That may be so, but there was one person that my Pa kept an eye on, and that was Mayor Todd. Pa always told me, 'Never talk about our family in the presence of Mayor Todd.' He never told me why, aside from not trusting the man," Richard said.

"Richard, Thurston, Ms. Ashley, we thank you for seeing us, for the lunch and for the history lesson of the Holiday Family. We should be on our way, but I have one last question, Richard." Taking the poster he borrowed from Sheriff Tull's office from his pocket, he showed it to them and asked, "Have any of you ever seen this man or know anything about him?" Buff asked.

"Nathaniel Pug," Thurston replied. "No, Marshal I haven't,"

"Neither have I," Ashley replied.

But Richard said, "Marshal, I won't swore to it, but he looks a bit like the man who designed the Holiday Mansion, if memory serves me right."

Hiding his surprise at this, Marshall Buff said, "Well, thanks again for everything, and here's hoping you all come to Cockapoo City real soon," Buff replied.

"Oh, Marshal, please tell Aunt Bea that the three of us will be paying a call on her tomorrow," Ms. Ashley said.

"I'll do that, Ms. Ashley," The Marshal replied.

Richard, Thurston and Ms. Ashley saw them to their horses. One of the ranch hands was standing there with the horses and said, "They've each been watered and fed, and they're ready to ride. They're very good horses." They each said thank you and rode off.

"So, Marshal, what about the Bar X ranch?" Dollar Five asked.

"What about it, Dollar Five?" Buff replied.

"Well we still need to search the Bar X, don't we? Or are you going to wire Dean and have him and Thad do it?" Dollar Five asked.

"No, the Bar X will keep until we get back to search it. Right now we've got much to do, boy," Buff replied.

Sheriff Tull looked over at Buff and said, "Palomino Canyon, Marshal?"

"You said it, Sheriff," Buff replied.

"Well if you fellas wanna go and get yourselves dead by a gang of outlaws and possibly even the Morgans, then I reckon I better go along and see to it that those wild cats don't drop any of ya. We can stop in town and send a wire to Mollie from there and let them know that Buff is determined to get us all dead, so they can head back to Cockapoo City when they get ready," Dollar Five joked.

"You know, fellas, I can take care of that for you. No need to ride back into Shepherdsville for that," Matt replied.

"Thank you, Matt, that'll save us time," Marshall Buff said. "You know, Sheriff Tull, the way me and my brothers got it figured, it's time we met the Morgans, and Dollar Five is going to see to it that we make it in and out of Palomino Canyon, right Dollar Five?"

"Well, like I said before, Marshal, I make no promises, but I'm pretty sure that can be arranged," Dollar Five replied.

Once they got some ways out on the prairie Sheriff Tull said, "Well, if you boys got good eyes you can see the Palomino Mountains from here."

"Wow! Look at all the colors. Beautiful, just plain, darn beautiful," Buff replied.

"You're so right, Buff. But if you boys look over to the left, you'll see buzzards flying, and we all know what that means," Chocolate replied.

"Well, I reckon we'd better mosey on over there and see what's up. Dollar Five, you lead the way," Buff said.

The men rode and rode, and the closer they got, the sorrier they felt for whomever it was lying beneath the black buzzards flying high above them. Then a horse came running towards them and it was running mighty fast. Chocolate and Dollar Five ran down the horse, and as they were bringing it back in, Sheriff Tull said, "Look here, boys, that looks like a brand on this side. Come have a look."

"Buff are my eyes playing tricks on me, or do you see what I see?" Gray asked.

"Your eyes are fine, brother Gray, and so are mine," Buff replied.

Chocolate said," Hey, guys, what on earth is the circle, 'LP' brand doing all the way out here?"

"What's the 'LP' brand?" Sheriff Tull asked.

"Well, now, Sheriff, I see you're not as sharp as you think," Dollar Five said, "but then you wouldn't have known it anyway. That brand is the same as the ones on Buff, Gray and Chocolate's horses."

"That's right, Dollar Five, and it stands for Logan & Potts. It's our family brand," Buff replied. "But what I want to know is how it got here?"

"I got one better than that Buff. How about, who rode it here?" Gray replied.

To be Continued in "The Adventures of Buff, Gray and Chocolate" series, Book Two.

Miner Binder

Miner Binder

GLOSSARY OF CHARACTERS

The Adventures of Buff, Gray, & Chocolate
The Series

The Potts Family

Charlie Potts: Purebred Standard Poodle with shiny black hair muscular build, struck it rich in gold, married Marian, and Pa to Annie Potts.

Marian Potts: Miniature Poodle with curly black and white hair, four-time beauty queen of Pittsville, married Charlie Potts and ma to Annie Potts.

Annie Potts: Toy Poodle with white wavy hair with black patch under chin, married Roy Logan, ma to Buff, Gray, Chocolate, Clay, and Fuchsia Logan.

The Logan Family

Russell Logan: Purebred Cocker-Spaniel struck it rich in gold with best friend Charlie, became Marshal of Pittsville, married Sarah Logan, one son Roy Logan.

Sarah Logan: Purebred Cocker-Spaniel former beauty queen of Pittsville, one title only, owner of Marian's Hat Shop, ma to Roy Logan.

<u>Roy Logan:</u> Purebred Cocker-Spaniel rancher married Annie Potts Pa to Buff, Gray, Chocolate, Clay, and Fuchsia Logan.

<u>Children of Annie & Roy Logan</u>

<u>Buff Logan:</u> Cockapoo, son to Annie and Roy Logan, Marshal of Cockapoo City.

<u>Gray Logan:</u> Cockapoo, son to Annie and Roy Logan, deputy Marshal of Cockapoo City.

<u>Chocolate Logan:</u> Cockapoo, son of Annie and Roy Logan, Middleton detective and deputy Marshal of Cockapoo City.

<u>Clay Logan:</u> Cockapoo, son of Annie and Roy Logan, rancher.

<u>Fuchsia Logan:</u> Cockapoo, daughter of Annie and Roy Logan, part owner of Marian Dress Shop.

<u>The Morgan Family</u>

<u>Asa Morgan:</u> Schnauzer family, farmer turned notorious outlaw, most wanted man in the Notorious Territory, married Sarah Ann Morgan, Pa of Gus Morgan, adopted Pa of Sophia Morgan.

<u>Sarah Ann Morgan:</u> English spaniel family, school marm, and wife of farmer turned famous outlaw Asa Morgan, Ma of Gus Morgan, adopted Ma of Sophia Morgan.

<u>Sophia Morgan:</u> Background unknown, adopted daughter of Asa and Sarah Ann Morgan, sister to Gus Morgan, but she never claimed the Morgan name.

<u>Gus Morgan:</u> Part Schnauzer part English Spaniel son of Sarah Ann and Asa Morgan, stepbrother of Sophia Morgan, born outlaw shot down on Front Street in Pittsville by Marshal Russell Logan, Pa to Pace, Lace, Billy Bob, and Bo Morgan.

Floleen Morgan: English Shetland Sheep family former saloon girl married Gus Morgan for money, Ma to Pace, Lace, Billy Bob, and Bo Morgan.

Pace Morgan: Oldest son of Floleen and Gus Morgan, member of Red Basset gang, shot in pistol play with Chad Shepherd in the Bobcat Saloon for the killing of Roy Logan.

Lace Morgan: Next to oldest son of Floleen and Gus Morgan, member of Red Basset gang, witness to Roy Logan murder, wife died from yellow fever.

Luke Morgan: Son of Pace Morgan, wanted outlaw, bank rubbing. Once Bar X Ranch cowhand.

The Russell Family

Jack Russell Sr. Purebred Russell, born lawman, founded the famous Canine Territorial Prison and only family to run the Canine Territorial Prison. (Deceased)

Jack Russell Jr: Purebred Russell, former warden of Canine Territorial Prison.

Jack Russell, I: Purebred Russell, son of Jack Jr., former warden of Canine Territorial Prison.

Jack Russell II: Purebred Russell, son of Jack Jr., current warden of Canine Territorial Prison.

Jack Russell III: Purebred Russell, son of Jack Jr., current warden of Canine Territorial Prison.

The Tessel Family

Hattie May Saints Tessel: Ma Tessel, married to Zachariah Bernard Tessel, both purebred Saint Bernard mountain folk.

<u>Zachariah Bernard Tessel:</u> Purebred Bernard. **(Deceased)**

<u>Raina Tessel:</u> Only daughter of Ma Tessel and Zachariah Tessel, purebred Saint Bernard.

<u>Lucky Tessel:</u> Oldest son of Ma and Zachariah Tessel, purebred Saint, sent to Canine Territorial Prison for shooting Marshal Ben Colby.

<u>Sandy Tessel:</u> Middle son of Ma and Zachariah Tessel, rough but no trouble with the law.

<u>Zack Tessel Jr.:</u> Youngest son of Ma and Zachariah Tessel, left home as soon as he came of age, whereabouts unknown, not on any wanted posters.

<u>The Greenwood Family</u>

<u>Thomas Greenwood:</u> Purebred English Sheep, white hair, tall build, founder of Cockapoo City, wife Elizabeth passed away, Pa to twin boys.

<u>Elizabeth Greenwood:</u> Purebred English Sheep, silver hair, stay home Ma.

<u>Charlie Greenwood:</u> Purebred English Sheep, oldest son of Thomas and Elizabeth Greenwood, mixed silver hair like Ma and black hair like Pa, twin.

<u>Matthew Greenwood:</u> Purebred English Sheep, youngest son of Thomas and Elizabeth Greenwood, twin, silver and black hair, married Ashley Holiday half owner of Greenwood freight and Cockapoo city stage-line.

<u>The Clayton Family</u>

<u>Thaddeus Clayton I:</u> Beagle on the short side, founder of Cockapoo City. Wife deceased.

Thaddeus Clayton II: Beagle, short, took over family business after Clayton Sr. passed on.

Jean Clayton: Basset, homemaker, married Clayton, two children.

Rebecca Clayton: Part Beagle and Basset, daughter, bank manager of Clayton Cattlemen, smart, friendly, short brown hair.

Thaddeus Clayton III: Part owner of the Cockapoo Eagle, part-time deputy of Marshal Buff Logan. Part Beagle & Basset.

The Holiday Family

Richard C. Holiday, Sr.: Richest man to have ever lived in Cockapoo, owner of gold mines, etc., one son, twin grandkids, one stepdaughter, married Martha Terrier.

Martha Terrier Holiday: Deceased wife of the late Richard C. Holiday, Ma to Victoria, step Ma- to Holiday twins, and home maker.

Richard C. Holiday, Jr.: Terrier, married a saloon girl, marriage disgraced, Pa of Ashley and Thurston, now living with daughter, son, and son in law in holiday mansion, whereabouts of wife unknown.

Ashley Holiday Greenwood: Married Matt Greenwood, Tibetan Terrier, twin brother Thurston, daughter of Richard C. Holiday, Jr.

Thurston Holiday: Successful businessman, shipping gold bullion, Son of Richard C. Holiday, Jr. Tibetan Terrier twin sister.

Victoria: Terrier Yorkie, Step-daughter of Richard C. Holiday, Sr., always hated the family and the Holidays, left out of ol' man Holiday's will, married Mike Eastern.

<u>The Colby Family</u>

<u>Marshal Lance Bay Colby:</u> Farmer turned lawman, and Ben's Pa, passed away.

<u>Betty Louise Colby:</u> Wife to Lance Colby Ma to Ben Colby, passed away.

<u>Marshal Benjamin Bay Colby:</u> Once marshal of Cockapoo, born Chesapeake Bay, he was part Retriever, loyal to the badge, married a saloon girl name Hope.

<u>Hope Colby</u>: Worked in a saloon called the Hide Out in Beagle Town until marring Marshal Ben Colby and moving to Cockapoo City. Background unknown.

<u>Main Supporting Characters</u>

<u>Dr. Arlington Ollie:</u> Veterinarian Doctor.

<u>Parson:</u> Spiritual leader of Pittsville, breed: Yorkie.

<u>Chad Shepherd:</u> Purebred German shepherd, six feet tall with black shoulder length hair, best friend to the late Roy Logan, once foreman of Miloh ranch, now Foreman of Logan Ranch.

<u>Nick:</u> Ranch hand on Roy Logan Place.

<u>Jason:</u> Ranch hand on Roy Logan Place.

<u>Ben Miloh:</u> Rancher, cattle and horse breeding.

<u>Jonas:</u> Owner of Pittsville General Store.

<u>Dakota Saint:</u> Barber of Cockapoo city, easygoing, real sociable, big fellow with black and brown hair from the Bernard family.

Judge Tuesday: Travels from town to town, his family is mixed with Terrier and Bull, intimidating at times, known to be an honest judge.

Mayor Todd: Middle height, black hair, from the Lakeland terrier family.

Mike Eastern: Married to Victoria, twin brother Ike, both short black and brown hair Yorkshire, banker.

Ike Eastern: Short black and brown, banking business with brother, Mike.

Doc Josh Stone: Graduated from Veterinarian school came back to home town Cockapoo City to practice doctoring, kin folk of the show business family Bearded Collie, Josh wanted work in medical field.

Dollar Five: Short with tan hair, owner of stable, kin to Aunt Bea, from the Terrier family.

Dean Moorhead: Owner of the Cockapoo Eagle, Dalmatian family, brown and white hair, black frame glasses, part-time deputy to Marshal Buff Logan.

Aunt Bea: Lhasa Apso, white hair kin folk to Dollar Five and Mollie, owner of Bea's Place.

Mollie: Owner of Mollie's Place in Poodle Town, sister to Aunt Bea.

Ms. Stella Siamese: Owner of Stella's Place, short lilac hair, blue eyes, nice slim figure.

Sam: Bar keep for Stella's Place, background known.

Ms. Peggy Waggy: Short height, long haired Javanese with vivid blue eyes, black jack dealer at Fatcat's Saloon.

Harrier: Barkeeper for Fatcat's Saloon, medium build, tan and white hair.

Napoleon Calico Fatcat Cobb: Brown and marble hair with shade of black, owner of Fatcat's Saloon, once called the Bobcat, owned by his uncle Bobcat years ago, known for his watered-down chicken broth and crooked card dealers.

Hollister Bobcat Cobb: Uncle to Fatcat and owner of the Big Top saloon in the town once known as Chow-Chow mining town and the Bobcat saloon in Cockapoo City and a thief.

Payton: Ranch foreman of the Bar X, now serving three years in Canine Territory Prison.

Hank: Stagecoach driver.

Sheriff Tull: Alexander (Alex) Tull, Sheriff of Poodle Town.

Dingo: Wino, reddish brown hair, Australian Hound pals with Dunker and Ned.

Dunker: Wino, Norwegian Hound, brown and black hair, pals with Dingo and Ned.

Ned: Town wino, background unknown. Pals with Dingo and Dunker.

Nation Middleton: Head of the Middleton detectives, detective son of Jonah Middleton.

Jonah Middleton: Nation Middleton's Pa and founder of the first organization of peace officers (The Middleton's Detective Agency) to rule the Nokota and Appaloosa territories, best friend of Marshal Russell Logan; retired.

Chet Basenji: Undercover agent for the Middleton Detective Agency, and plant at the telegraph office in Cockapoo City.

<u>Red Basset:</u> Once led the Red Basset gang; whereabouts unknown.

<u>Ben Elam:</u> Born in the Great Blue Dane Mountains, prospector and brother of Major Seth Elam.

<u>Miner Binder:</u> Born and raised in the Great Blue Dane Mountains, prospector and best friend of Ben Elam, Black and Brown short haired Yorkie, about ankle high. Pa to Kaleb Binder. Wife Beulah passed away.

<u>Jonesy:</u> Saloon barkeep in boomtown Cockapoo.

<u>Tobias (Toby) Bombay</u>: Messenger Boy for the Mayor's office in Cockapoo City.

ACKNOWLEDGEMENTS

First, I would like to give God all the glory for giving me the inspiration to write this book and the ones that will follow. God is truly amazing, and through Him all things are possible if we believe.

I would be remiss if I didn't thank the following people who stood by me during this writing process. Thank you for believing in me, especially when I did not believe in myself sometimes. They were my backbone, providing love and support daily:

My dog, Dillon, who I love. My 11-year-old cousin, Jeremiah for receiving an A on his book report and for using my book, and his sister Jayla - I love you both so very much. Terza Tessel, Beaethel Jackson-Terry, Kathleen Lemanski, Shirley Porter.

A special "thank you" to my cousin Cynthia Porter Johnson for being so supportive of my vision and her insight in helping me see more clearly! Kudos to you!

A special "thank you" to William Law, a dear and trusting friend for doing such a spectacular job of proof reading and editing my book.

To my illustrator, Ms. Lauren Kisich, "thank you" for delivering one of the most incredible Book Covers and illustrations I have ever seen, and for seeing my vision in the way God gave it to me. Your work is for the world to enjoy. You are indeed a jewel.

On behalf of the Logan brothers, Buff, Gray, and Chocolate, I would just like to say, Thank You, God!

Lionel James

EPILOGUE

Payton, Fatcat, and Luke each got sentenced to three years and joined Lucky in Canine Territorial Prison. Ms. Peggy Waggy walked out of the Marshal's office a free feline, promising to do no wrong.

Matt Greenwood talked Ashley Holiday into buying back the mansion and marrying him, and Thurston Holiday opened the Holiday Bank and Trust. The murder of Miner Binder is still unsolved. Gray's shoulder finally healed and he's back at work. Victoria Holiday Eastern's whereabouts are unknown.

Dean finally got the biggest story his newspaper had ever reported. Thad, Dollar Five and Dean had second jobs as deputies.

The Holiday Mansion was sitting on top of the biggest gold mine anyone in Cockapoo, or miles around, had ever heard of.

The Logan boys began to Tame the Wild West, Logan Style.